FRIGHT BITES

(A COLLECTION OF 29 CREEPY TALES: VOLUME 1)

To all my current and new readers:

I'm extremely grateful to each of you for your wonderful support.

Thank you,
Miracle Austin

ACKNOWLEDGEMENTS

Thank you all for working with me to bring *FRIGHT BITES* to life: Rebecca Jaycox, a.k.a., The Sledgehammer, and Debbie Manber Kupfer, my awesome editors; Linnea (lixxiiia.drawss) for creating my beautiful custom book cover art; and Temys Designs (temysdesigns.com) for the amazing interior design, formatting, full book wrap, and extra magic. Puzzle created by the fabulous Debbie Manber Kupfer. Please check out Debbie's website: paws4puzzles.wordpress.com

I wish to extend a huge thank you to my extremely supportive friends: Irenka Vlajnic, Erica Barfield (Lee), Natasha Wright, Rosario Ozuna (MLS Librarian at RGCGISD Grulla Middle School), Julie Warner DeCesaro (Teacher at Sterling Martin Middle School), Jacqueline E. Smith (author of the *Boy Band* & *Cemetery Tours* Series and other stand-alone books), Manuel Ruiz (author of the *Dead Club* and *Sugar Skull* Series), Lorelei Buckley (author of *Beyond The Graveyard* and other stand-alone books), Steve Parlato (author of *The Namesake* and *The Precious Dreadful*), Katelynn Rentería (author of *The Other Side Of The Law*), Ian Sputnik (author of *Food For Worms* and owner of Sanitarium Magazine), and Margie Longoria (MLS Librarian at Mission High School and editor of *Living Beyond Borders*).

My family at Sirens Call Publications (SirensCallPublications.com): Gloria Bobrowicz, Nina D'Arcangela, and Lee Andrew Forman: thank you all for the support you've given me over the years and continue to give. I'm extremely grateful to have my stories in your outstanding eZine. It's because of publications like yours that authors can share their works with others around the world.

A very special thank you to Mrs. Channing Raney who sends me inspirational messages about my stories, which she has either read or listened to via podcast, and how they've impacted her. Thank you also for sharing my works with others—it means so much!

Finally, Mama, thank you so much for sharing all your stories with me when you were a young girl growing up in Crawford, Texas.

DEDICATION

Mr. Walter McDonald

When I attended the Belton Comic Con a few years ago, Mr. McDonald strolled by my author's table. As I talked about my books with him, he told me how he wasn't much of a reader anymore. I challenged him to read the first page from one of my books. I wasn't sure if my book would be a good fit for him or not.

He ended up buying one. He contacted me a little later to share how much he enjoyed reading *Doll,* and how I recharged his reading interests, which made my day.

Since then, he's messaged me about how he's read the *Doll* trilogy several times and continues to share positive comments about the characters. It's a great feeling when an author can introduce a book to someone, and the person rediscovers how delightful reading can be. I'm so glad that I had the opportunity to do that with Mr. McDonald on that busy day. Thank you, Mr. McDonald, for allowing me to pitch my books to you. I hope you enjoy ***FRIGHT BITES***, which is dedicated to you.

In the inspirational words of my phenomenal librarian friend,
Mrs. Rosario Ozuna:

**"One Book or Novel at a Time... Remember,
everyone's a reader. Some of you JUST haven't
found the right book, YET!"**

MIRACLE AUSTIN

FRIGHT BITES

FRIGHT BITES

ISBN-13: 978-0-9986182-6-5 (paperback)
ISBN-10: 978-0-9986182-7-2 (ebook)

Editors: Rebecca Jaycox & Debbie Manber Kupfer
Interior Design & Formatting/Cover Designer: Temys Designs | temysdesigns.com
Cover Artist: @lixxiiia.drawss

Published by: Miracle Austin

PUBLISHING

Published in (United States of America)
10 9 8 7 6 5 4 3 2 1

INTRODUCTION

Proceed with caution... Once you start *FRIGHT BITES: VOLUME 1*, you won't be able to stop yourself from inhaling each tale. You'll want to know the endings to all of them. Go ahead, flip through the pages to determine if any of these stories are true or just part of the author's imagination. You get to figure that out because after all, you're the reader.

By the way, you'll want to check out the story I'm featured in. I would place it in the modern category inspired by a classic. Oops, there I go trying to claim my story is the best and making *FRIGHT BITES* all about me. Seriously, I'm not vain at all. Well, maybe a little.

Anyhow, I've read all these creepy stories more than once. I wish I could share more about them with you, but you're just going to have to find out on your own by reading each one at your own pace.

Oh, I almost forgot to mention, make sure your phone is charged... just in case the lights flicker off as you're reading *FRIGHT BITES*, and you need a flashlight to make sure a ***nightrunner*** isn't hiding somewhere in your room...

P.S.
A SECRET MESSAGE TO SOLVE AWAITS YOU, AT THE END.
—GRYSELDA

TABLE OF CONTENTS

The brilliant 'Master of Horror' said it best about the short story:

"...A short story is like a quick kiss in the dark
from a stranger."
—STEPHEN KING

PACHOOEE

(Paw~chew~ee)

Tossing and turning all night, I felt like an oversized catfish being reeled into its captor's boat. I kicked off my *Alien versus Predator* comforter. I attempted to close my eyes several times, but sleep failed me each time. My sheets were soaked in sweat. My ceiling fan was on full blast, and the air conditioner was set at sixty-three degrees.

Without any warning, a sharp pain side-kicked me in my jaw. I felt something throbbing under my jowl. I glided my hand down and felt a golf-ball sized swelling, which hadn't been there a few hours ago.

Jumping out of bed, I dashed to my bathroom and flipped on the light switch. The reflection in the mirror watching me didn't look like me. My tremoring hands accelerated upwards to cover it. When I counted backwards from five and looked again, the *monster* remained.

My face looked as if someone had whacked me a few times with a tennis racket—faint plum and bright, raspberry bruises splattered my cheeks. My eyes were bloodshot red, and my throat felt sticky. I went from worried to being super freaked out.

Something started moving around in my mouth. I leaned in closer to the bathroom mirror, but couldn't see anything. I moved my tongue up and down, side to side. Clear slime coated the walls of my mouth. I grabbed a bath rag off the side of the tub, fished out the slime, and chucked the rag in the trashcan.

Opening my bathroom drawer, I shoved a tube of toothpaste and hair clippers aside until I found a small flashlight. I flicked it on and shined it inside my mouth.

After about fifteen seconds or so, I noticed a short, perforated stubby tail and then two yellowish glowing, beady eyes staring up at me. Once the light hit its eyes, the strange critter shot towards the back of my throat and burrowed itself inside my right gum.

My booming scream caused the mirror to vibrate against the wall. It felt like someone had stabbed me with a hot poker. I dropped the flashlight on the floor and ran to my mom's room.

Flinging her door open without knocking, I yelled out in a high-pitch tone, "Mom, we gotta go to the doctor, right now!"

She popped straight up, flipping her *Murder She Wrote* eye-mask above her forehead. "Charlie, what's wrong?" she asked, reaching to turn on her bedside lamp and almost falling onto the floor.

"I don't know, but there's something inside my mouth, and it hurts." My eyes felt grainy and started tearing up.

She shoved her covers back and climbed out of bed.

"You're burning up," she said, rubbing my damp forehead with the back of her hand. She guided me to the end of her bed. "You're growing so tall. Sit down—let me take a look."

She turned on the ceiling-fan light while scrambling around the room to find her eyeglasses. She grabbed a flashlight from her top dresser drawer.

When she shined the light on my face, she gasped and said, "What happened, Charlie?" She stumbled back a step.

"I don't know," I said, drool spooling out of the side of my mouth. I wiped it with the collar of my T-shirt. "Mom, I look worse than the son of Frankenstein."

"Charlie, it's not that bad," she said, swallowing hard.

"C'mon, Mom, you know it is... You won't believe what I saw when I looked inside with the flashlight," I said.

Adjusting her glasses on her face, she asked, "What did you see?"

Pausing for a few seconds, I blurted out, "A tadpole-like thing, smaller than my pinky finger." Whenever I swallowed, my throat felt slick.

"Tilt your head back and let me see what the fuss is all about," she said, pushing my forehead back gently with her index finger.

Switching on the flashlight, she looked all around my mouth.

"Charlie, I don't see anything. Your gums do look really puffy and red."

"Mom, look again, I saw it, I swear," I pleaded, clenching the edge of the comforter with my hands.

She assessed it a second time and still nothing.

"I believe you may have an abscess—your jowl is really swollen." She turned the flashlight off and threw it in the middle of the bed.

Glancing at her clock on her dresser, she said, "Listen, it's almost eight. Get dressed, and we'll have Dr. Wind's Family Dental check this out."

On our way there, Mom told me to get two Tylenol pills out of her purse next to her. I tried to pick it up, but my hand quivered and I dropped it. I saw them on top. I attempted to unscrew the bottle—I couldn't. When Mom reached a stop light, she opened the bottle up, and shook two in my sweaty palm.

I popped them in my mouth, and they slid down my slippery throat without any need for water. I knew the only thing that was going to give me relief was removal of whatever that thing was from my mouth.

When we arrived, Mom signed me in and started working on the paperwork. The waiting room was practically empty, except a lady with her young kid.

The kid pointed at my face. I just stared at her. My mouth and jaw were pulsating. I scooted down inside the chair and pulled my retro *Dungeons and Dragons* hoodie over my head as low as I could to conceal my face.

The girl's mom whispered something in her ear. She stopped pointing and started reading from her book that her mom handed her.

I squirmed around in the chair. Mom finished the paperwork and returned it to the front desk. After about fifteen minutes, Sam, the dental assistant, called us back. She sat me down in the dental chair. Sam took my temperature and blood pressure. It was a 102.5 and 165/99.

"Those are some high readings, Charlie, you've definitely got something going on. Don't you worry. Dr. Wind will get this all figured out, and you'll be feeling better in no time, sweetie. Now, have you taken any medications this morning?" she asked, clicking keys on her computer board.

"He took some Tylenol. It doesn't seem to be working fast enough," Mom replied.

Tingling, sharp pains shot inside my mouth, and I closed my eyes.

"Dr. Wind is the best dentist in town," Sam said as she clipped a paper bib around my neck. "He'll be with you, shortly." She patted my shoulder lightly.

I could hear dental tools clanking as she placed them in a metal tray not far from me. My mom held my hand, and I squeezed it tight.

"Charlie, my little baby bear, you must be in so much pain. The last time you held my hand like this was when you broke your arm in little league baseball after you made that unexpected home run," she said.

Dang, Mom, please don't call me that in public, I wanted to reply back, but decided to save my energy for Dr. Wind's questions. I just gripped her hand even tighter.

Bigfoot sounding footsteps echoed down the hall. I opened up one eye before tears filled it up again.

"Well... well... I heard you have a pretty nasty infection, Charlie. You mentioned you saw something moving around in your mouth. It's in the back of your mouth, where I pulled your wisdom teeth last summer, right?" Dr. Wind asked.

I nodded.

Dr. Wind pulled a medical mask up on his face and added safety glasses on top of his eyeglasses. He slid purple gloves on both hands.

"Thank you, Dr. Wind, for seeing us so quickly," Mom said.

"No problem, let's see what's going on." He sat down in a wheeled stool and scooted over to me, pulling down the square, swinging dental light. He turned on the bright fluorescent glow, retrieved a mouth mirror in one hand, and a curved, sickle scaler in his other hand from the tray.

"Charlie, I'm going to lean you back, so I can get a good look inside, okay?" he said.

He immediately started poking around in my mouth. My arm flung up knocking the tray and everything on it up in the air.

I grunted, "I'm sorry."

"It's all right," Sam said. I watched her pick up the tools off the floor.

He continued poking around for a few minutes. A stream of milky, yellowish pus sprayed up towards the light fixture. He reared back and dodged the eruption. His hands were trembling, and he dropped his tools.

Sam scooped them off the floor and cleaned the light with an alcohol wipe.

"There's a lot of movement inside of your gums, Charlie," Dr. Wind said, breathing hard.

"What do you mean?" Mom demanded in a wobbly voice.

"Dr. Wind, did you just say something was moving inside of Charlie's gums?" Sam squealed. "What do you think it is?"

"Yes...I need to retrieve a specimen before I can determine that. Sam, please hand me a lidocaine shot." Dr. Wind held out his hand, and Sam placed the needle inside of his palm.

"Charlie, you might feel a little prick, but I'm going to need to make a small incision in a few minutes to really know what's inside of your gums, okay?" Dr. Wind said as he injected the drug inside my right lower gum.

I cringed and frowned.

"You have one of the severest infections that I've seen in a long time. The last one I saw similar to this was almost five years ago. I think I know what it could be," Dr. Wind said. He withdrew a handkerchief from the bottom of his scrub pocket and wiped sweat pellets from his forehead.

"What's next?" Mom asked, tapping her foot against the tile floor with a balled-up tissue in her hand.

"I need to complete my assessment," Dr. Wind said as he scooted back up closer to me. "Charlie, have you eaten anything exotic or been swimming anywhere in the last few days?" he asked.

I hesitated and didn't want to answer him. Mom would then know where I had been, then there would be more questions later on, especially about the *secret* I'd been keeping to myself for a while now.

"Charlie, we're waiting... Answer Dr. Wind, right now, young man," she commanded without a blink.

In a low and garbled tone, I said, "The lake with Joey and Oscar on Sunday night."

"Where?" he asked as Sam handed him clean tools.

"Charlie, I've told you over and over again to stay away from them after that accident a year ago with Molly's son. I know one of them was involved," Mom barked, shooting up from her seat. "They've been in juvenile detention twice. I'm sure they'll both end up in prison one day with their histories."

"Ms. Franklin, please, allow Charlie to answer my questions," Dr. Wind snapped.

"Sorry, Dr. Wind," she said, sitting back down.

"There are a few lakes in the area. Which lake, Charlie?" Dr. Wind asked, narrowing his eyes.

"Lake Pachooee," I said.

Dr. Wind almost slipped out of his seat. He readjusted himself quickly. "Did you or your friends do anything shameful that night at the lake?"

"Not to sound disrespectful, Dr. Wind, but why are you asking all these questions?" Mom asked. "I don't understand what a lake has to do with Charlie's mouth infection."

"It's important for Charlie to answer these questions because of what could be festering inside his mouth from the lake," he said.

"What... what do you think it could be?" Sam asked in a trembling tone.

"Sam, please be patient, and let me complete my assessment first," Dr. Wind requested, looking back at her then back down at me.

She leaned against the counter and kept silent.

"Okay, Charlie, what did you all actually do at Lake Pachooee?" he asked.

"We had a couple of beers, talked about girls, smoked, and Joey dared me to backstroke to the middle of the lake and back for fifty bucks, so I did. It was no big deal. I've won so many swim meets without even trying. The easiest money I've made in a while," I said.

"So, you were the only one who swam in Lake Pachooee?" Dr. Wind probed.

"Yes, why?" I asked.

Dr. Wind braced his hands on top of his knees and dropped his head.

"I know that look, Dr. Wind," Sam said, blinking.

"One of them knew," he said.

"Knew what, Dr. Wind?" Mom asked in a high pitch squeal.

"The curse of Lake Pachooee..." he whispered. "Are you sure you didn't do something bad with one of those boys that night, Charlie?"

I didn't respond.

"Do tell, Dr. Wind, I love reading and watching movies about curses. I've never heard of the Lake Pachooee one though," Sam said, rearranging some supplies in a cabinet and turning back around.

"Curses aren't real. I don't know why people believe in such nonsense," Mom said, rolling her eyes. "There has to be a logical explanation to what's going on with my Charlie."

Dr. Wind looked into my eyes without responding to my mom, and I felt as if he knew why I wasn't in a rush to disclose what I'd done. "The curse started over a hundred years ago between two feuding Native American tribes, the Wunni and Hakipaho people, who lived North and South of Lake Pachooee," he shared. "One late evening, a young Wunni girl was washing clothes in the lake and decided to take a swim. As she was emerging from the water, she caught a young Hakipaho boy spying on her. She started screaming as she swam back towards the bank."

He paused and continued to fix his eyes on mine. "The boy then ran over and jumped into the water in order to quiet her down. Before he knew what he had done, her half-dressed body was floating in the black water. He stole her silver and turquoise, double-wrapped bangle from her limp wrist and ran off."

"Who found the Wunni girl?" Sam asked.

"The late girl's grandmom. She asked the water to gift her the vision of how her granddaughter died. The grandmom summoned the *Pachooee*, a vindictive water spirit to wake up. The *Pachooee* resembled a twenty-foot royal blue serpent with glowing, canary-colored eyes. Slimy spikes protruded from her iridescent algae mane."

"Seriously, an angry serpent creature in a lake? This sounds a bit much and ridiculous. You really believe in this stuff, Dr. Wind, someone with your prestigious background?" Mom replied, laughing under her breath.

My palms started sweating more and my heart sped up. I didn't want anyone to find out who I used to be.

Folding his arms across his chest, he raised his voice. "It may sound that way to you, Ms. Franklin. If you only see what you think is real in this world you live in, then you're blind. Other worlds exist beyond ours. I've seen the *Pachooee* once, when I was in junior high. I know what she's capable of firsthand."

Mom's laughing stopped, and she lowered her head.

"You think you know who I am. I may look like you, but I'm half Hakipaho. I grew up with my elders telling me all kinds of stories about the *Pachooee*. They warned me to stay far away from Lake Pachooee to avoid becoming another victim of its curse since I carried the Hakipaho bloodline."

Dr. Wind rolled up his scrub sleeve and pointed at his tattoo—a ruby lassoed serpent. "This symbolizes my Hakipaho heritage. Wunni people showcase a golden, un-lassoed serpent on the side of their neck," he said.

Mom's head remained down.

"Please finish, Dr. Wind," Sam pleaded.

Unfolding his arms and dropping them to his side, he continued, "The grandmom begged *Pachooee* to use its resources to curse those who committed irreversible crimes. She wanted the cursed to experience pain like her granddaughter had suffered before her life was taken. The lake became more than a body of water. From that day onwards, it could sense any bad person."

"Did the grandmom ever find the boy?" Sam asked.

"Yes, and she lured him back to the lake with golden coins sprinkled in the woods on a path he traveled frequently and left something floating in the middle of the lake for him to seek. The boy swam out to the lake to grab the bag. He swallowed some of the water that contained the cursed *Pachooee* eggs, the same eggs that are probably dwelling inside of Charlie's mouth now," Dr. Wind said.

"So, baby *Pachooees* are cursed parasites?" Sam asked with her eyes locked on Mom and Dr. Wind.

Nodding, he said, "Exactly, a *Pachooee* can hibernate inside its victim's mouth and exude a numbing secretion to not be detected until it's ready to wake up. It's about the size of a pinhead and can grow to its maximum size in as little as a few hours and cause excruciating pain—even death."

Mom opened the rose gold locket I brought her a few Christmases ago, which had a photo of her holding me after I was born and a current photo of me holding her after Dad's funeral. Wiping a tear from her eye before it landed inside, she slammed it shut and stared up at me before turning around to look out the window behind her.

I watched her and thought how these could be my last memories of her as my lips quivered.

"So, what happened to the Hakipaho boy?" Sam asked.

"He died the next night from a massive heart attack," Dr. Wind said.

"Charlie, if any of this curse stuff is remotely true, then what in the hell did you do that night with those horrible boys for this so-called *Pachooee* to curse you?" Mom asked, tears streaking down her face.

I closed my eyes to review my last few years in high school and that night at the lake. I knew the answer to her question, and it had nothing to do with Joey or Oscar hurting others. It only had to do with me. I was the guilty one. If this curse was real, then whatever was pulsating under and around my gums was growing every second.

My head started pounding, and my heart started pumping faster. This was my payback for what I'd done. My punishment was being served in real time. There's no sense in me trying to keep my secret buried— someone would've eventually exhumed all of my sins. I needed to come clean and share my dirty little confession, while I still had some time left.

I was inducted into the **WBWH**, *Wild Boys of WestFalls High*, my sophomore year. It was like a secret high school fraternity—we all had code names based on our favorite movie characters. We were all good looking and Greek Gods in and out of the classroom. Most of the teachers at WestFalls High worshipped us—if we wanted a test on a different day, then it was done.

We did awful things to a lot of girls at WestFalls High, especially the freshmen because we could. They didn't deserve any of it, but back then I didn't care. They were the ones left with permanent reminders. We assigned them code names based on video games and kept tally of each one we slept with. When we thought a girl would resist, we made sure she was relaxed with a special drink.

Each week we met up to see who had the most names in our **WBWH** book. At the end of the month, the guys with the highest numbers would have their names thrown in the **WBWH** lottery pot, which was a combination of money, alcohol, gift cards, concert tickets, and jewelry. The lucky guy took home the winnings until the next drawing. I'd won three lotteries.

Joey's younger sister, Nodin, was written in the book under my alias. He must've found out somehow. He wasn't even a member of **WBWH**. After hearing Dr. Wind's story about the curse, it all made sense to me now and why Joey only dared me to swim in Lake Pachooee.

The viper-looking tat on his neck triggered my memory—he's a Wunni. Joey knew about the *Pachooee* curse and wanted to make sure it was introduced to me that night. Well played, Joey. No reason for me to be mad at him. I deserved it.

I just didn't want my mom to find out what I'd been doing or who I was back then. I dropped out of **WBWH** a few months ago, after Catori Love found out about our games off the field. She'd told **WBWH**'s leader, Nick Stryker, she was taking it to Principal Ordones.

Nodin found Catori's lifeless body the next morning, swinging from a bloody rope in an oak tree outside the football field. She ended up being sent to an inpatient psychiatric hospital for a while. I'd forgotten that they were good friends, which was Joey's second reason to give me the gift of the *Pachooee*.

Catori's death was later ruled a suicide by the local police, but I knew it wasn't and so did **WBWH**. Even though I wasn't there that night when Nick and a few others made sure Catori would never tell, I knew about it. I didn't go to the police. The **WBWH** brotherhood promise—to be loyal and to protect each other at all costs, regardless of what the consequence was for somebody else—meant more to me back then.

My loyalty gave me nightmares, where I would see Catori swaying in that tree with the noose squeezing her neck. She would talk to me while stretching out her blood-stained hands towards me. I never could understand her silent words. Catori was on my mind last night before the pain started.

Listen, I was trying to become a better person, but I may have waited too late. I chose to be in **WBWH**—no one forced me to be part of the pack. Looking back now, none of it was worth it. I wished I'd never joined. My mouth throbbed worse than before. I didn't want to and couldn't answer Mom.

Staring into my eyes, I felt as if Dr. Wind heard all my thoughts about my **WBWH** crimes. "Ms. Franklin, you two can discuss that matter another time. I really need Charlie's blood pressure to not rise any more than it already has," he pleaded. "I need to perform the procedure as soon as possible. The lidocaine should be good now." He adjusted the light above me and bent down closer to my opened mouth.

Dr. Wind made a small incision in my gum with the scalpel. He shouted, "What in the Sam Hill, Charlie boy! You must've had a really pregnant female enter your mouth. Your gums are infested with her eggs. I have good and bad news," he said, after being in my mouth for almost thirty minutes.

"Good news first then the bad," Mom said, clearing her throat.

"I was able to extract the female, and she's in here," he said, holding up a sealed dark plastic container. He handed it over to Sam and looked at Mom.

"Okay, bad news next?" Mom asked, staring into Dr. Wind's eyes.

"All of Charlie's teeth will need to be extracted right away. Charlie will be asleep of course. I'm going to have to dig all these eggs out, one by one. She laid them under his roots. If I don't, then they'll hatch and flow into his bloodstream straight to his heart until he takes his last breath," Dr. Wind gasped.

"Just do the damn procedure, right now!" my mom screamed, stomping her feet.

"Sam, prepare the surgery room," he dictated in a stern tone.

She flew out of the room.

"Charlie, the *Pachooee* is notorious about spreading havoc in other ways, such as harming those you care for, if given the opportunity. Did you come in contact with anybody else that night?" Dr. Wind asked.

"What do you mean?" I said, in a gurgled tone.

"A pregnant female could transmit via bodily fluids, if she emitted eggs prematurely, such as through kissing," Dr. Wind murmured, looking over his shoulder at my mom.

I paused for almost a minute.

Barely raising my head, I mumbled, "I did hang out with Justine, my girlfriend, for a bit and then went on home."

"Ms. Franklin, you're going to need to call Justine's parents for me, so I can explain the situation to them. Not sure if they'll believe everything I'm going to tell them." Dr. Wind sighed.

"She could be infected, too?" Mom asked in a shaky voice.

"Probably not, but I hope her parents allow me to examine her to rule out my suspicions," Dr. Wind said, adjusting his mask.

"Did you do anything else that you can recall when you came home that night?" Dr. Wind questioned.

"That's about it... Oh, I was starving after Justine's. I went straight to the kitchen to eat snicker doodle cookies and guzzled down some milk from the carton. I went to bed after, around one."

"Dr. Wind, I did have a glass of milk from the same carton Charlie drank out of, which I've scolded him time and time again not to do, around five this morning to calm my stomach... You don't think I could be infected, too, right?" Mom asked with rapid blinking eyes.

"Ms. Franklin, you had no direct contact with Charlie. I'm sure you're just fine," Dr. Wind said as he stood to help me up from the chair.

"Ouch!" Mom yelled as she inserted her finger inside her mouth. "I just felt something sharp graze over my tongue."

Dr. Wind looked at me with wide eyes.

THE END

A little extra from the author...

Charlie ingested two *Pachooee* parasites when he went swimming that night in Lake Pachooee —one was pregnant and ended up laying her entire brood inside his mouth, while the other one ended up inside the milk carton—and slipped into a temporary hibernation state from the cold temperature of the fridge—from his backwash. His mom later poured it into a glass and ingested it. Hers was dormant during its growth cycle for a while—until it woke up just before Charlie's emergency surgery in Dr. Wind's office.

Austin's inspiration—A recent dental visit; the Spur Posse of Lakewood, California; and a parasite called *Cymothoa exigua* that "severs the blood vessels in a fish's tongue, causing the tongue to fall off. It then attaches itself to the remaining stub of the tongue and becomes the fish's new tongue." Source: Wikipedia

Theme Song: "Voices Carry"
Artist: 'Til Tuesday

DARLA

Some will probably ask, "What did your brother, J. R. Hightower, do to deserve what happened to him?"

I'll tell you. He should've begged more before his finale, and the curtains closed.

One night, as I was searching for one of my favorite blankets in a hall closet, I reached up to the top shelf. Without knowing it, I pressed a button, and a secret door opened up.

A steep, metal stairway introduced itself to me as a cold draft slapped me in the face and ran her icy fingers through my natural, braided hair. She crawled into my ear and whispered, "Come, and you'll understand." My knees started shaking.

I pulled a *Cobra Kai* printed blanket from the shelf and wrapped it around my shivering body. I paused for several seconds before grabbing the pulsating rail and descended below, one step at a time.

My breath drew icy, deformed figures in the air. As I reached up to touch them, each shattered and melted away. Tiny, murky yellow torchlights scantily dressed the cobwebbed walls.

Upon climbing down the last three steps, I saw J.R. and all what he had done. A pile of bones, almost touching the ceiling, attempted to conceal its creator. I sniffed a faint salty and charcoal-like odor in the air.

Looking down at the blood-stained concrete floor, I spied a shredded purple collar. The faded name printed on it was still readable—Darla, my cat, whom I'd rescued from an animal shelter three years ago.

Several stainless-steel, sharp tools hung on one wall where an examination table rested. "J.R., what have you done?" I yelled, pointing at his collection and holding Darla's collar in my trembling hand. "Where's Darla?" Tears flooded my eyes.

Jerking his body around and wiping his gloved hands onto his black apron, he glided towards me. He peeled his plastic face-shield backwards, resting it on the top of his head. "Little sis, you shouldn't be here," he said, pulling one glove off and chunking it to the floor. A thousand scratches tattooed his outer hand and halfway up his arm. "You were never supposed to know about any of this."

I stepped backwards and fell into the mountain of bones. I scanned the temporary grave. They were too small to be human—these were animal. My entire body started jerking, and I felt cold.

He knelt over me, slurring a few of his words, and said, "Now, listen up, I had to stop them."

"What? I don't understand," I cried out and hid my face in my hands.

Rocking back and forth on his knees he said, "The dreams... they always come to me and gather around the foot of my bed and cry. They won't stop coming, and they cry and cry... The perpetual scratches against the back of my headboard are the worse, almost every night, all night until six in the morning."

"Who's crying and scratching?" I asked with a deep frown.

"The kittens... the kittens I placed in a burlap bag, alive. I threw them in the lake when I was thirteen years old. One of them clawed me so bad that I had to constantly hide my right hand or wear a glove."

J.R. narrowed his eyes at me then tore them away.

"Those voices in my head told me to do it," he said as sweat skated down his face and drops plopped down onto my cheeks.

"Told you to do what?" My heart throbbed hard against my chest.

"To hunt them down, skin them, and harvest their bones... the kittens. Then, they would leave my dreams, but the voices lied. The kittens' cries aren't gone. They've been with me now for over five years."

"J.R., did you kill my baby, Darla?" My heart beat faster, as if trying to escape my chest.

He didn't say anything.

"Did you kill her?" I gazed into his still eyes.

Licking his lips with his pierced tongue, he gave me a wide grin. "Yes... her raw heart tasted the sweetest out of all of them. She was my last one, but now the voices are telling me that I have to finish you. They know you'll tell on all of us. We can't have that. The pain will only last for a little while, I promise." He stroked my hair with his weighted hand that reeked of decayed anchovies and catnip.

Reaching from his back pocket, he pulled out a long blade.

I fumbled, grabbing two jagged bones on the side of me. Before he could drive the blade down, I stabbed him on both sides of his jugular.

Blood gushed out like wild fireworks all over me. He gurgled and spouted, "Thanks, Indigo... I... won't... hear... the... cries... anymore."

"Yes, you will. I'll make sure of it for all eternity." I rolled over and stood up.

His eyes widened, and he tumbled to the ground.

I tore a long strip of the blanket and wrapped his wounds tight, just to stop the bleeding enough to finish what I needed to do. I ran up the stairs to gather supplies. I placed a candle on the ground and lit it with a match.

Slicing his abdomen down the middle with his blade, I pulled his flesh back. He screamed so loud that a few of his tools slid down the walls. I entombed Darla's collar and several bones under his liver and saucy intestines. I sewed him up with a large fishhook-like needle and cloth string. I poured hot candle wax down his fresh incision.

Dabbing my finger in his seeping blood, I wrote a message on a sheet of paper: *Darla and friends, haunt J.R.'s rotting flesh and dead bones, forevermore!* Then, I balled it up and stuffed into his mouth. I pinned his lips together with large sewing pins and painted his mouth with fire ash.

Unwrapping the bandage from his neck, I finished watching him bleed out. Before he took his final breath, my nails on my right hand retracted, and curvy, crimson claws with snow-white tips extended from my fingers. I carved out his charcoaled heart and hurled it onto the ground. I slammed my shoe down hard until I saw all of his bloody remains squish out. My oval pupils transformed into neon green vertical glowing slits.

I waved my hands over the bones and J.R.'s body. They all floated up in the air in a speedy, circular motion for a minute. Clapping my hands together, they disintegrated and flew down inside the open glass jar. I screwed the lid on firmly and tied a white ribbon, drenched in his blood, around it.

Traveling in darkness, under the candlelight of the oxblood full moon, towards the lake, Darla's floating and translucent body found the perfect place to bury the jar. As I wandered away, I turned around and purred in the howling winds, "J.R., I always heard those cries and scratches... I just didn't know you were a monster, too."

THE END

Theme Song: "Superman (It's Not Easy)"
Artist: Five for Fighting

WAKE

What a cruel and disrespectful teen girl! That's probably what you'll think in the beginning. Go ahead and judge me, but I bet you'll think differently in the end.

My name is Judee Lee Tucker.

Lucille Night, my great-aunt died twenty-four hours ago, ruined what would've been the best weekend of the year—my thirteenth birthday celebration.

Six weeks ago, I won a school contest where I scored two all-access passes with photo-ops of choice for *Garga-Con*, the biggest comic convention in Texas. This was the year I thought I'd finally be able to meet Henry Cavill, a.k.a. Superman, my favorite superhero, with my bestie, Sadie Banks.

On Thursday morning, I decided to break the bad news to Sadie before class. She was sitting on the steps near the library, reading *Superman Vol 5: Under Fire* by Scott Lobdell. I took a few deep breaths as I approached her to sit down while slipping my fuchsia and black *Smallville* backpack off my left shoulder.

Sadie placed her book facedown next to her.

"I'm so excited about Saturday. We're going to make the most epic memories!" she shouted, tapping her feet in a rapid, rhythmic beat on the cement and whistling the *Superman* theme song.

Lowering my head, I said, "Yeah, about that. We need to talk."

"Why?" She clutched the top of her backpack and stopped.

Staring down at the cracked pavement for a few seconds before looking into her eyes, I mumbled, "Something happened."

"What... are you okay?"

Sadie's eyes didn't move until I shared why I had to bail on her.

"I'm fine. It's just my great-aunt died, and my mom is making me attend the funeral, which happens to be this Saturday."

"Oh... Sorry about your aunt." She bowed her head.

"Just hate that I won't be attending the con with you and meeting you know who."

"I understand, Judee," she said, releasing a long sigh.

Leaning in closer to her, I asked, "Hey, you're still going to have an awesome time and post pics, right, Sadie?"

"No, it won't be the same without you. I'm not going."

"You have to! When will you get another chance to meet Superman?"

"Never, but if you're not there, what's the use?" Her entire body bent over like a wilted flower.

"So, you're going to let the tickets just go to waste?" I screamed. Other kids stared in our direction, but I didn't care.

Sadie shrugged, dropped her book inside her backpack, stood up, and said, "I guess."

"Seriously, Sadie. You gotta be kidding me."

"Nope. Just wouldn't be right going without you." She started to trudge away.

I grabbed her arm. "Hey, would you just go for me?"

Her eyes focused on the ground for a minute before she looked into my eyes. "I don't know, Judee."

"Think about it," I pleaded, wanting one of us to enjoy our big chance. "Okay."

We went opposite directions. I watched Sadie head to her science lab, and I shuffled off to my computer class.

During our lunch hour, over a hot dog and cheesy fries, I finally convinced Sadie to attend and take her younger brother. She promised to take a photo of Henry by himself and get his autograph for me.

My mom contacted the school office later that day to share I would be out of school on Friday, due to the funeral services.

I tried to focus on my classes all day, but couldn't. Instead, I daydreamed of Superman's eyes locked on just mine out of everyone in the crazy crowd, as he levitated several feet in the air in his lit suit. Before his boots touched the main stage's floor, I noticed a huge Kryptonian bouquet of plum, turquoise, and tangerine Surrum Blossoms—singing flowers. A few Oregus flowers with golden, glittery tips were mixed in.

He flew down to my height. Then, he handed me his gift with a light kiss on my right cheek.

Dinner was super quiet the night before the trip. I rolled my peas around my mashed potatoes with my fork and stared down at the pile of food.

"Can I be excused?" I asked, refusing to meet my mom's eyes.

"You haven't eaten two bites off your plate. Judee, I know that you're upset," my mom said.

"Not hungry, and I really need to get some reading done for my history class before Monday."

"Okay, go ahead." Mom inhaled and pressed the glass of red wine against her chapped lips.

Grabbing my plate off the table, I scraped the food in the trash and washed my dishes.

Before I left the kitchen, Mom said, "Judee, you know that family comes first."

I jerked my body around to face her. "Why do I have to go to this stupid funeral, anyhow? I only met Aunt Lucille a few times. She always gave me the creeps," I barked. Her onyx, beady eyes seemed to follow me around like a venomous snake hunting for its next meal.

"First of all, you're being very disrespectful. Second, you're going to pay your respects, young lady, and that's final. Make sure you're ready to go by 8:30 in the morning—it's about a seven-hour drive."

Rolling my eyes with a deep sigh, I blurted out, "Don't worry, I'll be ready. Will Dad be there?"

"I doubt it. He never gave my family a chance."

"Can't blame him on that, and Dad wouldn't force me to go, if he was still living here," I grumbled under my breath.

"Excuse me, what did you say?" Mom asked, squinting her eyes at me and slamming her glass down on the table, causing all the dishes to rattle.

Grinding my teeth, I said, "Nothing."

I stomped off to my bedroom, slammed the door, and slid down the wall to sit on the floor facing my bed. A white eleven-by-seventeen box with a loose-tied pink bow rested in the middle of my bed. I crawled over to pick it up. My orange-and-black polka dot nail slid under both sides of the box and sliced the tape. The cardboard cover fell off, and I peeled back the tissue papers.

Once I uncovered it, I gasped. I then noticed a small card underneath, which read:

I know it won't make up for you missing the con, but thought it might help a little. Happy birthday, Buttercup.

Love Dad.

It was a genuine Superman cape. I pulled it out of the box and flung it around my shoulders. Kal-El would be very proud of this glistening Superman logo on the back. Standing in front of the mirror across the room, I saw it perfectly fit me, not too long or short. It barely touched the top of my ankles. I spun around and around until I collapsed to the floor and giggled to myself.

I grabbed my cell to text Dad.

Me: I love it. thank u so much! I wish u were here

After fifteen minutes, he responded.

D: Hey there, Buttercup! Glad you like your gift.

Me: will u be at Aunt Lucille's funeral on Saturday?

D: No

Me: why?

D: Long story. Sorry about you not being able to attend the con.

Me: ur the only 1. Mom only cares about the funeral, not my feelings

D: She cares—just hard for her to show, sometimes.

Me: no kidding!!

D: Hey, what if I make it up to you?

Me: what do u mean?

D: I've been researching some cons and found a few where Henry Cavill will be making an appearance in a few months.

Me: really?

D: Absolutely, my treat!

Me: ur the best! luv u

D: Love you too. Get some sleep. Long drive to your aunt's place tomorrow.

Me: don't remind me. goodnight

I packed my suitcase with my toothbrush, toothpaste, socks, tennis shoes, pjs, jeans, Superman T-shirts, and a black dress with matching flats. I folded my cape and placed it on top before zipping it up.

The alarm on my phone went off at seven-fifteen. I snoozed it just once before I got dressed. I opened the front door and carried my stuff out to the car.

Upon re-entering the house through the front door, I saw Mom at the kitchen table.

"Want some cereal?" she asked, pouring milk in her bowl.

"I'm good. Ready?" I snatched a protein bar out of the cabinet and a bottle of grape juice from the fridge.

"It's not even eight-thirty yet," she said as she crunched down on the cereal.

Throwing my empty hand up in the air, I shouted, "The earlier we can get on the road, Hillary, the better, right?"

"Let's talk, Judee." Mom stopped eating. "Please address me correctly or not at all."

"You know, I'm just going to grab my phone and wait for you in the car." I jammed my hands in my front pockets and started heading back to my room.

"Look, I'm doing my best here. It hasn't been easy at all for me. I've been working late shifts at Rolling Hills Healthcare and Rehabilitations Center. I used up all of my vacation time for meetings with my lawyer and court. I know you think your dad is a hero, but he's not even close."

I stared at her for a minute then retreated into my room to grab my phone, charger, and earbuds.

"See you outside, Mom." Tears filled my eyes. I went to the car, wiping my face with the back of my sleeve.

After a few minutes, Mom came out of the house and locked the door.

"Sorry I unloaded on you back there. I shouldn't have said that about your dad," Mom said as she slid into the car.

I placed my earbuds inside my ears and scrolled down to my New

Kids on the Block, Lizzo, and Pink mix playlist on my phone.

Mom reached over and jerked out one of my earbuds.

"Didn't you hear me?" Mom asked with a huge scowl on her face.

"Yeah, I heard you. Let's go already."

I replaced the dangling earbud in my ear and texted Sadie as Mom backed the car out of the driveway.

> Me: u at school?
> S: yes. u on the road?
> Me: yep, lucky me
> S: hope funeral goes ok
> Me: rather be there with Henry and u, tomorrow
> S: I don't have 2 go
> Me: Sadie, u gotta go for both of us. Anyhow, I talked 2 my dad last night and he plans to take me to another con soon.
> S: that's great news!
> Me: u have a blast and post pics, ok? talk more later
> S: k

The hours drifted by. We stopped to get gas twice and at a restaurant to eat a late lunch. The conversation was minimal.

We were almost thirty minutes out from late Aunt Lucille's place when I turned down the volume and asked, "Why isn't Dad coming down for the funeral?"

"It's just best this way."

"Mom, it's been almost three months since you and Dad divorced."

"Judee, please, there's just a lot of things you don't know, and I plan to keep it that way. Drop it. By the way, I'll be glad when your dad starts buying you more mature birthday gifts."

"Whatever! I know your family never liked Dad because..."

"Say it," she shrieked, squeezing the steering wheel tight. I could see a few fingerprints on the soft leather whenever she moved her hand out of the way.

Pulling one bud out, I said, "You know why. I don't need to spell it out for you. I've been dealing with kids snickering behind my back at school and making jokes of how I look since first grade. First, it was the nasty comments from the kids at school about my curly hair and how lucky I am to have a suntan year-round. Some of your family has even said similar things to me, sometimes meaner. You know deep down inside that they're repulsed that you married Dad, and then you had me. They destroyed us, not Dad!"

"Judee..."

"Don't pretend Mom, you know I'm right." Tears streamed down my face as I turned the volume up.

Mom shook her head. She went to touch my hand. I moved it, and leaned my body against the door, staring out the window.

We didn't speak any more on the trip.

Aunt Lucille's house rested on top of a hill. Tall, twisty trees encircled it, casting a darkness over it. Her house reminded me of the one in that old *Psycho* movie—my dad loved to watch it every Halloween, and I would watch with him. It was Victorian style minus the *Bates Motel* nearby.

I'd never noticed any flowers growing around the house or near it. Come to think of it, whenever we had visited, there were always these huge biting horseflies inside the house. Her house always reeked of mothballs and burnt cabbage. I swear she kept a box in every room, even under the stairs outside.

Mom parked. There were more than a dozen cars wrapped around the side of the house. We started up the creaky wooden stairs. A cockroach, almost the size of my hand, raced down the metal-sided rail. I cringed and jerked my hand back in the nick of time.

"Why are there so many cars, here?" I asked.

"Oh, I forgot to tell you. Aunt Lucille's wake is at seven tonight."

I stopped on the third step and asked, "A wake, what's that?"

"It's when the close family comes together to view the body," Mom explained.

"Like view the dead body where?" I could feel my heartbeat revving up.

"In Aunt Lucille's house, silly girl."

"Mom, you're telling me that there's a coffin inside with her dead body?"

"Yes, it's an old family tradition. Aunt Lucille always wanted to have a wake in her home. The funeral home will reclaim her body from here tomorrow morning. Her graveside service will then be held late Saturday morning."

I took a few deep breaths as sweat sprinted down my forehead.

Mom patted me on my shoulder and went ahead in front of me up the stairs. "There's nothing to be afraid of. You're safe here. It's not like she's going to get up and bother you tonight." She laughed.

My eyes expanded. I paused for a few seconds. "I'm going to go ahead and get our bags out of the car."

"Okay, don't take too long. There are a few relatives I want to introduce you to. I believe Beaver will be around."

I hadn't seen my cousin Beaver since two summers ago. Beaver was shorter than me and chubby with braces and eyeglasses, which resembled the bifocals old people wear. We were the same age.

He loved to collect weird insects in glass vessels and kept them in his basement lab. Whenever we had to visit Aunt Lucille, he made me feel comfortable with no judgments. He was different, in a good way. Beaver always made my visits way more interesting and less creepy.

Opening up the back car door to grab the bags, I slipped my mom's oversized tote bag, which felt like she had packed a couple of bricks inside, over my shoulder. I stumbled backwards and regained my balance. Then, I pulled the handle of my suitcase. Before it dropped to the ground, I heard someone call my name. Heavy footsteps came up behind me.

"Hey, Judee! What's up, girl?"

Blinking my eyes a few times, I refocused. It was Beaver, and he must've morphed into a different boy. He was a few inches taller than me and slimmer, without any metal or thick eyeglasses. His hazel eyes seemed to sparkle, and his voice seemed deeper, too. My mom's bag slid off my arm, and my suitcase fell over as soon as I let go of the handle.

He came up and swung his muscular arms around to hug me. I didn't smell the familiar old dirt or a cesspool on him, instead a scent of warm pumpkin spice and fresh pine saturated his skin and Einstein T-shirt.

I pushed him away and stepped back. "Whoa, what happened to you?"

"What?" He picked up both bags like he was picking up two pillows and tossed them over his shoulders.

"You know what I'm talking about, Beaver." I placed both hands on my hips.

"Umm, I guess Connie Bosak." He wiggled his eyebrows, followed by a huge smile. "You like?"

"She must be something special," I said, smiling.

"You could say that..."

"So, you're attending the funeral tomorrow, too?" I asked.

"Yep... my mom is making me go."

"We got that in common."

Beaver nodded in agreement. We made our way through the dry grass towards the house.

"Happy birthday, Judee."

"Thanks. Had plans to meet Superman." I pressed my lips tight.

"Bummer, you have to be here." Beaver squeezed my shoulder with his warm hand.

"Tell me about it. I so didn't want to come here."

"If you want, we can hang out tomorrow evening," he said.

"Would like that. Maybe I'll get to meet the girl who changed Beaver." I snorted.

A huge grin appeared on his face.

We paused for a few seconds before we stepped over the threshold. A coldness climbed up my legs and arms. I jumped and bumped Beaver from behind.

"Judee, you okay?"

Bending over, I shook from my head to toe. "Yeah, I just felt something funny go over my entire body."

He stuttered his next words and blinked his eyes a couple of times, until I could understand what he was trying to say. After taking a few deep breaths, he whispered, glancing over his shoulders and back at me, "She did it."

Glowering at him, I stood back up to face him, "Whom are you referring to?"

"You know who." His eyes twitched.

"Aunt Lucille?" I twisted my mouth.

"Yes, her."

"Whatever, it was probably just a draft."

"Sure... that's all it was, a draft." Beaver arched his eyebrows and strolled towards the kitchen.

The wood floors made loud popping sounds with every step we took.

A group of adults, mostly strangers, were gathered in the enormous, open kitchen. Mom looked up and pointed to her right down the long hall.

An ebony coffin was planted in the middle of the room, maybe a hundred feet from the bedroom I would be staying in.

Beaver leaned down next to my ear and mumbled, "That's her." He pointed his index finger at the coffin.

Rolling my eyes up to the ceiling, I said, "Who else would it be, Sherlock?"

We made our way into the bedroom where I would be staying. Beaver placed my mom's bag next to the door, tossed my bag near the bottom of the antique, four poster bed and sat on top of it.

"Hope you don't have to go the bathroom tonight," he said.

"Why?" I asked.

"You don't remember?"

I leaned against the tall dresser to face him. "No."

"There's only one bathroom on this floor, and it's through there." He pointed over to the coffin.

"So? I'm not scared." I slid my trembling hands inside my pockets.

"You should be. Look down."

When I did, I saw several deep scratches embedded in the floor.

"Big deal." I shrugged my shoulders.

Beaver kicked his shoes off, jumped on the bed, cupped his hands behind his head, and stared up at the ceiling for about a minute without speaking a word. He then turned toward me and whispered, "Wanna know how the scratches got there, and why they're all over the house? I bet you never noticed that before."

I flopped down on the bed next to him with my legs crossed and begged, "Please, spill it."

He turned his head to face me, "Don't wanna freak you out... You gotta stay here tonight."

"Just tell me. You're not gonna freak me out." Sweat pooled down my lower back.

"Well, Aunt Lucille was a *bruja,* or witch, and I heard she was no Samantha Stephens from that old *Bewitched* show my mom makes me watch with her. She had these super long toenails, she refused to cut them, and she wore special shoes when she had to leave her house. Her toenails would claw the ground every step she took and made an awful sound like someone dragging Freddy Krueger nails down a wet chalkboard during the day. At night, when no one was around, she would float inside her house, practicing spooky magic spells."

"Okay, you know your story sounds crazy, right? Plus, how do you know all of this?"

"My grams told me about her, and how her younger brother saw her floating in the air one night."

"I don't believe it. Just some stupid story." I swallowed a big gulp of air.

"Judee, you might think different in the morning, if she doesn't drag you inside her coffin tonight." Beaver's bulging eyes locked on mine.

Scanning the room, I replied, "Yeah... right... *Bruja*, if you're real, then prove it."

"Wow, you're braver than I'll ever be," Beaver said. "I would never say that out loud. You just invited her to come out."

"You're nuts! I don't believe any of this." I was biting my lower lip.

"Guess you'll just have to find out on your own."

My mom entered the room. "Dinner time. Come on, you two, five minutes."

Before she exited the room, she turned around and asked, "What were y'all talking about?" She picked up her bag from against the door.

"Nothing," Beaver blurted out.

We both hopped down from the bed. He went ahead of me.

Beaver turned around. "Whatever you do, don't go to the bathroom after three in the morning. She likes to roam around the house about that time, especially in there." He glanced down the hall towards the coffin.

I patted the side of his face with my hand and said, "Whatever, Beaver."

He placed his hands on my shoulders and muttered, "You'll see."

I slid out of his grasp. I tried to dismiss his nonsense, but I couldn't completely.

Several family members were present for dinner. Mom introduced me to second and third cousins who didn't mean anything to me. We all ate, and I drank four glasses of raspberry punch. Beaver stared at me a few times and shook his head.

Everyone left soon, after viewing Aunt Lucille's body—an invitation I skipped.

It was almost nine and the sun was fading. I opened the door to my room and tiptoed all the way from the bedroom to the bathroom, passing you know what, to take a quick shower and brush my teeth.

The coffin remained in its same location as I tiptoed back. Halfway to my room, I peeped over my shoulder, and it was still there.

When I opened the door to my room, someone came up behind me and touched the back of my neck with a cold hand. I jumped. It was Mom.

"Judee, you okay?" she asked, staring into my eyes.

"Of course, why wouldn't I be?" I said as my eyes jittered around.

"You look nervous."

Faking a yawn and stretching my arms up, I said, "I'm fine, just tired, that's all."

"Well, good night."

"Night." I shut the door behind me. I spotted a lock above the doorknob and turned it until I heard a click. I vaulted into bed and pulled the covers over my head.

A few hours passed. I woke up and checked my phone. It was almost 3:30. I tossed and turned a few times, my bladder aching. Almost forty-five minutes had passed, and I knew I couldn't hold it until the sun came up. The bathroom called my name, so I slid on some fuzzy orange socks and put my cape on.

Unlocking the door, I crept down the middle of the hallway. A bright beam of moonlight illuminated my path. I looked at the coffin. It was the same as before. I took a few deep breaths, counted to ten backwards, and darted past the coffin into the bathroom. Once I flipped the lights on, I slammed the door, locked it, and did what I needed to do.

When I opened the door, I looked out and noticed the coffin had moved from its center placement, and its lid had opened up a few inches. I thought... *did I bump it somehow, maybe... nope, I didn't. How did it open? No time to play Nancy Drew, Judee.*

I dashed from the bathroom and slid in my socks across the floor to the open bedroom door with my cape flying upwards. I closed and locked the door. Leaping into bed, my cape wrapped around me by itself, and I fell into a deep sleep in no time.

My alarm went off at seven-thirty, an hour before the arrival of the hearse to retrieve the coffin from the house. The sunlight peeked through the half open curtain. I tossed the covers off.

Placing my feet down on the bare floor, I felt something cold and sharp pierce the center of my foot. I jerked my bleeding foot up and covered my mouth with both hands to silence my scream. My eyes rounded as I glanced down, and I lowered myself to the floor onto my wobbly knees. The cape billowed out around me in slow, rolling waves.

A ten-inch long, curled-up black toenail with razor-sharp edges rested in front of me. I examined it closer. Beaver was telling me the truth about her after all. Swiping the nail over to the side with my hand, I noticed something written on the dusty floor in backward smoking, squiggly letters, which read:

I ALMOST ATE YOU BEFORE DAWN...
LUCKY, LUCKY GIRL... WITH THE RED CAPE...

THE END

Theme Song: "Jealous"
Artist: Ingrid Michaelson

PLUCKED

You don't see me.

Yet, I see you.

Melted chocolate chip morsels, peppermint, and root beer lollipops ooze from your perfect pores.

I can smell you six feet away.

For 237 days, I followed you.

You didn't even notice me.

I'm a chameleon who blends in anywhere.

A thicket of trees, loud football games, or crowded malls would surround me with their wings of protection.

I watched you each day as you gather in a huddle with those spiteful girlfriends who didn't deserve you.

You shouldn't waste your time with them.

The countdown started Monday until game night again, Friday.

My anticipation grows to see you perform your incredible double round offs and standing back tucks.

That purple and gold skirt seemed as if Botticelli painted it on your 5-foot-1-inch frame.

I waited until I knew it was just right to introduce myself to you, when no one was around to interfere.

Your scent was off tonight, not your usual.

Hmm, you're going to make me guess, aren't you?

I leaned back on the hood of my Mercedes SUV in the ebony distance under the full moonlight.

Inhaling deeply, I dissected your scents—beef jerky, methanol, ammonia, nicotine, and warm beer from your chilled lips.

Who touched and kissed you?

My nails dug into my palms.

I noticed crimson droplets splatter onto my car.

A water bottle rested in my seat. I grabbed it, unscrewed the lid, and poured it inside my hand.

I dressed my wound with ointment and a bandage from the first-aid kit in my glove compartment.

The wolf drove you home in his dated Porsche.

Of course, I followed you both, staying a few car lengths behind.

He parked in front of your house. I did the same, two houses down.

I saw him pull you closer to contaminate you again with his sickening poisons and unruly hands.

My steering wheel squealed as I squeezed it with my hands, wishing it was him instead.

After several minutes, he finally released you.

You jumped out, grabbed your poms-poms from the backseat, and scurried away from his car.

He drove off before you even reached your door. He didn't deserve you, either.

This is exactly why I must introduce myself to you before dawn.

11:45PM...
1:30AM...

Now, it's time.

I slipped latex gloves over each hand, folded a large duffle bag under my arms, and maneuvered my way around to your back window.

You should've closed and locked your window, but you didn't.

Thank you.

As I stared down at you sleeping like Snow White in the fairytale with sheer baby pink sheets draped over your *Jem* pajamas, I knew you would be mine forever.

I would be your true Prince Charming like no other.

Kneeling down next to your face, I sniffed your hair and those toxins had disappeared from earlier.

I snipped a lock of your hair with a pocketknife, stuffed it in my back pocket, and pulled out a syringe. I pressed it against your neck, where his claws once claimed.

By morning, I've removed your precious body gems, including the extraction of all your teeth.

A permanent home waited for you in my garden, so I lowered you down slowly.

Mounds of dirt devoured you.

A dead stag was placed on top and buried with you.

Belladonna and hemlock seeds showered your grave on Halloween Eve.

I took a long, hot shower, dressed, and sipped a pumpkin spice latte with extra whipped cream and mint chocolate sprinkles from my insulated mug.

Once I arrived at work, I reviewed some papers on the edge of the stage with my drink next to me.

Someone opened up the door, but I couldn't make out who it was, due to the intense glare of the sun.

The student ambled towards me and whispered in a soft, stuttering tone, "E-excuse me, Mr. Bardot," with a violin in her trembling hand.

I straightened my plaid bow tie as my finger grazed the folded lock of your hair tied with a red ribbon pinned in its back mid-section.

"Why, Miss Olivia, you haven't thrown in the towel after all," I said, staring into her dazzling, emerald eyes. "Are you ready to play Paganini's Caprice No. 24 again?"

"Yes, sir."

"Well, don't just stand there, please take the stage and begin."

My fingers tapped the rim of my cup to the swaying rhythms that echoed against the golden walls.

Traces of ripe raspberries and coconut sprinkles drowned my palate.

Without hesitation, my eyes froze on her.

THE END

Theme Song: "Torture"
Artist: The Jacksons

STILTS

There was a young girl named Eleanor Krinkletoe.

You could say she was a recluse by choice and a tad agoraphobic and very coulrophobic.

A therapist had diagnosed her when she was eleven years old, after Eleanor had told her how a clown had volunteered her for the dunking booth at a local fair in Bumblebee, Oregon. He laughed and laughed as he yanked her by her arms and shot a confetti gun in her face several times.

Eleanor had cried and tried to pry the heavy and hairy clown's hands from hers, but he wouldn't let her go. He'd placed his hands on his hips and with slurred speech, he said, "Stop being a sourpuss." He'd stooped over, tossed Eleanor over his shoulders, danced up the stairs, and strapped her in the seat. He'd sang out loud to the crowd. "Oh, little Miss Sour Puss, turn that frown upside down. We're all here to have fun, fun, fun! No Debbie Downers today, only happy times." He skipped down the stairs.

She moved to Whistle Moon, Texas, the year she entered high school and restarted her therapy.

Eleanor took her medications as prescribed, most of the time.

Whenever she skipped them, she swore she saw that clown climbing on her ceiling at nighttime and singing that awful song. It gave her insomnia. She told her parents and therapist, but they all dismissed her worries. Her therapist reminded her that visual and auditory hallucinations were known consequences of skipping her medications.

However, every year when her best friend, Tamera, asked her to attend the annual carnival, she declined.

One day in a therapy session, the carnival subject came up.

Her therapist, Ms. Berry, asked her why she avoided her friend's invitations, although she already knew why.

The therapist decided to try a new technique with Eleanor.

> *Session #27: Ms. Berry showed her a picture of a clown.*
> *Session #28: A stuffed clown was placed on the table in front of her.*
> *Session #29: Ms. Berry picked it up and held it in her hand.*
> *Session #30: Eleanor was asked to touch the stuffed clown where she felt most comfortable, so she touched its blue oversized shoe.*
> *Session #31: She was asked to pick it up and hold it for a minute, until a total of fifteen minutes was reached.*

Session #32: The stuffed clown sat next to her for the entire session.

Sessions #33-61: Eleanor was shown short videos of clown performances. Her vitals were monitored. They were high for the first fifteen minutes or so, and they slowly dropped to normal range. Her legs continued to shake off and on.

Ms. Berry collaborated with the circus owner to make a special arrangement on Wednesday night before the grand opening on Friday. She convinced Eleanor to attend the carnival with her to watch a circus show together. She explained to her that no other spectators would be present—just them.

Eleanor agreed with a long sigh. Her knees began to knock together as she exited her therapist's office on Monday.

Ms. Berry met Eleanor at the front gate. The owner gave them free range and returned to his office. He assured Ms. Berry that none of his staff would interfere. She promised Eleanor that she would be near her at all times. They explored the grounds and enjoyed cinnamon funnel cakes, corn dogs, and ice-cream before it was time for the special show.

A clown on stilts paraded inside the tent. He was dressed in a bright lime, puffy suit with pink, white, and yellow flower-shaped buttons in a row down his chest. He had ropy rainbow-colored hair. His sheet-white face was accented with black eyeliner painted under his eyes and large candy-apple red circles decorating his cheeks. His orange lips and red nose glistened.

Ms. Berry whispered, "He's walking towards you. Just remain calm and know he's friendly and won't hurt you. I'm right here. Remember, your breathing and tapping exercises."

Her heart felt like it was trying to claw its way out of her chest, and Eleanor's entire body felt heavy and stiff.

The clown walked closer and closer towards her on his wobbly stilts. He stood more than ten feet high.

Eleanor's legs began to tremble, and the metal bleachers made a loud, clanking sound.

Ms. Berry looked at her and shared, "You're doing great, Eleanor. I'm so proud of you. You've come so far in your therapy. I just need to observe your reactions from a distance, near the entrance. You're safe. Nothing is going to happen to you."

Eleanor exhaled deeply. "You promise?" Her words stumbled out as her wide eyes blinked uncontrollably.

"Absolutely, I'm just going to be right over there. Now, take in a deep breath for me and let it out. Again..." Ms. Berry instructed.

Eleanor completed her request.

Pointing near the open tent, Ms. Berry said, "After tonight, you'll be able to take Tamera up on her invitation, and come back this weekend, and have a great time together. I'm discharging you soon. This is your final test."

"Really?" Eleanor asked with a trembling smile.

Ms. Berry nodded and said, "If I sense you need me, then I'll return quickly. Deal?" She held her hand out.

Eleanor shook her hand. "Deal."

"At any time you feel overwhelmed, what's the safe word we practiced a few sessions back?" Ms. Berry asked.

"Firefly," Eleanor whispered.

"Good, I'll see you in no time," she said and headed to the observation area.

The clown was pretty close to her now. He had a high-pitch voice and spoke with a lisp that made her ears ring, "Hi there, my name is Stilts! I heard this is a therapy session. I'm going to make it unforgettable, just for you."

Eleanor's lips felt cold, as if the temperature had dropped thirty degrees.

He bent down, winked, and pulled out a blue and white polka dot balloon bouquet from behind his back. He held it to her face, pushing a button on one of the stems. A light mist blew over her face. She attempted to yell out 'firefly,' but she couldn't.

The clown waved and smiled at Ms. Berry and gave a thumbs up, mouthing, "She's doing great." He tapped a button on his collar. The song, "Send in the Clowns" by Judy Collins started playing from the surrounding speakers in the tent. He shook out his legs and did a sloppy version of the Charleston dance.

He twirled and danced around to face Ms. Berry. She clapped and smiled. He inserted a stick with rattlesnake rattlers glued on it inside his mouth. A dart flew in a twirly pattern in the air—blue smoke shot from behind it. Ms. Berry stopped clapping and attempted to run towards Eleanor. The dart struck her lower neck, and she dropped facedown, melting into a pile of fleshy Jell-O.

Eleanor's lips trembled as her tear-filled eyes remained on him. She attempted to scream. Nothing came out, only a low murmur.

He laughed and shouted, "Bingo, another dumb therapist down.

When will they ever learn?"

Stilts focused back on Eleanor. She tried to move, but couldn't. It was as if she was glued to her seat. Tears skated down her face. His hot breath carried saliva bullets that penetrated her jawline.

Near her ear, he whispered, looking around with his bug-eyed, bloodshot eyes, "You've had every reason to be afraid of us all these years. Miss Sour Puss from Bumblebee, right? I've been waiting for you to visit me for a long, long time. You should've kept taking your medicine. Nighty, night, Krinkletoe." He twirled his stick around his fingers like a baton.

Eleanor felt herself finally loosen in her seat. She punched him in the eye with her fist. He stumbled backwards and screamed out, "Ouch... that's going to leave a shiner."

His snake stick flew up in the air. Eleanor snatched it and blew one of his darts into his other eye. He hit the floor with an echoing thud. She jumped up and stood over him.

"Miss Sour Puss, I underestimated your capabil..."

He transformed into a massive pool of bubbly, slimy tar-like slush before he could finish the last word. Eleanor smashed the snake stick in half on her knee, tossed it over her shoulder, and strolled out of the flapping tent entrance, singing, "Send in the Clowns" as she traveled home in a zigzag pattern on her electric moped.

THE END

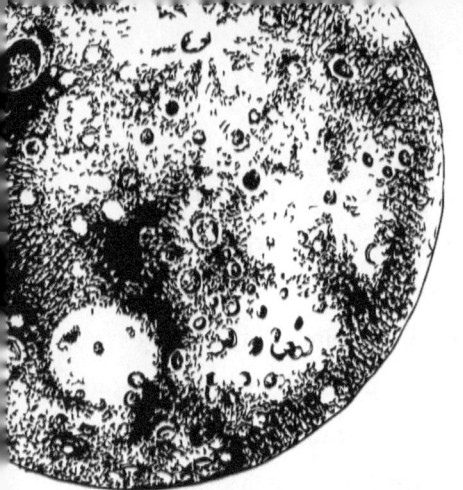

COOTIES FROM MERCURY

lithering, itsy-bitsy fiends crawled down Nathelee's parched throat, leaving a trail of bloody, yellow scales, and sucking out all of her oxygen until her lungs collapsed. She crumbled into a pile of fiery ashes.

Upon tumbling out of her vacant mouth, they stretched out their moth-eaten wings. The mighty winds escorted them fifteen miles to Nathelee's school, Gingersnaps Elementary, where a group of second graders were flying in swings and surfboarding down slides—the children's laughter ricocheted against the metal.

A thousand poisonous mini scarlet dart-shaped seeds fired out. They flew in and nested inside the little ones' eyes, noses, mouths, and ears.

Within ten minutes of lining up from recess and marching back to class, their legs locked, and they all fell down.

THE END

Theme Song: "Close Your Eyes"
Artist: Kim Petras

THE LATCH

A s Ruth Ann planted snapdragons in her grandmother's flowerbed, her gloved hand brushed over a jade metal box. She tried to dig around it with the hand trowel, but it remained stuck in its tight spot.

Focusing on the box, she began to dig the dirt from around it with her hands. It took several minutes until the box popped out of its fitted home onto Ruth Ann's lap. After she blew loose dirt from the top, some strange, shimmering Greek letters and Egyptian hieroglyphics appeared.

She recalled the summer after her sophomore year of high school when she'd spent half of her summer in Greece and Egypt with her aunt and cousins. Ruth Ann decoded eleven words and read them out loud: *Unleash us, and we promise to cure your grandmother's terminal illness…*

Exploring the box, she found a latch underneath. She turned it over, and her fingers commanded her to open it. Her grandmother stumbled out of the back door and shouted, "No, Ruth Ann! Stop!"

She jumped and tried to push the latch down, but it forced itself open. It made loud, hissing sounds followed by a thunderous growl. The box flew out of her hands. It levitated above her head, rotated on all its sides in the air for more than a minute, and vanished.

Her grandmother shuffled over to her. She placed her hand on her shoulder for support and dropped to the ground, one knee at a time. She stared into Ruth Ann's eyes with her wrinkled, watery eyes.

Lifting her tattered lace apron to her face to wipe it, she whimpered, "Typhon and Echidna, who were once buried, will be awakened. They won't cure me. This time, they'll wipe all of us out, permanently."

THE END

Theme Song: "Bust Your Windows"
Artist: Glee Cast Featuring Amber Riley

VERONICA'S FIRE

Music echoed down the hall as the bass pounded against my chest. Couldn't wait to meet you at the Lambda Chi Delta All Hallow Eve's Annual Party.

I'd given you my *irreplaceable gift* the weekend before. We'd been dating since our junior year in high school...

Arriving in my prettiest dress—off the shoulders—the retro cream one with tiny butterflies dotted along the waist and strappy red sandals. I clicked my heels twice and ran up the stairs to find you.

My heart started pounding harder and harder. I had to place both hands over it... Or it would've exploded into a gazillion pieces.

Standing there in the hallway, I watched you.

Your hands ran through her long, strawberry hair and down her thin spine.

A strand of hair soared under your nose, and you caught a whiff of her cheap, enchanted scent.

Opening your mouth, your lips drifted down to her plum painted and juicy lips.

I saw those unfaithful hands of yours keeping up with the rhythm of "Truth Hurts" by Lizzo—dancing over her gyrating hips.

After you tasted her flavors, you licked your cinnamon lips and spun around towards me. Your eyes captured mine, immediately.

You knew that I knew...

Falling back against the wall, my head started spinning, and I slid down in a zigzag motion.

A rainfall of tears gushed from my eyes, saturating my chest and dress.

You were motionless.

I stared down at the sterling silver *crescent moon* ring you'd given me last November.

You swore with that ring to be true and never dishonor me.

Why did you think I stayed with you that night?

Yet, you committed your cold-hearted and merciless crime against me, again.

Standing up, I walked towards you as our song, "Always in My Heart," by Tevin Campbell, played in the background.

I jerked the ring off my finger, and my heart's pounding slowed down, as if your torment spell had finally been lifted.

My locked shackles dropped off from around my bruised wrists.

The strange girl saw me and backed away from you with a red plastic cup in her hand.

Looking at me, you began to speak my name, "Veronica..."

An untrue apology was about to be vomited out of your lips with the lingering Corona scent of your hot breath swirling in the air.

Followed by several long blinks from your sparkling midnight blue, bedroom eyes.

My index finger pressed up against your lips while I dropped your ring in your open hand.

I turned around and headed out without looking back.

As I ran down the twenty-one cement steps, a tall guy was leaning against the brick wall and blowing a cloud of smoke from his cigarette up into the air.

Don't think I'd ever seen him before that crestfallen and crisp night.

Zipping away with wet mascara encircling my eyes, he pointed towards a row of field hockey sticks resting against the house.

How did he know about my catacombs of betrayal?

I belched out a shrieking whistle, and four of the hockey sticks lifted off the grass. They cartwheeled high up in the air above my head towards the tinted windows of your cranberry vintage Corvette.

Clapping my hands twice, your car burst in roaring flames.

A smile curled up on my face, as I clicked my heels and wandered into the yawning fog.

THE END

NAUGHTY OR NICE

All was never calm in my late Aunt Mavis's house at Christmastime. Cousin Devin Holt's black furtive eyes made extra sure of that with his undressing games. His octopus hands were an extra annual Christmas bonus for me each year.

So many fake people filled her house. The only good things that I looked forward to were Aunt Cat's delicious brownies, and her spooky stories from when she was younger. I wished that Aunt Cat could've been my mom instead of Karen the Scrooge, whose dark and cold heart would never change, even if she was visited by ghosts. It seemed I could never do anything that met her standards.

Criticism danced off her lips every time she spoke out loud about anyone, especially me, her primary target. My weight became the big issue when I didn't make the cheer team in fifth grade.

Ever since then, she'd attempted to control everything I ate. The holidays were the worst for me. If she ever caught me eating something off her approved list, then I would hear, "Drusella, now, you don't want to become a *Drusella-Puff* like my sister was around your age. You'll never get a nice-looking boyfriend." She poked me in my tummy with her finger, and a deep Joker-like laugh followed. She was only missing the green hair, milky-white face paint, and sinister smile.

I cannot count how many times I cried myself to sleep from Karen's cruel remarks about my body. My dad used to tell me that I was beautiful, and I didn't need to change anything unless I chose to, which really pissed her off. He's been gone for more than six months now.

Dad was called off for a classified military assignment in Afghanistan. I'd written him several letters, but no responses back yet. Karen told me that I was wasting my time because he'd forgotten about us. I didn't care what she said, I knew he loved me, and he'd answer me when he got the chance.

So, as you probably could guess, I wasn't looking forward to the road trip with her and my younger brother and sister, Sam and Gertrude. I could deal with them just fine, just not Karen.

As we drove, the snow started falling hard to the point where Karen had to turn on the windshield wipers at the highest speed. Through all the years I'd traveled to great Aunt Mavis's home, I'd never seen snow like this.

I was a huge Stephen King fan, and I'd read nearly all of his books. In fact, I was rereading *The Girl Who Loved Tom Gordon*. This snowstorm reminded me of *Storm of the Century*.

Karen despised me reading. She made comments how I could be exercising rather than absorbing calories in my non-active state. I had to sneak and read, mostly at night with my cell phone flashlight under my covers. I kept my books hidden in a special place in the attic, where she would never discover them.

Aunt Cat always slipped my Christmas gift to me—usually a Barnes & Noble gift card—either in person or by sneaking it into my backpack. She told me how she couldn't keep up with my reading list, so it would be best for me to pick out what I wanted. I usually purchased four or five books from the card she gave me each year.

I happened to notice the sign as we slowly drove by—thirty more miles to Hollowsville, Vermont. Karen was driving about fifteen miles per hour, and the other cars were driving a little slower than she was. I looked back. Sam and Gertrude were both asleep with their iPads on their laps, so I reached back to turn their movies off. Karen reminded me to eat the frozen meals and snacks that she packed just for me.

Almost an hour had past, and we were still a few miles away. Gigantic snowflakes slammed against the window and burst into a thousand frozen pieces before the windshield wipers swooped them off.

Lighting up her cancer stick, Karen cracked the window a few inches. As I reached over to let my window down, she slapped my hand and gave me the look. My window remained closed.

The smell of nicotine made me nauseous. I tried to hold my breath as long as I possibly could before I'd have to exhale. She would sometimes blow smoke in my face on purpose and laugh under her rum-marinated breath.

Before she could finish, we arrived in front of the house. It was just like I remembered it from last year—two stories crying for a fresh paint job and vomit-green shingles that needed to be replaced. Most of the cars were completely covered in snow.

Colored Christmas lights decorated the entire perimeter of the roof. I opened the door, so I could finally breathe. Snow covered my *Monster High* rain boots, almost to the top of my knees. Wetness began to seep through my leopard-print leggings. Sam and Gertrude woke up.

Karen peeled Gertrude from the seat and tossed her on her hip. I walked to the back of the car to help Sam. I turned around, and he jumped on my back. He wasn't that heavy yet. I carried him until we reached a cleared sidewalk, which was being shoveled by Devin. Sam slid down and ran over to give him a hug. Karen winked and embraced him a little too close. She kissed him near his purple lips.

He looked at me and motioned me over. I took my time. I would've liked to have given him a swift kick you know where, but Karen stood next to him, and a few family members watched from the large windows like visitors at a zoo.

Devin pulled me in really close to his chest, which reeked of heavy cigar smoke and cheap aftershave. His sticky tentacles ran down over my shoulders as he squeezed them hard, then down my back, and almost near... I pulled back. I didn't know where the large icicle came from. It pierced his right hand. Blood squirted out onto the snow, the crimson bright against the white.

Stepping back, I noticed Karen's pale face. Devin yelped and pulled a gray furry scarf from around his neck, wrapped it around his hand, and scurried inside the house, Karen following behind him. As I walked by the stained snow, I noticed two bloody words:

SOON, SINNER.

My leg muscles tightened up.

I looked towards the window and pointed at the snow. The spectators shrugged their shoulders and mouthed, "What? There's nothing there." Cousin Ryan came out. I trusted him—I always felt comfortable around him. He hugged me and went to our car to retrieve the bags and gifts. He strolled right past the bloody snow and said nothing.

When I looked again, the words had vanished, but the bloody stain remained, soaking farther down, deep into the snow. I questioned myself if the words had actually been there. Shaking the snow off my boots, I entered the house. My fuzzy blue thermal socks were dry. I decided to change clothes before I found Aunt Cat.

Before I could reach one of the bathrooms, several family members stopped and hugged me. A few planted wet kisses on my cheeks. I wiped the saliva residue off with a tissue from my pocket. It was the best I could do until I could lock myself in a bathroom in order to perform my personal decontamination.

After passing about twenty family members or so, I finally saw an opportunity to grab my suitcase and backpack. I found a bathroom upstairs to perform my Christmas ritual. I felt refreshed after a shower.

As I was brushing my hair up in a ponytail, I noticed something outside the window. I walked over to get a closer look. It was a huge black widow spider, frozen against the windowpane.

Stumbling backwards from the white oval bathtub with silver bear claw feet, I recalled a story that Aunt Cat had told me about finding a similar frozen spider on her window when she was around my age. I couldn't remember the details, but I knew it was a sign for something awful. I hung my wet clothes on an empty towel bar behind the tub, tossed my bath essentials inside my cosmetic bag quickly, jerked the door open, and sprinted out of the bathroom.

Aunt Cat always allowed me to stay in her room during the two days. I headed down the hall and made a right. Her room was adorned with dragonfly decorations. A plush rollaway bed with extra blankets was set out for me. A red envelope and a clear-wrapped brownie rested on top of a fluffy pillow.

Shutting the door, I placed my suitcase in the corner and sat down on the bed. My backpack rested near my feet. I opened up the envelope and pulled out a card with a folded sheet of paper.

It was a Christmas card from Aunt Cat and inside was her usual gift, a fifty-dollar gift card from Barnes & Noble with a black key taped onto the front of the gift card. The card made sense, but not the key. I opened up the letter and read:

Dru, something terrible, has happened here again... The sinners will soon be punished by Frau Perchata, a powerful witch who hands out gruesome punishments to sinners, starting tomorrow, Christmas night. You'll not want to be here when she unleashes her fury. A snowmobile is waiting for you in the barn with further directions in a green envelope located inside the right compartment and appropriate gear. You'll find a rope ladder outside your window. Go! Don't worry about Sam and Gertrude—I'll take care of them. Get away from here now! I hope to meet up with you, soon. Remember, all the stories I've told you during our past visits. Be careful, and trust no one...

Love, Aunt Cat

Folding the letter up in the card, I placed it and the brownie inside my bag with my shivering hands. I knew what I needed to do from Aunt Cat's letter. The smell of smoke crept under my doorway, and I started coughing. It was coming from somewhere in the house. I peered down at the door—it was locked from the inside. I threw on my coat without zipping it up and slid on my boots. Grabbing my backpack, I opened up the window and tossed it down. I heard Devon calling my name from the hallway. I climbed on the windowsill dangling my legs outside. I placed one foot in a rung and my other foot in the other one. I repeated the process until my feet were buried in the snow.

The snow was falling heavier than earlier with high, screeching winds. I hoisted my backpack onto my shoulders and treaded through the snow. Halfway to the barn, I heard the kitchen screen door slam open and shut. Startled, I whirled around. Ryan was standing on the porch. I threw my hand up to wave.

He was dressed in a hooded camouflage snow bib, black gloves, and goggles rested on top of his head. He pitched a door key away from him in the snow. He scowled at me, and he ran in the knee-deep snow in a crooked pattern towards the barn with a cold, sneering smile frozen on his face. I bolted towards the barn door.

THE END

Theme Song: "Creep"
Artist: Radiohead

CHASER

ish I could tell you that all of us made it back home and the underdog, Golden Grizzlies, won the football state championship that night against the Texas Red Rattlers, 39 to 41. My freshman band members and I loaded onto the bus with our heads lowered. A few convertible mustangs and chargers swarmed around the bus.

The drivers and passengers yelled out, "Red Rattlers are unstoppable! Hibernation time, Grizzlies. We're number one... we're number one!" Their piercing laughter filled the crisp December air.

I noticed the football players' heads bowed down too as their bus drove off, kicking up swirls of dirt and rocks.

We all buckled up. No music or loud talking on our one-way trip. Instead, most focused on their cell phones with ear buds planted inside their ears.

Our bus was the last one to drive out of the mega-sized graveled parking lot. Mrs. Pinkerton—Mrs. P—our bus driver didn't follow the other buses towards the main highway. She took the back road. I figured she knew a short cut.

As I was reaching down to grab a book from my backpack, I heard a loud pop, which echoed against the metal interior of the bus. My head almost slammed into the musty smelling vinyl seat in front of me.

There were no cars in front or coming towards us that I could see. The bus swerved wide to the left and then to the right. Mrs. P gripped the oversized wheel with both her hands and guided the bus towards the grassy side of the road. It came to a complete halt.

"Everyone okay?" Mrs. P yelled out. Her face was painted scarlet with a steady stream of sweat running down. Her hands trembled against the steering wheel. She unbuckled her seatbelt and slid out to stand.

All the students nodded.

My backpack slid a few feet towards the front end.

Our band teacher, Mr. Casey, lightly jogged down the aisle to check on us. He then went back up towards Mrs. P. "Looks like we got a flat."

Mrs. P pushed the handle out near the wheel, flinging the bus door open.

"Y'all stay put. We're going to assess the damage. All will be okay, and we'll be back on the road in no time," Mr. Casey said.

I looked at my friend, Link, and he did the same. We both shook our heads.

Half of the students were texting, playing games, or watching movies on their phones while the others watched Mrs. P and Mr. Casey outside. I noticed Mr. Casey walking towards the back of the bus to retrieve the spare tire.

After ten minutes, he rolled it back towards the front of the bus to start changing it out. We sat down. I found my backpack and returned to my seat.

Link, the class clown, turned around in his seat and stood up on his knees. He always wore his Grizzlies baseball cap backwards. Link turned on the flashlight on his phone and placed it under his face, projecting an eerie blue glow.

"Anyone want to hear a true story that happened on this very road?" he asked while rotating his eyes back and forth like a pendulum.

A small group turned around to face him and tuned in. I watched them. Their eyes were fixed on him like he had placed a spell on them.

"Cut it out, Link! When will you stop with your crazy, make-believe stories?" Link and I had been friends since second grade, and he always told weird stories, mostly for attention, in my opinion.

"Let him tell the story, Chuck," Kim begged. She possessed the prettiest golden-hazel eyes you'd ever seen; I promised they twinkled whenever she smiled. Plus, you would've thought an angel was playing the flute when you heard her perform.

I leaned back in my seat and folded my arms across my hunter green Vibranium T-shirt. "Okay, tell us," I commanded.

"Y'all sure?"

We nodded. I raised my eyebrows, lifted my hands up in the air, and he started.

"Promise... this one is true," Link whispered with a slight grin.

I turned my head to stare out the window and observed Mr. Casey mounting the wheel back onto the axel while Mrs. P held the flashlight.

There was something strange that night when I think back now... I hadn't noticed any other traffic traveling on this road since our tire blowout.

Link started his story.

"My older cousin told me about the *Per-se-gui-dor* when we went camping last summer at Lago Fantasma—Phantom Lake, almost fifteen miles from here."

"Per-what?" I asked with a frown.

"Chuck, you need to start paying attention in Mrs. Z's class. It means *Chaser* in Spanish," Kim popped off with a slight wink at me.

Link's flashlight from his phone started flickering. I joined in to listen like the others, unfolded my arms, and rose up in my seat.

"Almost a year ago, two best friends—Wilbur and Antonio—around the same ages as us rode out here on their BMX bikes on a night just like this. They made a pact to capture the *Chaser*, a creature that upon first sight resembled a large rolling tumbleweed."

"What, a tumbleweed, Link?" I asked, scratching my head and squinting my right eye.

"Come on, Chuck, let him tell us," Kim pleaded.

"It could roll almost ten to twenty miles per hour towards you and then shapeshift at will into a seven-foot half-werewolf (upper body) and roadrunner (lower body) with huge talons, feathers, and a long snout with fangs. It had claws, sonar hearing, pointy ears, and glowing maroon, slit-shaped eyes."

The entire bus was silent. Everyone gathered around to listen.

"Wilbur and Antonio packed their backpacks with a large fishing net, heavy-duty gloves, flashlights, a sling-shot, and quarter-sized silver pellets," he said.

I started laughing out loud. "I must say, Link, this is probably one of the best stories I've heard from you so far. A hybrid werewolf/road runner, really? Was Wile E. Coyote around, too?"

Others laughed as well, except for Kim. I glanced up at her. She stared at me with her wide eyes. My laughing ceased.

"Okay, let's pretend for a moment that your story is true. Why did Wilbur and Antonio want to catch it?" I asked.

"To prove that it existed and claim the undisclosed monetary award that's been accruing since the Battle of San Jacinto! *Chasers* had been feeding on humans for a long time," Link said.

"Well, did they?" Kim asked without blinking her eyes.

"If you're asking if they caught the *Chaser* that night, then..." Link said, dragging out each word.

"Don't leave us hanging," I shouted.

"You don't believe anyhow, Chuck," Link barked.

"Whatever, man... I may not, but it looks like you have a crowd that does."

He continued, attempting to sound like the Crypt Keeper. "Wilbur and Antonio waited for it for over an hour. It finally showed up, a few feet away from them. The *Chaser* then rolled up on them crazy fast. They froze for several seconds before they remembered what was inside their backpacks, but Wilbur and Antonio were too slow."

Link paused and stared out the window for a minute.

"The next morning, the local sheriff and his deputy found their mangled bicycles with ripped leather seats and discarded backpacks. A trail of blood led off the road and into the woods. On the ground was one twelve-inch burgundy and mocha tinted feather. Wilbur and Antonio were never found... not even their clothes... or their bones."

Kim's face turned pale.

Link turned off his flashlight and slid down into his seat with a sly, crooked smile.

All of the sudden the bus began to rock back and forth, almost tipping over. High screams saturated the air, and more screams could be heard from outside.

I held on tight to the back of the seat in front of me, stood up, and looked out my window. I didn't see Mrs. P or Mr. Casey anywhere, only the flashlight spinning in the middle of the road.

A loud boom sounded from the roof of the bus. Something moved from the back towards the front. We all looked up and noticed sharp claws piercing through the metal with ease. All the kids screamed and ran toward the front of the bus.

Link stared at me. "I told you the *Chaser* was... Oops, I mean *Chasers* are real."

My eyes grew double in size as my teeth began to chatter.

His green eyes flickered a few times and transformed into shimmering maroon, slitted eyes. Two razor-sharp, glistening fangs crawled out of Link's trembling mouth.

"Oh, man... Link, we're good buddies, you know that, right?" I begged, nearly wetting my pants.

He howled and jumped into my seat. I tripped backwards and landed on my back on the floor. He pounced on top of me and buried his claws into my sides. I yelled and pretended to close my eyes as I turned my head to the side.

In a growling tone, near my face, he said, "Chuck, you never believed in any of my stories—you always laughed. Wilbur and Antonio surely did, when I accepted their invitation. Let's see if you believe me, now!" Warm saliva cascaded down my neck.

THE END

Theme Song: "Animals"
Artist: Maroon 5

NIGHT TOUR

O nce upon a time, my best friend and I attended one of the best concerts and after-parties ever, but I was the only one who made it out in one piece. It all started two weeks ago when DJ Precious, the smoothest disco jockey on the radio, made the announcement one night while "Thinking Of You" by Usher played in the background:

> *"Hey there, all my cool dolls and gents... Y'all know what time it is. That's right... The lucky caller to dial me up, and answer the trivia question right will not only score two front row tickets to see the hottest R&B teen*

*heartthrob around, Tomorrow, on his Night Tour—
one of the highest selling-out tours in America—this
Halloween night, but the winner will also get two VIP
passes to the after-party. At the party, the winners will
get a private, serenade from Tomorrow! You heard me
right—a serenade. Tomorrow must be a true fan of
Shakespeare. Okay, start flexing those fingers... This is
going to be a tough question. You must be a huge fan and
follower of Tomorrow since the beginning to know the
right answer. He's only mentioned it once in an interview
before he blew up. Ready: one, two, and three... What's
Tomorrow's favorite song?"*

Beatrice—a.k.a. Bea—my bestie, had the station's number
programmed into her phone. "Okay, you got this, right?" She held her
phone up in the air, pressed the dial symbol, and hit speaker.

An entire playlist of songs ran back and forth through my head. I was
pretty sure I knew Tomorrow's favorite song. I rocked back and forth on
Beatrice's carpet floor next to her bed. A buzzy signal echoed in the room.

"Crap," Bea huffed.

"Do it again," I commanded.

"Well, folks, I've received over twenty calls, and no one has
answered it right yet," DJ Precious said. "Come on, I know somebody
out there knows it."

"I do! I do!" I yelled.

Bea hit the dial button the thirteenth time, and she finally got a ringtone.

"Oh my gosh, oh my gosh, we finally got through," she said, rubbing my shoulders with her hands and looking me in the eyes as if I was about to enter the ring and box. "Now, if you get it wrong, then I guess I'll live afterwards." She flopped back on her bed.

"Don't worry, I know the answer," I said in a reassuring voice.

"Are you sure?"

"Yes, are you doubting me?" I questioned her. "Why don't you answer it then if you think I'll get it wrong?"

"Oh, no, it's just that you have only one chance to get it right. You keep up with stuff like that better than me," she said, popping up from the bed and twirling her hair up in a messy ponytail.

"Hello, there. Who do I have the pleasure to be speaking to?" DJ Precious asked.

I couldn't talk. This was so not me. I was a talker. I talked all the time, but for some insane moment, my voice froze up. Bea shook me.

"Hi, DJ Precious, my friend just needs a quick moment," Bea begged.

"Is she okay?" he asked.

"Oh, yes, she certainly is," she responded.

"She has exactly ten seconds to answer before I go to the next caller," DJ Precious replied.

Bea whispered, "Come on, snap out of it." She opened up her multi-colored leopard Tomorrow water bottle, pointed it, and squirted it in my face.

I shook my head and blurted out, "It's 'Little Bitty Pretty One,' by Frankie Lymon."

"Well, well... All you radio listeners out there—I finally have a winner. Who am I talking to, please?" DJ Precious asked.

"Redford Wilson," I said.

"You stay on the line for a quick commercial break. We'll be right back." DJ Precious chortled.

Bea stood up on her bed and started jumping up and down. I thought I was Tomorrow's biggest fan, but Bea had me beat by a few. I mean I kept up with everything about him, and she collected anything related to him.

Posters of him were plastered all of over her room, including inside of her closets and bathroom—mini ones served as liners for her drawers. She possessed Tomorrow shoes, T-shirts, leggings, purses, bed sheets, comforters, pillowcases, towels, slippers, socks, backpacks, undies, lip glosses, tumblers, denim jackets, bowls, plates, ice-cube trays, and so much more. This girl couldn't fall asleep or get ready for school in the morning without listening to one of Tomorrow's songs.

I couldn't even tell you how many times she'd gotten in trouble at school for listening to music in class. You guessed it, Tomorrow. We'd attended probably four of his concerts since sixth grade. Yet, we never had a chance to see him up close. This was one of the best things that could've ever happened to us, especially for Bea.

"Welcome back, Redford. Now, that's an unforgettable name," DJ Precious said.

"Yes, I know. I hardly ever use it unless I need to, so please call me Red."

"Red, I like that, and you got it. Now, who'll be accompanying you to the concert at the Billie Holiday Concert Hall and VIP party next Friday?"

"My best friend, Bea," I said.

"She's there with you, right?" he asked.

"Yes," I stated, holding the phone up in the air towards her.

"Hi, you have no idea how excited we are!" she screamed and jumped off the bed. She side bear hugged me. I couldn't breathe. She retreated.

"I think I have a pretty good idea. Well, listen, when I take a break, we'll work out all the details. Before we go to another commercial, Red, what Tomorrow song would you like for me to play in honor of y'all winning tonight?" DJ Precious asked, humming.

We looked at each other. Tomorrow had more than a hundred songs and most of them were hits. "DJ Precious, 'Girlie, Got Me Falling,' please." It was one of our favorites with drums, violins, piano, and guitars—a moderate paced melody. He'd won a Grammy for this one, when he was only fourteen years old. He was now sixteen. I turned sixteen the night after the concert—this was going to be the best birthday gift ever.

First thing, we had to score cool costumes. Bea found a Maleficent and Selene mash-up outfit that fit her perfectly at the local thrift store. I couldn't find anything that was calling my name. There was less than a week left before our big night. I had to find something fast. DJ Precious's envelope with the tickets and passes arrived.

Since the days were flying fast, I begged Mama to drive me out to the country so I could spend the weekend at my MeMe's farmhouse. I knew she could help me find something. Mama agreed. I loved going out there. MeMe lived in a white two-story barn-like house with fifteen acres of land surrounding her. The animals and feral cats were the best. As soon as Mom drove up in the car, I saw MeMe standing on the porch.

Mama stepped out and waved. I jumped out the car with my Tomorrow backpack, and she drove off right after. She and MeMe had a complicated relationship. Something happened when Mama was a teenager. I'd asked her to tell me about it, but she refused. MeMe wouldn't share with me, either. She said once, "I'll tell you when I know the time is right."

I ran up the steps and wrapped my arms around MeMe. She always smelled like cinnamon and honeysuckle. Denim, cuffed overalls with a vintage T-shirt and tennis shoes were her go-to outfit. She wore a long, thick purple braid over her shoulder.

"MeMe, you have to help me," I said looking into her gray eyes and lightly freckled face.

"Of course I will. Is it about Duncan Wheeler, the boy you've had a crush on since third grade?" she asked, cupping her pillow soft hand around my face as she brushed my curly, burgundy and mocha hair with her other hand.

"Oh, no. I'm so way over Wheeler. I need a costume for this huge concert event that I won on the radio. Bea is my date, and she's already found hers," I said, casting my eyes down.

"Honey, don't you worry about that. I've been working on something very special for you over the last few weeks for your birthday. We're just going to celebrate early," she shared.

Lifting my eyes up to her, I replied, "Seriously, MeMe?"

"Absolutely," she said.

After I helped her feed all the animals, we ate a home cooked dinner and talked for hours before I drifted off to sleep. I woke up on Saturday after one in the afternoon. I found a note taped to the oval mirror in the bathroom. It read:

Come downstairs for your birthday surprise.

As I was getting dressed, I brushed my teeth and washed my face. I slipped on my tennis shoes and tied them up. I almost grabbed my cell. I descended the stairs and headed towards the kitchen, where I could smell brewing vanilla coffee, blueberries, and chocolate.

There were blueberry and chocolate pancakes, my favorite, waiting for me with a large glass of iced milk. Floating balloons, a card, and a huge black box with a big, red bow sat in the chair next to me.

"Happy early birthday, Red!" MeMe said, sitting in a chair across from me and sipping her coffee. She pushed a playlist on her phone, and it was none other than Tomorrow's greatest hits.

I gasped. "Wow, all this for me? Thank you, MeMe." I stooped over and hugged her neck. She patted my arms.

"Eat something and then open," she said.

After I cleaned my plate with two helpings of pancakes, I pushed the plate to the end of the table. I grabbed the box from the chair and sat it on top of the table in front of me. I lifted the top off. Layers and layers of tissue paper covered the surprise. I tossed handfuls out on the floor.

There it was. I'd never seen anything as beautiful as what was staring back at me. I glanced up at MeMe and back down at my gift. "MeMe, is this what I think it is?"

"Yes," she nodded. "Try it on."

I stood up and pulled it out, slowly. I waved it around before wrapping it around my shoulders and snapping the golden buttons. The ruby hooded, half cloak reached over my hips. I twirled around like a ballerina on stage. It even had inside pockets.

"This is perfect. Thank you so much, MeMe."

"Oh, honey, you're very welcome. It'll come in handy this Friday night at the concert. The weatherman shared that there's a strong possibility of a cold front coming in that morning with temperatures falling to the low thirties."

"I have the perfect maroon jeans, and an old-fashioned peasant blouse I scooped up at a garage sale for a dollar, last month to pair this with. Mama has this small picnic basket she found at an estate sale a year ago. She's never used it. It's just collecting dust on a top shelf in our garage."

"Red, there's one more thing I have to give you," MeMe said. She scooted the chair back and went into her bedroom. She returned with a small pink gift bag and handed it to me.

"MeMe, you've given me more than enough," I protested.

"Just a little something extra I wanted you to have—it'll give me some peace of mind, when you're away from home. There's so much that goes on nowadays. You can never be too careful," she explained. "Young girls are vulnerable, and you never know when a predator is watching... waiting to take full advantage of a situation," she said.

"You're kinda freaking me out, MeMe. I think I'll be pretty safe at a Tomorrow concert. The security is always extreme," I said, giggling and brushing the sides of my new cloak.

"Well, it's better to be safe than not. Open, open," she commanded with a smile.

I reached into the bag and grabbed something round. I unraveled the paper around it. It was a thick gold and scarlet colored bracelet with a clear octagon-shaped center. I noticed my initials dangling from it and a tiny button under the bottom. "MeMe what's this button for?" I asked, twisting it to the top of my wrist.

"That's for if you're ever find yourself in a serious pickle." Her mouth twitched. "All you have to do is press it once. It has my number programmed inside of it, including the police department as secondary. This little gadget is perfect in case you don't have access to your cell phone or worse, someone takes your phone."

"Wow," I said. I secured it on my wrist.

"The bracelet also acts as a mood sensor. It changes colors based on your emotions. Deep brown indicates danger. If you're unable to tap the button for some reason, then it'll automatically alert me or the police of your exact location, in case you're in trouble or something," she said.

"So, it's like a GPS on my wrist?" I asked.

"Exactly," MeMe said, grinning.

"Where did you get this?" I asked, examining the bracelet closer.

"I have a high-tech buddy. She creates neat gadgets in her spare time," MeMe replied.

"Thank you for giving me the best gifts," I said.

"You're welcome. Remember, wear your bracelet from here on out, promise?" she stated.

Hugging her, I whispered, "I love you."

"I love you too. Enjoy your concert and don't forget to tell me every detail, especially about the great Tomorrow."

"Oh, I sure will," I said, admiring my bracelet more.

We spent the rest of the day on a long stroll around the farm and fishing in MeMe's huge tank a few feet from the house. When she cast her reel, I observed MeMe wearing the same bracelet as I was.

"MeMe, did someone gift you one, too?" I asked, baiting my hook with a bright pink lure.

"Yes, someone sure did. My first one didn't have the technology as mine and yours possess now," she said, looking down at hers.

Squinting my eyes and looking over my shoulder at her, while keeping my eye on the bobber, I asked, "Is there something you've been hiding from me?"

She cleared her throat and focused on the water. She giggled softly and replied, "Oh, my sweet girl, can I take a raincheck on that one?"

"Sure thing. I won't push this time. After all, you helped me to complete my outfit for my big night."

We laughed out loud together and stayed outside fishing until sunset. MeMe drove into town later that night, and we ate dinner at Gert's House, a Mom and Pop's local restaurant. We both went to bed early. The next day arrived, and the time for Mama to pick me up came too fast.

I hugged MeMe tight, and she did the same.

"I'll see you soon," I said as I strolled backwards with my bag and box under my arm.

She waved at me. I opened the back door and sat my bag and new treasure in the backseat. I climbed into the passenger's seat. "Hey, Mama," I said as I buckled myself in. I dug a tube of Tomorrow's sour apple-berry lip gloss out of my front pocket and dabbed my lips.

Mama threw her hand up at MeMe and placed the car in reverse.

"So, what did she get you for your birthday this year? I'm sure it'll top mine again," she mumbled, focusing on her rearview mirror.

"Why do you say that every year? I appreciate your gifts, too." I sighed.

Mama was nearly out of the winding driveway and a few inches from approaching the road before she slammed on her brakes. "Is that what she gave you?" she inquired, jerking her shades off her face.

"Yeah, isn't my bracelet pretty and different? I love it. I also have my costume for the concert this Friday night. MeMe really knows how to save a girl just in time. You wanna see it?" I asked with a huge smile.

Replacing her shades back on her face, she said, "No. I don't need to see it. I'm sure she gave you a genuine hand-sewn cloak. Did she tell you that she gave me the same gifts when I turned sixteen?"

"No, she didn't. I think that's a cool tradition. I've never seen you wear yours?"

"I got rid of both of them a long time ago," she replied.

"Why did you do that?" I asked, looking at her and fidgeting with my bracelet.

She gripped her steering wheel and paused for a few seconds. "There are so many things you don't know about Gryselda Durham, and I'm not getting into all of that right now, Redford."

"That's fine. It doesn't surprise me that you don't want to talk about her. By the way, that's the first time you spoke her name out loud," I said.

The drive home was silent besides the car radio and my fingernails tapping the armrest. There was no use of me trying to bait my mom to talk about MeMe. I've played that game way too much, and I always lost.

I went about my school week as fast as I could. I told Bea all about the gifts that MeMe gave me over the weekend. I found my favorite burgundy jeans on the floor of my closet on Thursday night, under a pile of clothes next to my Gwendolyn Brooks poetry and Nancy Drew book collection. I threw them in the washer and called Bea.

She answered after the second ring.

"You know what tomorrow is?" she squealed.

"Of course," I shouted, falling on my back on the floor and then flipping over to my stomach. I placed her on speaker.

"So, you're coming over after school to get ready at my place and spending the night, right?" Bea asked.

"You already know it. Will you do my make up?" I begged. "You do the best cat eyes."

"I got you, girl," she said. "I can't wait to see your outfit."

Mama opened my door and whispered, tapping her watch, "Wrap it up. Remember, I'm leaving early in the morning for my two-day work conference trip in Arizona. Dad will drop you off at school in the morning."

I nodded.

"Hey, it's getting late, and we're going to need all the rest we can. We're not going to sleep at all after the concert and party," I explained.

"True. See you in the morning," she said. "I hope I pass Mr. Palacious's geometry test. He's tough, and he doesn't believe in the curve."

"Me too, good night," I replied.

"Don't let the bed bugs bite." She snickered and hung up.

I went to the laundry room and tossed my jeans in the dryer. I returned to my room, showered, and started packing an overnight bag for tomorrow night. I hung up my cloak in a hanging bag. I retrieved my jeans from the dryer, grabbed the picnic basket off the shelf in the garage, and turned the lights off. I added the jeans to my overnight bag and went to sleep.

When I turned on the radio station the next morning, Tomorrow's songs were playing back-to-back. I placed the tickets and passes inside the picnic basket ready-made purse. I entered the kitchen with my bags and backpack.

"Happy early birthday, Kiddo," Dad said as he stood up from the island eating his breakfast—a plate of assorted muffins sat in the center. He stepped near me and leaned down to kiss me on my forehead. "I heard you have a big night planned." He grabbed my bags.

"Thanks, Dad. Yes, Bea and I are so excited!" I screamed with a slight jump.

"I understand. I can still remember when I first saw my favorite band, Phoenixx Stingrays, an all-girl rock/country band, my freshman year in college. What a night! That's when I first met your mom," he said. "Good times. I'll have to let you listen to one of their CDs. I think you may enjoy them—they have a different sound than what you're used to, but I think you may like them. Well, we better get going, don't won't to be late."

"Whoa, you had to wait until you were out of high school to see your first band?" I asked, stuffing a chocolate muffin in my mouth.

"Sure did. My parents, your grandparents, were really strict. I didn't have any freedom like you have now," he said.

I spotted a card and small box on the counter. I thought about opening them, but tossed them in my backpack to open up later. I grabbed a milk bottle out of the refrigerator. I followed Dad to the car. He slid my bags in the backseat, and I hopped in.

As he drove to my school, North Raven High, I guzzled the milk down.

I'd been thinking about Mom's comment about MeMe. I asked, "Hey, Dad, what happened between Mom and MeMe when Mom was my age?"

Rubbing the back of his neck with his hand, he asked, "Um, your mom hasn't mentioned anything?"

"Nope," I fired back.

"Red, all I can say is that it'll be best for your mom to explain everything that happened between them. I can tell you that their relationship has been strained for years," Dad explained.

"That I already know. All right, I plan to ask her again, but I don't think she'll share much of anything with me as she never has," I said, screwing the top on the empty bottle and dropping it inside the cupholder.

"I believe she will. You're older now..." Dad replied. He paused and said, "It's time for you to know certain things. Make sure you open up our gift before the concert—your mom picked it out for you. Have a great time and be safe. I'll pick you up from Bea's on Saturday evening. I'm sure you both will be sleeping in."

Bea and her mom were parked and waiting for me. I transferred my bags into her mom's car. "Thank you, Mrs. Hummings," I said, bending over the open passenger's window. Bea stood next to me, tapping her feet as she listened to music from her headphones.

"No problem at all. I'll pick you girls up, right here, after school. I'll put your bags in Bea's room," she said.

I elbowed Bea and pointed towards the window.

"Bye, Mom, I'll see you later," Bea said with a half smirk. "Ouch, you hit really hard."

"Oh, come on, don't be such a baby," I said.

She rubbed her arm with her palm as we entered the front door. Bea pulled up her sleeve and barked, "Look, it's already turning a deep purple and blackish gray."

"Impossible!" I yelled. "A bruise like that takes a few days or so to look like that. You must've already had that one."

"No, this just happened. At least my arms will all be covered up tonight. I wouldn't want Tomorrow to see this ugly thing," she said.

"Hey, if I did that, I'm so sorry," I offered.

"You're probably right though. I bet I ran into something and just forgot about it," she replied, wrapping her arm around my neck.

Before I knew it, the last bell had rung. Bea's mom was right where she said she would be. We both made a run for the front seat. Bea won.

"How was y'all's day?" her mom asked.

"I bombed my geometry test. I guess my mind was on the concert too much, and what Tomorrow would be wearing," Bea said. "I think he's going to wear the purple outfit for his opening act. You know the one with all the sparkles and lights."

"He might. I'm betting on the orange jumpsuit," I said.

"None of it matters. Whatever he wears, he's going to look so beautiful singing his songs to us tonight, right?" Bea said, turning around to go give me a high-five.

It was almost four, and the concert started at seven. Bea's mom stopped at a drive-thru to pick us up some dinner and drinks. My mind stayed on what Dad had said. I almost texted Mom. Instead, I concentrated on my big night.

We ate and raced upstairs to Bea's room, shutting the door behind us. She worked her make-up artist magic, creating a candied-apple cat-eye for me with golden sparkles surrounding it, and secured a Tomorrow iridescent temporary tattoo on my face cheek that read: *Tomorrow's Girl*.

Bea painted a classic black cat-eye for herself with silver sparkles. Thick mascara followed. She secured two *Tomorrow's Girl* tats on both of her cheeks. She hot curled her hair while I was getting dressed in her bedroom. We both sung along to his songs from her phone.

She stepped out of the bathroom and clicked the light off. The black leather, long-sleeve shirt and pants with an attached skirt fit her slender body like they were made for her. She placed the curvy horns on her head, which she'd covered with various Tomorrow stickers and emerald, green glitter. She handed me a giftbag.

"Thank you," I said, peeking inside.

"Happy birthday, bestie of mine. You're the reason why we have front row tickets and VIP passes," she replied, singing the happy birthday song to me.

I lifted the gifts out from the bag and unwrapped them—a brown leather corset with matching bracers and gloves. "Bea, oh my gosh, what made you get these for me?" I questioned and hugged her at the same time.

"When you told me what your MeMe got you, I had to buy them for you. Every cloak requires the necessities, and you're welcome," she replied with a bow.

"Whoa, your outfit looks so much better on you than the rack. That headpiece completes it. I think you're going to take first place," I said, slipping on my tennis shoes. Standing up to fasten the corset and place the bracers on both of my arms, I peeled the cloak off the hanger and swung it around my shoulders. I snapped the buttons, tied the two ribbons in a bow around my neck, and slipped on the gloves. I danced around and rocked my hips back and forth to one of my Tomorrow faves, "Can't Go." A fast beat with Caribbean drums. The cloak ballooned around me.

"No, you're going to win the costume contest. Your cloak with all the extras are on fire, Red," she said, approaching me and stroking the material. "Your MeMe really made this?"

"Yes," I replied and ceased my dancing.

"I've never seen a cloak like this. It's beautiful and that hood totally sets it off. Hold on, you're missing something." She paced around me twice, tapping her index finger under her chin. "I got it." She wandered over to her top dresser drawer and returned with a thin long, mahogany belt. She wrapped it around my waist twice and fastened it. "There... now, you're outfit is perfect." She smiled and twirled me around to face the full-length mirror on her closet door.

Bea was right. Her last detail to my costume made it pop. I hugged her and said, "Thank you."

"No problem, just wait until Tomorrow sees us. He's going to have to invite us on the stage," she shrieked. "Let's get out of here. It's after five. Mom should get us there in forty minutes, adding the traffic downtown and Tomorrow being in town." She removed her headdress.

We exited the room as I grabbed my basket with the most important things inside—the tickets and passes, including my card and gift.

Bea's Mom drove with the traffic. "Don't worry, girls, I'll get you both there safe." She focused on the highway as several cars zipped in and out between us. Snowflakes started falling. I flipped the wooden flap of my basket over. I removed the card and opened it first. There was a picture of colorful balloons floating up in the air, the card read:

I hope you and Bea have the best time. I'm sorry I've been distant after you asked me about your MeMe. When I return, we're going to have a long talk about everything. Have a great birthday weekend. Be safe, Red.

See you soon, Mama.

The box dropped on the floor as Mrs. Hummings hit her brakes. A car flew out of nowhere in front of her. She swerved. "Sorry, girls. Maniac drivers are everywhere tonight," she squawked.

Picking the box up from the floor, I started opening it.

Bea turned her entire body around and asked, "Oh, what's in the box?"

"Not sure yet," I said. "It's a gift from Mama."

"Hurry up, we'll be there in less than ten minutes," she said.

I slid my nail under the tape to break the tight seal. It popped open. I placed the lid next to me. As I uncovered it, I found a necklace. I lifted it up to examine it closer. It was a mini axe with a silver head and rubies embedded along the front and back handle.

"Well, I wasn't expecting that from your mom," Bea said. "It matches your outfit perfect. Every Little Red Riding Hood needs an axe to keep all the *werewolves* at bay tonight, right?" she said and laughed, clapping her hands.

"Yeah, it completes my gear. I really didn't think Mama would buy me something like this. She's never been a fan of MeMe's gifts," I said as I bent my head down to clasp the necklace behind my neck.

Within seconds, we neared the concert hall. It was so packed. There were ten lanes and like a hundred cars in front of us. I knew we would miss the first couple of songs. It was nearly seven.

A stocky guy dressed in all black with a gold badge on his matching jacket tapped on Mrs. Hummings's window while holding a clipboard. She rolled it down. He asked, "Tickets, please. We're scanning them here. One step to make it faster. This is the busiest concert I've ever worked—that Tomorrow fella must really be something."

Bea and I just looked at each other, grinned, and stomped our feet. I handed the tickets and passes to her, and she handed them to her mom. The guy ran a scanner over them. He instructed, "You'll drive in this lane behind me to be escorted through a side door and will then be seated quickly. One more thing, according to your special tickets and passes, one of us, could be me, will transport you both to the group after-party once the concert ends. Have a good time at the concert." He pointed us in the direction with no congestion.

Looking back at him, I saw him pull a walkie-talkie out of his back pocket as he stared at me without blinking. Mrs. Hummings found the side entrance and another security guard tapped on the glass.

"Bea and Red, if you both feel uneasy about anything tonight, then please don't hesitate to call me. I'll pick you both up. I just find someone escorting you to a different location strange," she explained, biting her nails.

"Mom, you're doing it again. It's a part of the radio contest. Everything is safe!" Bea snapped.

"What?" Mrs. Hummings asked.

"You promised that you would stop being overprotective. You're trying to ruin my biggest night probably ever in my life with my bestie," she said, sniffling, as if she was about to cry. I placed my hand on her shoulder. She grabbed it and squeezed my hand.

"No, I'm not. I just don't have the best feeling about that part," she mumbled. "I can drive you both to the party and just wait in the car."

"Whatever—you're insane! I don't want my mother waiting for me in a parked car," she shouted, throwing the car door open hard. Snatching her headpiece off the seat, she said, "This is why I hate you most of the time." She shot out of the car and slammed the door. She waited with the guy until I could climb out of the back.

I whispered, "Sorry, Mrs. Hummings." I patted her shoulder.

"Oh, Red, thank you. She's always had a short temper with me. You two are so very different. Promise me that you'll watch over her tonight," she begged as tears fell. "Have a good time and happy birthday."

I nodded and left. In front of me, a full scarlet moon seemed to follow me—something I'd never noticed before. I wrapped my cloak around me tighter. Bea skipped ahead and I followed. I looked back, and Mrs. Hummings was still there. We descended a flight of stairs and could hear voices and music, which seemed to increase with every step we took. I tapped Bea on the shoulder. "Why the blow up back there?" I fixed my eyes toward the ground.

"She makes little comments like that to me all the time. She always think something bad is going to happen. She watches those true crime shows constantly. I've never heard of anything awful happening at an event like this. Mom just needs to calm down."

My fingers massaged the axe on my necklace. "I think she's just worried about you. She's being a mom, you know."

"The big bad wolf isn't going to gobble us up," she said softly with a light laugh. "Listen, I'm fine. This is your birthday weekend. No more talk about parents, deal?"

The guard directed us to our seats. There were six sets of winners. We were just twenty feet from the surrounding netted stage—we had the best seats. Bea raised her hands in the air. My eyes swept the entire hall, and there were probably more than twenty thousand people—not one empty seat. Only the floor lights and rotating ceiling white lights lit up the dark oval stadium.

A waving, sky background with lots of stars, tall trees, grass, various birds, butterflies, deer, and squirrels decorated the stage. The wildlife were mechanical, but the colorful butterflies were real. A cushioned stool and standing microphone were positioned near the edge of the elevated stage.

When I looked up, more than a dozen aerial performers with glow-in-the-dark body suits flew around the entire building. Their performance lasted about fifteen minutes before smoke, which resembled cumulonimbus clouds, saturated the ceiling. The acrobats seemed to be swallowed up in the smoke.

One of my favorite Tomorrow songs, "Abnormal Energy," started up—electric guitars, harps, violins, and piano. It was him singing, not the record. Everyone stood up from their seats and searched for him. He wasn't on the stage or on the floor.

Before everyone thought to look up in the air, a glowing green swing was lowered down, and Tomorrow stood in the oversized seat. Screams came from everywhere in the place. Bea and I jumped to our feet as did all the other guests. Bea shouted so loudly that I couldn't help, but laugh, but my eyes never left Tomorrow.

He was dressed in a white space suit, half of it covered in purple and the other in orange rhinestones—his favorite colors. It was tailored to his hot body. He was more than six feet tall without shoes. He had an eye mask of the same material. His long and curly raspberry hair with gold and silver glitter highlights flew in the air. His luscious hair made my heart beat so fast.

Tomorrow sat down, and the swing lowered up and down into the crowd. Fans attempted to touch his hand. Some were successful. A few fainted for a moment. He finally traveled towards us. He jumped off and landed on stage while completing three back flips in a row. He just stood there with his arms extended as the screams roared on and on.

He adjusted the stool, grabbed the microphone, and sung a mix of his hottest tunes ever recorded. Bea and most of the real fans were on our feet the entire time. Bea would sometimes grab my hand, and I would hers.

Tomorrow sounded great on his recordings, but seeing him perform live was no comparison whenever we attended one of his concerts. This time was way different than any other time—we were watching him up close. His smooth and energetic dance moves made me feel woozy as I swayed to his music.

"Hey, out there, all my beautiful fans!" Tomorrow hollered. "How are you all doing tonight? Do you wanna hear another song?" He ran to the right and slid on his knees on the stage floor and jumped up—he did the same on the opposite end of the stage.

The crowd went wild and replied back with loud screams.

Bea yelled out, "Tomorrow, I love you. I'm your biggest fan, me, me!" She stood on top of her seat. I pulled at her to get down before one of the security guards saw her, but it was too late.

One spotted her and headed towards our seats. She refused to get down. Tomorrow called the guard near the stage and whispered something in his ear. The guard resumed his trek to us. Bea finally jumped down. The guard waved us to come up front.

"Well, it was good while it lasted, Bea," I mumbled.

"You think they're going to kick us out?" she asked, tears pooling in her eyes.

"Um, yeah," I replied.

The guard guided us, and then he punched a special code on a panel near the stage. A platform with rails appeared. "Get on," he commanded.

Bea and I looked at each other.

"Wait, we're not getting kicked out?" Bea asked.

"No, you both are going up there with Tomorrow," he said, punching in the code again as the platform started levitating in the air.

Bea shook me by my arms, and I did the same to her.

"Hold on to the rail," the guard said in a deep tone.

Within seconds, we both faced Tomorrow, staring deeply into his light, umber eyes. My legs started wobbling, and Bea nearly fainted in my arms. Tomorrow caressed our faces with his hands and whispered between us, "Are you both okay?" His hair and body smelled so good—a combination of tuberose, jasmine, orange blossoms, cedarwood, and warm vanilla. He was intoxicating from head to toe.

I wanted to wrap my arms around him and never let him go. Bea stepped towards him, and I wrangled her back in and whispered, "Down Girl... if you do anything, you'll be all over social media, and we'll definitely get kicked out. Forget the after-party, too." She retreated and took in deep breaths.

"You both know what time it is, right?" Tomorrow asked, staring at Bea with his dazzling purple microphone in his perfect hands. His nails were manicured and shiny.

I shook her, and she did what she promised she would never do—froze up on me. She felt like a statue. So, I answered, "For what, Tomorrow?" I stared into those *don't ever wake me up out of these dreamy eyes* of his. They locked on mine.

"The costume contest, ladies..." he said. "You both are killing it with those costumes. You're both winners. I love her horns. By the way, is your friend okay?" he asked, covering the top of the microphone with the palm of his hand.

"Yes, she'll be fine, just starstruck over you." I giggled, keeping my eyes on him.

"It happens a lot," he said with a smile. He had the whitest and straightest teeth I'd ever seen. His breath smelled like fresh mint and strawberries.

"Can I ask you a question?" he asked, brushing his hair back out of his face.

"Tomorrow, you can ask me anything," I said, and I knew my eyes were twinkling and everyone in the audience probably knew it too.

"Where did you get your cloak? I haven't seen one like that," he said.

His question took me by surprise. "My MeMe gave it to my for my birthday. She made it."

"Wait, your birthday... when is it?" Tomorrow asked.

"Actually, in less than three hours," I said.

He announced into the microphone, "We got a birthday girl in the house. You know what that means, right? May I kiss you?" he asked, clicking his glowing boots together.

Of course you can kiss me, I thought to myself, *Red, did you floss and use mouthwash earlier?*

Fanning my face with my hands, I yelped, "Yes!"

His hand touched mine. *Redford, stay calm, don't freak out. Breathe in, breathe out, like that video on relaxation techniques MeMe shared a few months ago,* I instructed myself.

I parted my lips and closed my eyes. I waited for Tomorrow's magic lips to perform the rumba with mine.

He bent down and slowly pressed his lips against my right cheek. I could feel his hair tickle my face. He returned back to his personal space. I tell you one thing, this cheek would never, ever be washed again. I touched it, and I could still feel the warmth from his velvety lips. My ears felt really hot.

"You both aren't only the costume winners tonight, but also winners of a special gift."

"Seriously!" I shouted, which woke Bea out of her spell.

"What did I miss?" she asked with a slight stumble towards me.

"I'll catch you up later," I replied.

"Give them an applause," he requested from the crowd. They followed his request and clapped. Two guards walked from behind the curtain, carrying two white sashes and a bag. Tomorrow placed them over our heads and handed me the giftbag. The sashes read in bold orange letters: *Tomorrow's Forever Girls*

Before the guards ushered us off the stage, Tomorrow said, "I'll see you both at my after-party, along with the other radio guests."

We stepped back on the platform to be lowered back down to our seated area and found our seats. Bea and I watched his remaining performances. He sung more than seven of his hits, plus interspersed conversations and games with the audience throughout the night. Several costume changes accompanied each of his themes. Tomorrow's last song, "Lost in Love/Talking To The Moon," a mash-up of the New Edition and Bruno Mars's songs had everyone up on their feet with their cell phone flashlights waving in the air.

After that, he took several bows, and he ran to the middle of the stage to strap himself into a special rope vest. The ropes lifted him way up into the air, and he vanished out of the building.

It was after ten. The lights came on, and a guard accompanied all the ones headed to the after-party out in a secret door, hidden from the crowd. We rode in black Tahoes. Bea and I were together. I told her everything that happened on the stage with Tomorrow. The first guard we met ended up being our chauffeur. As we drove out of the city, I looked behind me. The other SUVs were gone.

"Hey, what happened to the other cars following us earlier?" I asked, biting the side of my lip.

"Tomorrow's special, special guests attend a one-on-one party with only him. You both were awarded Tomorrow sashes tonight, right?" he questioned as he looked at us from the rearview mirror and sipped on a straw from a paper cup. "Afterwards, Tomorrow and you both will make a special appearance with the other special guests at a different location."

"Yes!" Bea shouted. "You know what this means?" she asked, facing me without a blink. "We get to spend time with him without sharing him with anybody."

I dropped my voice. "Bea, maybe your mom was right?"

"About what?" she asked.

"Keep your voice down," I whispered, pointing my finger towards the driver. "I don't want him to know what we're talking about."

"Don't even go there. You really think we're about to enter stranger/ danger territory," she replied.

"Come on, Bea, the signs are pretty obvious—the special sashes and now we're being driven out to who knows where," I said, rubbing my hand up and down on my arm.

"Listen, I'm here with you. Nothing is going to happen to us. This has all been arranged by the radio station and record company. They wouldn't risk trouble with the police and press. Relax and let's have fun, okay, bestie," Bea said in a reassuring voice. She pulled me into her and caressed the side of my face with her hand.

I took a deep sigh. "Hey, you're right. I don't know why I get so worked up sometimes."

"OMG!" she yelled. "How much longer?"

"Not much, maybe five more minutes," the guard replied.

She rummaged through the bag on the floor next to my legs. She dug out two *Night Tour* T-shirts and a new CD.

"Oh, please, please, can I have it?" she asked in a pouting tone.

"Sure," I said. My mind drifted back to Bea's mom's concerns as I stared out the window into the unknown darkness, picking at my fingernails.

"Let's keep them here. No sense taking the gifts with us inside to the party. They may get misplaced," she said, powdering her face, adding fresh lipstick, and a few squirts of a light cologne all over her, which reminded me of fresh rain and pink lemonade.

We were near Shadow Lake, almost an hour from the city. Bea and I stepped out of the car. There was a two-story log cabin standing in front of us. A thousand pine trees and the glistening lake surrounded it and us.

"I'll be back to pick you both up in about an hour and drive you both to the other party. Have fun, you two," he said and drove off, kicking dust and small rocks up from his tires.

Bea grabbed my hand as we ran up the wooden steps. Bright, motion porch lights turned on. I pushed the doorbell. I looked down, and I noticed a red smudge that resembled a handprint on the step next to my outer foot. Before I could get Bea's attention to confirm what I just discovered, we heard light footsteps approaching the door.

It opened wide. A young girl in zebra leggings and a cut-off top, probably thirteen, peeked from behind the large door. She had long black hair, nearly touching her thighs. She wore lime green cat-shaped eyeglasses.

"Come on in… you must be Bea and Red?" she said, tapping the edge of the door with her glittered white nails.

"Yes, this is my bestie, Bea, and I'm Red. We won—"

"I know the winners to DJ Precious's special contest and the big sash winners at the concert tonight... blah... blah... blah," she said, rolling her eyes. "My brother, Tomorrow, is upstairs. I'm Camila. He's been waiting for you two." A smirk painted her face. "By the way, I need your cell phones or no serenade show." She held a cotton drawstring bag open in her hands.

"What for?" I asked with a frown.

"No temptation for pictures or recordings to be uploaded. It's one of the rules on the back of your VIP passes. Didn't you read the fine print at the bottom?" she asked.

Bea looked at me. I leaned over to her and whispered, "I didn't know there were rules like that, and Tomorrow had a little sis."

She said, "I could care less. This is our big chance, and what a way to begin your birthday morning." She dug her phone out of her pocket and tossed it in the bag.

Camila led us to the staircase and pointed up. I stalled for a bit before I handed her my phone.

Before I placed my foot up on the first step, Bea flew up the steps without me. I cried out, "What happened to us going together?" I looked back, and Camila was gone.

Bea stopped at the top of the high staircase and threw her skirt back and adjusted her horns. "I'm sorry, Red. You don't love Tomorrow like me. You're a fan of his and all, but nothing like me. Don't act shocked now. Just be a good friend and let me have my seven minutes in heaven with him. You've already been kissed by him," she pleaded and headed toward the lighted path.

Inhaling deep breaths and grabbing the ends of the wooden banister with my hands, I heard a cracking sound and noticed the wood split. I studied the damage. I couldn't have done that. There must've been weak areas. My hands glided up the rails, and they felt sturdy. How was I going to explain this—ruining stuff in Tomorrow's lake house? I lowered myself down to the bottom step and sat.

My head hung between my legs. *Abandoned by my bestie*, I thought to myself. I thought about the entire night, and how Bea wouldn't be with me when it turned midnight in a few minutes for my birthday. We'd always stayed up late on the eve of my birthday for the last seven years. I stared at my reflection from the polished floors for a minute.

Something inside of me told me to check out my surroundings. I stood up and paraded slowly around the grand living area decorated in leopard, cheetah, and zebra prints. A mounted Kodiak bear, black rhino, Sumatran orangutan, and an African forest elephant's stuffed heads hung in between hundreds of glass cases on the high walls.

Examining the cases more, I noticed what was inside of them. Axes of all sorts, as if someone has been collecting them for a long time. Some seemed to be really old like back during the Salem Witch Trials. Suddenly, my wrist felt really warm. It was the bracelet MeMe gave me. The stone had changed into a murky, brown color. I remembered what MeMe had told me.

The cloak wrapped around my chest and then unloosened from me. I whispered to myself, "What the heck?" I looked down at my necklace, and it started emanating bright light.

Something was definitely not right about all of this and me. Mrs. Hummings was on target from earlier. I could feel tingling in my toes and fingers. My hairs stood up on my bare arms. I heard Bea screaming, and it wasn't the boy-crazy kind.

Running up the stairs and pressing the button on my bracelet, I surfed down the long hallway; my feet levitated a few inches off the ground. Somehow, I completed a flying kick, shattering the two sealed doors. "How did I just do that?" I mumbled to myself. I dropped down to my knees with my cloak billowing around me.

Looking all around the oversized study with tall, stacked bookcases and floor, I didn't see Bea. A wet and sweet, rusty odor penetrated my flaring nostrils. There was blood smeared all over the floor. Not just any blood, but Bea's blood. I could smell it was hers, somehow. How, I wasn't exactly sure. Tears gushed down my face. I didn't know where all these capabilities of mine were coming from, but Bea's body wasn't anywhere to be found. A trail of blood led to a closet and stopped. I started that way until I heard something from outside the open, balcony doors.

I rushed onto the balcony, and I looked down to the ground. Then, I heard a tapping on the roof. My eyes shot in that direction. There he was. He was dressed in black loose pants and a matching shirt with one of his legs up against his chest and the other extended out. His hair was tied in a loose bun.

"Where's Bea?" I demanded, baring my teeth.

"It's Red, right?" he asked. "Listen, this had to happen tonight."

"What are you talking about?" I asked, keeping my eyes on him.

"The *scarlet moon ceremony*. There's always that one over-hyped fan, and tonight it was your best friend. The radio contests draws fans out like you, and your now-dead friend," he explained, sliding down from the roof and landing on all fours and turning his head at me. His eyes changed. They started gleaming a neon violet.

Backing up into the room, I discovered more axes in cases. He stood up and dusted himself off. He circled around me with his hands behind his back. "Now, I can tell you that I serenaded Bea and sung one of my new songs, 'Mine Tonight,' to her before I slit her throat. I'm a poetic kind of guy. I thought she deserved to hear it before she faced her fate. Wouldn't you agree?"

My heart pounded as if it was about to double somersault from my chest. I clenched my fists and all the affection I once possessed for Tomorrow, extinguished. His once smooth hands transformed into hairy claws.

He flipped my cape up with his claws, ripping part of it, and sniffed my hood. "You're one of them. I thought your kind were all extinct. My great-grandad told me on his deathbed that he'd slaughtered the last hunter family," he said as he slithered around me followed by a faint growl.

"Hunter family... what are you talking about?" I asked.

He stopped in his tracks. "Wait, no one has ever told you about your family history, and what happens on your sixteenth birthday? That's why I couldn't pinpoint your scent on stage—your transformation was incomplete."

"No... wait, transformation? I asked, widening my eyes and glaring into his. "You're a liar and murderer. Stop it!"

Stooping down, he gazed up at me, and said, while licking his fangs, "My, my, poor Little Red has no clue of what she truly is. Let me help you out by telling you the short version... You're a hunter of my kind... werewolves. Your family bloodline has been murdering my ancestors for countless centuries, although you carry werewolf DNA from a slight mishap that happened many centuries ago."

"What?" I shouted, his words making no sense.

He growled loud, baring his long, razor-sharp, shimmering fangs. "Please let me finish... that's how you can use the gifts we gave you to hunt us, when you complete full transformation. My bloodline thought we finally killed the last Durham Hunter, almost eighty years ago. My great-grandad missed someone." He stood up with his claws pointing at me.

"So, you're going to eat me, too?" I asked, exhaling and inhaling hard.

His claws retracted, and he burst out in laughter. "I did kill your friend, but I'm not going to eat her. I'm allergic to her blood type. Camila is going to eat her. She hid her in the closet. She's waiting so I can have dinner with her. I'm going to gobble you up and find the rest of your family and do the same—before sunrise."

Camila dropped from the ceiling onto her hands and knees, her words slurred through her bloody fangs. "Your friend tastes so delicious!" She stood up, rubbing her stomach with her bloody claws.

They both started slowly stalking towards me. "You're trapped, Little Red. We're going to enjoy tearing you apart, piece by piece," Tomorrow roared, saliva dripping from his protruding fangs as he popped his hairy knuckles. Exposing her shiny fangs, Camila smiled. Blood smudges painted around her mouth.

He twisted my arm behind my back and pulled my hair up with his claws. Breathing hard, his hot breath no longer smelling fresh. With a slight howl, he whispered close to my ear, "I'm going to mount your head on my bedroom wall to always remember the night I terminated the youngest in the Durham Hunter Family."

Jerking my head from his firm grasp, I met his soulless eyes. It seemed to catch him in a temporary trance. I shifted my body around quickly and elbowed him in the face. He dropped to the ground. Camila ran over to him and kneeled down to help him.

I looked behind me and noticed two massive bookshelves towering over me. I stood on top of a desk shoving the nearest bookshelf down towards them. I climbed the other bookshelf and slammed my bracer into the glass and snatched an axe from its case. I held it with both my hands and dropped back down to the desk.

By now both Tomorrow and Camila had managed to throw the bookcase off of them and were howling in fury. They leaped in the air towards me. I cartwheeled high above them and swung the axe at them. Just like that, I landed on the ground and both of their heads tumbled to the floor close to my feet. I turned around, and their bodies collapsed like stuffed scarecrows.

Breathing in and out harder than before, I heard footsteps down the hallway. I gripped the axe, preparing for another werewolf to enter the doorway. I wiped my sweaty forehead with the end of my cloak and planted my feet firmly to the ground. I held the axe up on its side and prepared to swing. My hands were shaky.

"Red, Red..." MeMe called out.

Dropping the axe down between my feet, I watched as she entered and examined the crime scene. She pulled me to her and hugged me. I backed up from her. "MeMe, why didn't you tell me about all of this and the things I can do. I'm so confused. Bea's dead." I fell into her arms and started sobbing hard.

"Let's get out of here. I'm going to tell you everything and so is your mom," MeMe said, caressing my upper back with her hands.

As we descended the stairs, I said, "The cops are going to come looking for me."

"No, they won't. I have many connections that you wouldn't believe," she replied. "Just as the *Were-Nation* has to clean up their nasty messes."

Before we exited, I asked, "How am I going to explain what happened to Bea to her mom? Her mom asked me to protect her, and I failed." Tears streamed down my face as I lowered my head.

MeMe lifted my chin. "Honey, you didn't know. This is my fault. I should've told you everything way before now. You weren't the one who hurt Bea, it was the beasts, as it's been as long as I can remember. I'll take care of Mrs. Hummings."

Opening the car door, I asked, "So, I'm a hunter? Does Dad know?"

"Yes, if you choose to be. Your dad is aware. He was told before he married into the family. Your mom didn't like it after she made her first kill at your age," MeMe said.

"Mom's a hunter?" I asked, arching my eyebrows.

MeMe shook her head, getting into the car. She pushed the button to start the ignition. "You won't hurt my feelings at all if you wish not to partake in this life. It takes someone who has a passion for it. Your mom didn't. Believe me, I'll understand."

"How long have you been hunting?" I asked.

"Ever since my *hunter transformation* on my sixteenth birthday, just like you. I loved it without hesitation. My mom explained it all to me early on, so I was prepared. Your mom thought it would be best to keep it hidden from you. She asked me not to tell you after you were born. You had the birthmark under your right foot unlike her. You were meant to be a hunter. I told her that I wasn't sure if I could honor that. That's when she stopped coming around. She didn't want you to be traumatized," MeMe explained.

"Birthmark?" I kicked my shoe off and peeled my sock off. I pulled my foot into the seat and turned on the car light. I'd never paid attention to it before now. Yet, there it was—a mini, disfigured axe. "I wished you would've told me way before now. I'll be dealing with the trauma of losing my best friend, beheading my idol, and his little sis." I took in a long breath, closing my eyes tight. I rested my head against the window. All of this was way too much to process.

MeMe looked at me before backing out of the driveway. "Me too and you're correct. I'll make sure to connect you with a good therapist specialized in new hunter transformation with associated traumas. I'm so glad you wore the bracelet and cloak together tonight. They activated everything inside of you. Honestly, Red, they *saved* your life."

"Can I ask you a question?" I asked, gazing down at the axe next to my legs.

"Please ask me anything, darling," MeMe said.

"What's up with all the axes in there?" I pointed at the cabin.

"Like witches use wands, hunters utilize axes. Axes are a hunter's primary weapon. For every hunter killed, some werewolf species or families collect them for trophies," MeMe explained.

As we drove under the moonlit road, I gazed down at my glistening necklace and the axe's ruby handle. I knew right then that I was meant to be a hunter. I wanted to be a hunter to avenge Bea and maybe save a few other Beas in the world. I destroyed all of my Tomorrow stockpile within a few days after Bea's funeral. I didn't want anything associated with him.

Two *weres* down and more to go, right after MeMe gave me the true Durham Family history lessons—especially the part Tomorrow was rambling on about werewolf DNA crossing with a past hunter—with training sessions to hone my hunter skills.

My therapy sessions were helpful, but I knew my heart would never heal from everything I experienced that night, specifically losing my Bea. It was a birthday that I'll never forget for as long as I live. I still attended concerts now and then, not much as a fangirl anymore, but as *Red, The Hunter*...

THE END

Theme Song: "Pretty"
Artist: Ingrid Michaelson

JANIE

Many asked why she did it...

I knew, and they did, too.

Closed eyes and music turned all the way up inside their runaway minds.

Noise can only drown out so much, especially aching and blood-curdling screams night after night, right around 2:13 a.m.

I almost unlocked my door once, but I quickly retreated back into my coward skin.

She tried to tell me about a year ago, how he was a *monster*.

Laughter from me filled the air while streaming tears fell from her loaded hazel eyes.

One night, her dark cries stopped.

The next morning, I pulled my curtain back and noticed cop cars, an ambulance, a county coroner vehicle, and a special crimes van—a strange imprint on the side—surrounded her house.

Thoughts raced through my mind... *I should've believed her that day*.

My eyes began to swell. I knew she'd received her death invitation.

After forty-seven minutes, the door opened.

To my surprise, I saw her walking behind the sheet covered gurney, unhandcuffed, followed by two policemen.

Her blood-splattered, white knee-length gown rippled around her.

As the gurney was rolled down the steps, a large gray shaggy arm flopped out.

I noticed twelve-inch opaque, curved claws.

My heart started pounding.

Her scarlet stained face and wet eyes seized my stare.

Before the EMT lady assisted her into the back of the ambulance, Janie exhaled and did something I'd never seen her do until that moment—smile.

THE END

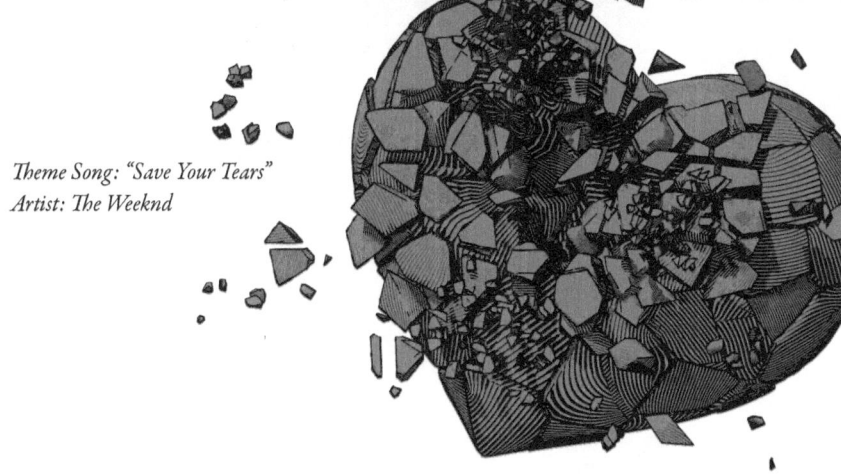

Theme Song: "Save Your Tears"
Artist: The Weeknd

BREATHLESS

You reached inside of my frail chest and snatched my heart out to wrap chains around it.

I collapsed, and you buried me under the weeping willow tree in my backyard.

You tossed the bundle of blood-stained letters I wrote to you in junior high onto my still body.

Thirteen feet of dirt and snow covered me up.

Next spring, no flowers bloomed.

My endless teardrops rained down onto my grave until my body was exhumed for all to witness...

THE END

Theme Song: "Precious Hewie (Haunting Ground)"
Artist: Rod Herold

SHADOW GROVE

My mother told me a story.

When I first heard it, I dismissed it.

The tale goes...

In a little country town almost sixty-three years ago, an hour before her uncle's funeral, the blue sky transformed into an onyx blanket with golden stratus clouds floating above the church on the hilltop in Shadow Grove.

Her uncle, she said, never attended church.

He'd spoken openly to her and others about how he'd wanted a graveside service only.

Yet, his family hadn't honored his last wish.

The day of his funeral the ushers lifted his coffin trimmed with copper out of the hearse and began to march towards the church.

Before they reached the steps, my mom, who was around fourteen years old then noticed high winds.

A powerful shower of leaves from a nearby oak tree blew inside the church, almost knocking her down; she braced herself between the sides of the doorway.

The ground began to shake.

She stumbled and fell backwards.

A dust storm rolled in out of nowhere.

The coffin rocked back and forth.

Its handles spewed bright cherry flames.

The pallbearers couldn't hold on to it. They dropped the coffin.

Her uncle's coffin rested several feet away from those steps.

The ground cracked wide open and swallowed it.

Within seconds, the sky returned to blue, the dust storm vanished, and the sun appeared gleaming down onto the church.

A burnt charcoal, zigzag line remained on the ground.

When I was driving to Mom's house, I decided to take the scenic route and drove to Shadow Grove to visit the church on the hilltop.

It appeared to have been treated with a fresh white coat of paint.

I parked and headed towards the church steps.

At first, I noticed no evidence of her silly story, but then a sharp breeze cleared out a pile of golden and raspberry leaves in front of my feet.

That's when I saw it—the zigzag line.

Stooping down, I touched it, and I jerked back—something burnt my hand.

I stood up.

Mom wasn't pulling my leg, I thought to myself.

It really did happen.

THE END

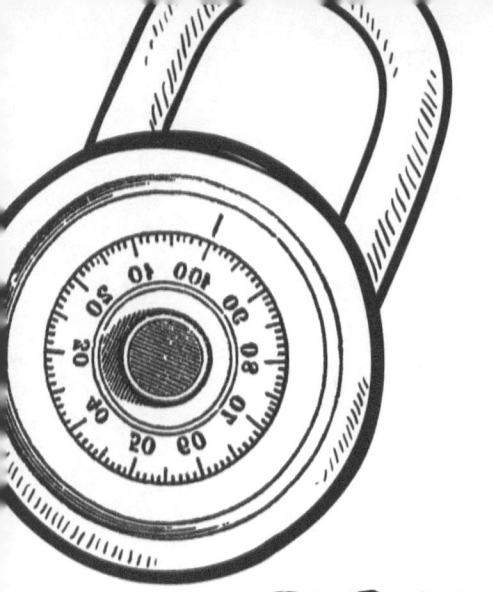

Theme Song: "Cell Block Tango"
Artist: Chicago (the musical)

FORGOTTEN

Mr. Marty Jenkins never made time for himself to clean or sort through his polluted basement until one Halloween weekend. He'd retired from being a middle school librarian for more than forty years. He unburied a black and golden chest, almost half the size of a twin bed, from underneath a gigantic pile of vintage clothing and warped boxes.

It had three combination locks—one in front and two on both sides. His body started shaking. A book flew off a shelf and landed into his open, trembling hands. The pages flipped to the last page where sets of numbers and crooked initials of his late teen sister, RJ, appeared at the bottom. Something pounded on the inside twice, and guided him to open each swinging lock. It was overdue...

THE END

Theme Song: "Maneater"
Artist: Daryl Hall & John Oates

PROWLER

Tick, Tock...

Tick, Tock...

It slithers around trees and in between leaves.

Spiraling up and down rooftops, it hovers above in its twisted invisibility.

After lavender sunsets, it dances while summoning black rains to wash away the hidden, gurgling screams.

Where any heartbeat races, it watches until the time is right.

Anticipation to strike is its favorite pastime while waiting to capture its prey.

Most don't think it's real.

So, if you're up for a little scare dare, then follow these simple directions.

Prepare a candlelit room and leave one window open.

Don't forget to hit the record button on your cell phone.

Then, repeat this out loud:

One

Two

Three...

I see you staring at me...
Show me what you are!

You'll feel a lingering chill climb up your thighs then towards your shivering spine.

A wet, musty odor will saturate the air and extinguish all the candle flames.

Once you feel something scratching at the back of your throat, close your eyes tight.

Your mouth will open automatically, and it will climb deep down to suck out your shattered soul before your lifeless body collapses and dissolves into a pile of sand.

It'll fly away into the onyx lights, devouring the gifts you surrendered.

I used to be a nonbeliever just like you until I found my best friend's phone buried under his powdery remains and viewed the video.

Be careful, it may just find you... next.

Tick, Tock...

Tick, Tock...

THE END

Theme Song: "Nighttime Hunger"
Artist: Overcoats

SUMMER OF 1989

Chopping Mall
>   *A Nightmare on Elm Street*
>   *Wolfen*
Friday the 13th
Basket Case
Re-Animator
Night of the Creeps
Howling
Vamp
Sleepaway Camp
Halloween...

Triggered my night terrors each night I drifted off to sleep.

I tried to stop watching them and others, but I couldn't.

My addiction to horror was my reality.

Each night, I would do the same thing—pollute my mind with horrific images.

In my dreams, the monsters always seemed to find me... no matter how hard I tried to hide.

When I woke up soaking wet from my sweat, I continued saturating my mind with those dark visions.

I should've locked them inside an impenetrable box a long time ago and buried it a thousand feet, deep down in the Mediterranean Sea.

Instead, my transformation began...

Chains nor cages could hold me.

I became pieces of those creatures I watched.

My passion to hunt cancelled my redemption.

I tried to leave clues for the police to find me, but it never worked.

An untouchable armor meshed into my once human flesh.

My internal destruction grew and grew into a voracious appetite.

I could never satiate it—I wanted and craved more.

Instead, I waited for my new victim to exit her dorm room.

Darkness gifted me the perfect opportunity to snatch her.

Loose papers flew from her satchel.

Shredded pages from her books carouseled into the wind, as her blood shimmered on the pavement from the bronze moonlight.

THE END

Theme Song: "Girl on Fire"
Artist: Alicia Keys

ROUNDUP

Priority #1:

　　Pushing the button, so I could exterminate all of them.

Priority #2:

Leaving Cydrastearea-S709 as fast as I could to prevent mass infection.

"Rain! I can't let you kill them," Shane shouted.

Staring at her, I thought back to over four months ago, when I lived on Earth with Mrs. O and the bunch. No worries like the ones I faced now.

MRS. O YELLED, "COME DOWN QUICK BEFORE YOU MISS IT, AGAIN."

Grabbing my backpack, I slid down the stair rail and jumped off before she caught me.

"Don't think I didn't see that, Rain Stephens. Come watch with me."

I flopped down on the couch next to her. She punched a button on her cell and a hologram appeared. The guy didn't look over thirty. He sported shoulder-length, black curly hair, deep blue eyes, and dimples. He sat on top of his desk decorated with awards and spoke:

> *"Salutations on August 20, 2099. I'm Dean Woolfe of Cydrastearea-S709. Are you ready for something amazing that only happens once a year? I bet you are. If you're between the ages of fourteen and seventeen, then you're eligible to apply to become a Cydrastearean Cadet and travel to Cydrastearea-S709—Cydra for short—to join a special program to improve your cognition and physical abilities.*
>
> *Cydra is a magnificent planet between Zahadd and Vuumeon. It's full of natural beauty and incredible wonders. If you're selected and complete the program, then you'll be able to choose the university or specialty school of your choice back on Earth with a full ride and a generous monthly stipend until you complete your studies.*
>
> *Your parents or guardians will also be handsomely compensated. A one-time payment will be deposited into their personal accounts, once you sign the contract. So, what are you waiting for? Apply today to the Cydra Cadet Program. It's easy—just complete the mini application in your hologram direct message box. You'll be notified within*

twenty-four hours or less if you've been chosen and detailed instructions will be linked to you. Your school principal will also be contacted.

Before I close, take a look behind me at Cydra for yourself. This could be your new future!"

Humongous bay windows showcased turquoise, rose, and violet skies with thousands of stars beaming down. Burgundy, castle-shaped mountains outlined the wide landscape and colorful loopers—a two-headed hummingbird species—zipped back and forth. Cascading orange and plum palm trees blew in the wind. I'd heard about this planet and program from teachers and kids in my class. I'd even done some research for my astronomy class a year ago about Cydra.

About ten years ago, a satellite discovered Cydra, which was way outside our solar system, and within a year, a classified group of astronauts landed there to study it. They found the planet had some similarities to Earth, and humans could inhabit it with proper essentials. A multi-billionaire created this program; he wanted to give youth exceptional opportunities.

"Mrs. O, I'm not sure about leaving Earth to go to some unknown crazy planet that could be infested with Xenomorphs, Predators, or worse... alien zombies."

She laughed and said, "Rain, there's no such thing. You've been streaming too many of those make-believe movies. Plus, this could be your ticket out of here. No more foster homes for you. You're always talking about what would happen, if you had a chance to attend Winfrey University. If you get selected and complete the program, then there's a full ride with no strings, like Dean Woolfe said."

"It sounds really good, but nothing in this world comes without strings," I said, taking in three deep breaths. I think I knew that better than most kids my age after being dropped into ten foster homes since I was seven.

"You're right, however, some strings are worth it, like this one. Just apply and see. Your chances are pretty slim, right?"

"Yeah... I guess," I said, shrugging my shoulders and grabbing my lunch bag off the counter.

"You have nothing to lose."

Standing there, I thought about what Mrs. O had just rattled off. A place like that wouldn't want some poor, foster girl who had nothing to give back. I applied anyway from my phone.

Opening the front door, I slipped on my scuffed-up, hot pink and black Jetters—flying high-top, tennis shoes with butterfly-shaped motors attached to the back of them—helmet, goggles, and knee and elbow pads. I touched the buttons on the sides and hovered above the ground and then shot into the gray sky towards school. Mrs. O had told me stories about how the sky used to be bright blue years ago.

During lunch that day, I heard several students talking about how they applied to the Cydra Program. I ran into Rubee Goldstein in the bathroom. She would be voted the *Stuck-Up Bitch* of Class 2100 at Fern Valley High, if that was an actual category.

Looking down at my Jetters, she rolled her eyes and said, "Those are practically three seasons ago, Stephens. They're filthy. Surprised you made it here in one piece with those poking out wires."

She was right. I barely had. I'd stopped at least three times to rewire. I almost crashed into a Supreme Telsa-ZX433 next to me. I'd somersaulted over it just in time. The driver honked at me and sped past while shouting, "Stay out of the airlanes, if you don't know how to operate your flight gear," as he zoomed away.

Rubee glanced over at me as her transparent cosmetic plate floated up in the air. She tapped on a shade of plum with a wand and pointed towards her mouth, and it appeared on her perfect lips. "I know I'm a surefire to get in the program. My daddy knows Dean Woolfe, personally."

I was silent and turned away from her to dry my hands under the cherry infrared lamp.

"Didn't you hear me, Stephens?" she barked, still staring down at my shoes. "I'm wearing an early release pair, Moon Jetters 2101 signed by the Takibi Star Moon, an ultra-female gymnast/ice-skater/archer/, who won several gold and silver medals in the 2084 Olympics. These are faster and smoother—very expensive and way out of your league."

Maybe my Jetters should've stayed in the trash heap when I found them a few months ago. I stared back at her and said, "Good for you, Rubee. I hope you don't get attacked in those pretty Moon Jetters on the planet when you land there."

"Attacked... what the hell are you talking about?" she hissed, spraying saliva in my direction.

I ducked to my left.

"C'mon, you know every planet has its weird creatures. Cydra has these crazy aggressive, venomous flying red lizards with hairy bodies and six legs called drazosnappers. They're about the size of a squirrel with golden whipping scorpion tails and protruding fangs. If one of them even scratches you with its tail or grazes you with one of its fangs, then your survival rate is less than three percent, if antivenom isn't in reach."

"Whatever!"

"Hey, you can hologram me if you make it, right?"

Rubee huffed and stomped out of the bathroom. Her cosmetic plate remained floating in the air.

That evening when I returned home, Mrs. O was taking out a huge pan of lasagna. The other kids—Joe, Mike, and Myrtle—were in the living room. Joe and Mike had despised me ever since I'd invaded their so-called home, but Myrtle, eleven and the youngest in the O foster family, had welcomed me.

Myrtle ran up to me. "Are you leaving us, Rain? Mrs. O told us that you applied. I'm really going to miss you."

"I haven't heard anything yet, and I probably won't. Listen, Myrtle, I'm not getting in, so don't worry. Girls like me just don't." I started up the stairs.

Myrtle caught my hand and whispered, "Hey, maybe a girl like you just might." She smiled, hugged me around my waist, and joined the rest of the kids in the kitchen.

"Hurry back down, Rain. You know my lasagna seems to evaporate around here," Mrs. O said as she untied her apron and smiled at me.

Pausing for a few seconds, I continued climbing the stairs to wash up.

I was about to go back down when a glowing blue message image appeared on my ceiling. I hit the play button on my cell phone. "You have one hologram message from Dr. Woolfe."

My mouth dropped. I froze for a moment. I ran out of my room and yelled downstairs, "Mrs. O, please come quick!" I listened again to make sure I'd heard it correctly the first time.

Mrs. O dragged herself into my room out of breath, and the other kids were right behind her. Myrtle made her way over and stood next to me.

"What's wrong?" Mrs. O asked, panting.

"I have a message from Dr. Woolfe," I said in a trembling voice.

"Oh, Rain, this is so exciting. Have you listened to it yet?" she asked.

"No, I wanted you all to be here when I did."

"Play it!" Mrs. O urged.

Before I could touch the play button, Myrtle did it for me.

A full hologram of Dr. Woolfe appeared in the middle of my room. He stood there with both hands on his waist.

> "Miss Rain Stephens, congratulations! You've been selected to become a Cydrastearean Cadet. Your flight will depart tomorrow morning from your local airport and then transfer you to a special transport with your travel companions. Your travel plans are attached to this message for you to download, including the contract.
>
> Report to your check-in at 0700. Don't be late, unless you want your alternate to take your place. Congratulations again, Miss Stephens. You're about to embark on a new adventure that many can only dream about. I look forward to seeing you tomorrow night during the reception.
>
> Please only bring three items—apart from your cell phone—that can fit in an 8x10 space. I'll discuss our communication protocol more at the reception. Return your signed contract to me this evening. Until we meet, Miss Stephens, I bid you your last night on Earth."

His hologram vanished and so did Mike and Joe. Myrtle grabbed my hand. "Rain, I don't want you to leave me, but you were chosen, so you gotta go. A girl like you made it in!"

"You really think I should go?" I asked, scanning all the pictures in my room and looking into Myrtle's eyes. Earth was all I'd ever known.

She nodded, released my hand, and exited my room.

Mrs. O sat down on my bed.

"I guess this is it. It happened so fast," I said.

Standing up, she walked towards my open window and pointed towards the sky. "You're going to be way up there somewhere, Rain. You know other kids I've taken care of have applied, but were never chosen. You're the first." She turned around and hugged me. "Now pack your bag, download your flight information, sign that contract, and send it back, immediately. We'll leave the house around 5:30 in the morning, so you'll be there early. There's no way anyone else is taking your spot. Get some rest. Your life won't be the same after tonight."

On our way to the airport that morning, I thought about how Mrs. O has taken care of me over the last year. She'd been the best foster mom I'd ever had. I knew I would miss her and Myrtle. The car floated a few inches from the curb. We all stepped out. They hugged me. I didn't want to let either one of them go. I thought I could block my tears. I was wrong. We were all crying together. Mrs. O dug through her purse to find tissue and handed Myrtle and me a few.

We embraced until Mrs. O whispered, "Rain, it's time for you to go. I'm going to miss having you around the house. I'll especially miss scolding you for sliding down the stair rail. You learn all you can on

Cydra. Don't forget to holo-message me, if you're not too busy."

"I'll be messaging you both."

"Be careful out there," Mrs. O said, wiping tears from her face with one of her hands.

I nodded. As I started to walk away from them, Myrtle yelled, "Check your bag when you get to Cydra. Love you!"

Dropping my bag down to the ground, I turned around and brushed my tears away with my hands. "I love you too. I'll see you soon."

I watched them until they were out of sight in the clouds. I picked up my bag and entered the airport. I checked in and boarded the crowded flight soon after. I wanted to know what Myrtle had added to my bag. It still felt the same, no lighter or heavier. I'd packed a picture of us at the beach from last summer, a faded vintage Charles Jackson French T-shirt, and my lightning rod stud earrings. I pressed down and could hear paper crinkling.

After a few hours in the air, the plane landed at Chicago O'Hare International Airport III. I followed the instructions to head to Terminal CDY-S9, located in a deep end of the airport. Upon arrival, I noticed secure glass doors. I retrieved my paperwork from my pocket, and I glanced down at it. I found a code to enter into the keypad.

Seven other girls around my age were huddled up and talking. They were all dressed in mango and turquoise jumpsuits embossed with shiny letters, which spelled out Cydra Cadet 3, and assigned Roman numerals printed on the back. One girl looked up at me but didn't say anything. A young lady on a levitating power scooter came up to me with a glowing green clipboard and pen in front of her.

"Greetings. My name is Miss Daphene York, and I'm the intake director. May I see your paperwork?" she requested.

I handed it over to her, and she scanned it with the pen.

"Thank you and welcome aboard, Miss Stephens. Please wait here."

She returned with a bag.

"You'll find your uniform inside. Change and join the other ladies. In the next thirty minutes, we'll complete a quick health scan on each of you, and then you all will be on your way to Cydra."

"What kind of health scan?" I questioned, clenching my hands.

"Oh, it's nothing to be nervous about. Just a little finger prick for a blood sample and a walk through that scanner over there," she said, pointing over her shoulder.

After I changed into my comfy jumper, I noticed a shoe box at the bottom of the bag. I flipped off the lid and pushed back the red and white polka dot tissue paper. A shiny pair of silver and yellow Jetters rested inside. They looked like Rubee's, but sweeter—these were autographed by Wicked Crimson, my favorite and one of the coolest girl bands around. I kicked off my old ones and slipped them on.

Staring down at my new shoes, I started thinking how I wouldn't be returning home after my last marine biology class today to show them to Myrtle. Instead, I would be somewhere far away in space for months, which also meant no more late night talks with Myrtle. She was probably the closest I'd ever had to a best friend—still there were things about my past that I'd never share with her.

I didn't hang out with anyone at school. I guess after you'd been hurt so many times, you just start avoiding people. I placed my hand over my heart, and I could feel it beating faster than usual. Tears flowed down my warm face. I wiped it with my shirt and threw it in the bag. I knew this was an opportunity that I couldn't throw away for me or them.

Upon my return to the sitting area, I noticed that all the girls were standing in line waiting to be scanned. Triple, elliptical rings spun around each girl's entire body as they stepped into the middle of the platform. When scanning was complete, we all ran our right index finger down a square glass on the side of the scanner's panel. Miss York tapped our fingers with a bandage pen that terminated the bleeding and a clear bandage wrapped around our fingers.

Only one girl was left to be scanned and when she gave a blood sample, loud sirens sounded off along with twirling, bright lights. We jumped, looking around. Miss York ushered the girl out quickly to a side door, where a guy in a suit and dark shades escorted her from the area.

"Is she okay? What happened?" I asked in a tremoring tone.

Miss York said, "She didn't pass the test—she'll become very ill within a year or less. Her replacement will arrive tomorrow and travel in her place to Cydra."

I wondered if I'd made the right decision to be part of this program after what I'd just witnessed. Could I still back out? If I did that, then Mrs. O wouldn't receive her compensation, and I really wanted her and Myrtle to be taken care of. I closed my eyes tight, counted backwards from twenty, and envisioned Mrs. O and Myrtle enjoying themselves on the beach.

"Ladies, it's time to board. Now, if any of you are having second thoughts and wish to terminate your contract, this would be the time," she said and gazed at each girl.

No one volunteered, including me.

"Okay, please locate your assigned seats and follow the instructions from your captain. I hope each of you succeeds on Cydra and beyond. We'll *not* meet again. I bid you goodbye." She placed her scooter in reverse and faded out of sight.

We traveled down the spiral walkway and boarded ivory stairs. The aircraft we boarded wasn't a rocket, but a Hyperboloid spaceship with rotating wings. The interior was all white with blacked-out windows. Each seat had Roman numerals that corresponded to the ones on our jumpsuits. I looked all around for the exit signs as both of my hands squeezed the seat armrests. A soprano voice spoke from the speakers.

"Good morning, ladies. My name is Captain Batwana. You'll find a magenta band secured on the arm of your chair. I'll need you to place it on your wrist and fasten your seatbelt in the next five minutes. Once you see green lasers shooting up and down the ceiling, you'll begin to feel sleepy."

I unsnapped the thick band and examined it in my shaky and sweaty hands.

Captain Batwana continued, "The band will release a dual medication into your bloodstream that will slow your heart rate and place each of you into a temporary sleep paralysis. This is necessary as you couldn't survive traveling from Earth to Cydra without it. This process was included in the contract that each of you signed. I hope you didn't skip that part. So, any questions?"

I didn't hear a chirp from any of the other girls, even though they sure were Chatty C-3POs earlier in the airport. Although I did read the contract, I couldn't recall the medication stuff now. I pressed the yellow call button.

"Yes, Miss Stephens, how may I assist you," Captain Batwana replied.

"Umm, the medication bracelet, any weird side effects we need to know about?" I asked. I felt as if heated eyes were targeting me.

"No. The medications are safe and have been through a series of tests before the program was initiated. You all will be just fine, and I assure you that you all are in good hands. Anything else?" she asked.

I tapped the button once more.

"Yes, Miss Stephens," she said with a slight giggle.

I hesitated then asked, "I don't think I'm the only one that's noticed, but why are there are no guys on board with us?"

"Cydra possesses many rules. Some I'm not privy to. I recommend you take your question up with Dean Woolfe," she explained in a calm tone. "Do you have any other concerns?"

Staring out into the black abyss, I said, "No, I'm good."

"One more thing, ladies. Each band has been downloaded with your personal playlists and memories—from the information each of you shared on your application—which will accompany you during your rest," Captain Batwana said. "All right, I'm about to begin the flight plan. I'll meet each of you once we land."

I pulled my seatbelt strap around my waist and was about to fasten it, when I felt multiple taps on the back of my headrest. I leaned over to my left. A freckled-faced girl with a midnight-blue pixie haircut waved at me.

"Hi, I'm Shane," she whispered.

"Hey," I replied. "What do you think so far about all of this, especially no boys allowed to fly with us?"

"I'm sure Cydra has it's reasons for separate gender flights. I think it's going to be exciting. I can't wait!" Shane smiled.

The lasers danced on the ceiling.

"It's time. I'll see you on Cydra when we wake up," she said.

"Sure."

When I woke up, I recalled how I'd dreamt about when I'd first arrived at Mrs. O's home, and how she'd welcomed me in. I could even smell warm strawberry and lemon cookie drops from the kitchen. She'd never questioned what happened at my previous fosters. There was no judgement. That was the first time I'd felt safe in my life. Did I make a mistake by going through with this? Would I need to be on watch every night again to protect myself?

"Finally," a heartfelt ballad by Wicked Crimson, continued to play in my head, which was a good distraction for me to hold on to, even if it was temporary. We'd traveled for many hours. Yet, I felt as if I'd just been napping. All the other girls around me were still in their deep sleep. I peeked back and noticed Shane's seat was empty.

Footsteps approached. I watched a petite lady with a bald head wearing neon green goggles and matching boots make her way toward each girl to ensure she was awake. I figured this had to be Captain Batwana. A badass Medusa tattoo decorated her muscular upper arm.

"Are you feeling okay, Miss Stephens?" she asked me and stooped down as she ran a thick, mahogany wand with buttons down my forehead and chest. She tapped a button on it—my vitals and heartrate readings all popped up in front of us with my name, weight, and birthdate underneath. "All clear. You're good to exit. Now, keep your band on, or you'll float away when you're outside. If your band malfunctions for some reason, then those special Jetters you have on will also prevent you from flying off to who knows where," Captain Batwana said with a grin.

"Thanks. Umm, where did the girl behind me go?" I asked.

"She woke up first. She's probably preparing for the reception tonight with Dr. Woolfe and the faculty."

"I almost forgot about that."

"That's a mandatory event, Miss Stephens—make sure you attend. You can exit how you entered, and an XC37 robot guide will be waiting to escort you to your living quarters."

"Can I ask you a question?" I said as I stood up to collect my bag from the compartment above me.

"Of course."

"Is there anything I need to know about?" I asked, frowning as sweat ran down my back, around my hairline, and down the sides of my face.

"Not to my knowledge. In fact, since I've been transporting cadets from Earth to Cydra, no one has ever requested to return to Earth." She pushed a button on a seat panel. A drawer of medical supplies slid out. She pulled out a box of tissues and gave me a few. "After you get to your room and have a nice shower, I think you'll feel a little better."

"Thank you, Captain Batwana."

"You're very welcome." She pressed the button and the drawer slid back and closed.

That seemed strange, that no one had wanted to return back to take advantage of the offered scholarships and opportunities. Were things so good here that they never wanted to leave?

"Enjoy your reception tonight and time on Cydra. I bid you

nothing, but good fortunes here, Miss Stephens." She bowed and stepped away from me.

I thought about remaining on the ship for a short moment.

A slender, bronze robot, which reminded me of an ancient standing fan I'd found in Mrs. O's attic last spring, guided me as I exited off the ship. "Follow me, please," it said in a choppy, metallic voice.

I paused for a minute to look back at the ship, then I exited onto Cydra. I gazed in awe at its multiple moons and iridescent skyline that seemed to glisten. I'd never seen anything like this before. The ground was full of lush white sand with lilac crystals. A looper landed on my shoulder for a moment and dashed away, leaving shiny flakes circling around my face.

The robot demanded, "Please follow," as it made clunky sounds strolling down the pathway. A gigantic dome covered the entire campus, possibly the size of three professional football fields. Four floating ultraviolet, medieval-like castles appearing to be made of sea glass were nestled inside the protective covering. Sparkling streams ran between them. Each castle possessed several towers with turrets.

One tower matched the color of my jumper and that was the direction we were headed in. The robot pulled out a burgundy flute from the side of its arm and played a classic song, "Memories" by Maroon 5. The castle lowered itself down as a transparent travelator levitated in front of us. The robot rolled in front of me onto the moving walkway. "Come." The robot secured the instrument back into its location.

I followed. As we approached the shield, I lifted my hand to touch it. The robot swatted my hand away. I jumped back. The robot rotated its head around to face me and shouted, "No touching, ever! It'll cause severe burns, if not worse." The robot continued to punch the code into the number pad. A portion of the force shield opened up and immediately closed once we were inside the Cydra campus. The hallways were massive and empty. Camera drones flew up and down, high above me. We traveled for several minutes before we arrived at my room.

"This is your new home, Cydra Dorm #3. Your attire for the evening is in your closet. The start time is 1730 hours. I bid you goodnight," the robot said and rolled away.

Once I entered my room, the door slid closed. I noticed two bathrooms, twin beds—a bag placed on one—and heard water running from one of the bathrooms. I inspected the room. I found a stiff A-line dress with the same colors and assigned Roman numerals as the jumpsuits, hanging in my closet with almond heels.

There were two glass desks, plus, doors to separate bathrooms on each side of the room. When I touched the glass desk with my hand, personal memories of Earth flashed all over it. I could even rearrange them. I thought about a concert I attended last Halloween, and those memories popped up. The desk was reading my mind. My heart started beating faster.

I backed up and sat on the bed, thinking how I wasn't on Earth anymore, but on Cydra with all this awesome technology around me, waiting to be explored. Glancing down at my bag, I remembered Myrtle's gift. I unzipped it and dug it out.

If you're reading this, then you're on Cydra. I bet that place is truly something. I'm sure it's not polluted and overpopulated like Earth. I knew you would be selected. They need someone brave and strong like you, Rain. Don't worry about me and Mrs. O. We'll be fine. Just do your best and do what's right, like you've always told me. I hope we see each other after your training is complete. Take care.

Love your little sis, Myrtle

P.S. I cannot wait to hear about everything. You can't leave anything out!

Tears crept down my cheeks as I folded her letter up and placed it back inside my bag. I thought to myself, *Myrtle, I sure do hope I made the right decision filling out that application and accepting this invitation. Plus, who's my roomie? Will I have that loathsome girl that forces you to move out?* I wiped my tears away, scanning the floating digital clock. It was getting close to the time for the reception. I took a quick shower and dried off. As I zipped up the back of my dress, the other bathroom door opened.

"Hey, it's you, again," I said. "I didn't think I would see you this soon."

"Anything is possible on Cydra, Rain," she said, tightening the towel around her chest as she refocused her eyes on me.

"Shane, right?" I asked as I placed my feet into the heels. I felt the hair on my arms standing up.

"You got it. Shoot, I better hurry," she whined.

Handing her dress to her, I said, "You'll make it."

"Thanks, roomie."

"Welcome."

Shane slid her dress on and zipped up just in time before the door slid open, and a XC37 entered to escort us down to the reception area.

It was packed. Twinkling white lights hung down like swinging, jungle vines and starlight from the open, multi-level triangular, ceiling made it look like a magical prom night. Shane and I found our seats. As robots served dinner, I looked all around the room in search of Rubee, but she wasn't here. None of the popular, rich kids in my district were either.

Shane nudged me. "Are you okay?" she asked.

"Yes, I just thought a classmate of mine would be here," I said, squinting my eyes.

"She just wasn't Cydra material, but we are," she said and chuckled.

"Guess so... Hey, there's no male students here. Why are the only males in the room faculty?" I asked, staring down at the plate of shrimp scampi that had a red, slimy sauce drenched all over it.

With her mouth full as she chewed, Shane said, "Boys distract... Isn't this good?"

I was about to answer, but Dr. Woolfe began his speech:

"Welcome to the future and more. Each of you were hand selected to be part of our unique program on Cydra. Your school curriculums will consist of intense art, reading, writing, math, science, flight training, martial arts, horticulture, yoga, mindfulness training, and special weapon training, which will be taught by the brilliant faculty behind me.

A very strict diet will be followed for all your meals, especially ritual vitamin shakes in the mornings. These shakes are mandatory to your training and time here. Daily digital readings by your assigned XC37 will notify me if you've skipped any. Skipping more than three may mean immediate expulsion from Cydra, including recall of the entire monetary gift given to your guardian with harsh punishments to be implemented, if repayment is late.

Once you complete your studies here, you'll be given the choice to return back to Earth to pursue your dream college or special studies, paid in full, or you may remain on Cydra, as long as you wish. One more thing, no hologram communications until the end of your program. Enjoy your evening and sleep well. Your training begins early in the morning. I bid each of you much success here."

"Is he insane? No hologram communications and daily vitamin drinks! I don't remember him mentioning anything about that before," I said, raising my voice.

"That part is in the contract," Shane said in a calm tone.

"Well, I just don't remember, and I don't like it! I promised Mrs. O and Myrtle that I would holo them."

Looking up at me, she asked, "Your mom and sister?"

"Sort of. I'm a foster girl," I said as I moved the shrimp around with my utensil.

"No way, Rain, I'm a foster too."

"What?" I dropped my fork in my plate. "You understand what foster life can be like."

She nodded and continued to eat, slightly shifting her eyes away from me.

"Hey, you okay?" I asked, placing my hand on her shoulder.

"Yes... bad flashback. I'm just so happy to know we have something in common. By the way, you can email your family."

Twirling some pasta onto my fork, I said, "Just not the same as seeing someone." I sniffed it, and placed in my mouth. "Shane, if those shakes taste anything like this fishy crap in my mouth, then I may just get kicked out of here."

"You won't. I'm going to help you get through all of it, even the no holo communications, and you're going to do the same for me, roomie. Eat up. We have a big day ahead of us tomorrow."

I thought about what Shane had said that night and convinced myself to do what I needed to do for four semesters and one summer. I read Myrtle's letter each night after classes to inspire me to keep going. I emailed Mrs. O and Myrtle often, and they always sent me emails with pictures of where they had traveled to. Mrs. O had even purchased a new vehicle, which she'd been needing for a long time. They looked really happy. I knew that I'd made the right decision.

The days and weeks flew by—we were nearing winter and our second semester. The education that I received on Cydra was mind blowing. I was learning complicated acrobatic flight moves in my Jetters, growing strange plants, practicing Wing Chu and Hapkido, and reading books that had been banned on Earth, such as the *Goosebumps* series by R. L. Stine, *The Weight of Blood* by Tiffany D. Jackson, and *Cemetery Tours* by Jacqueline E. Smith.

My friendship with Shane blossomed. We assisted each other with our studies and practiced martial art training techniques together. She slipped me *Imag Tabs* for those sour and bitter daily shakes. If faculty knew we had them, then we would be expelled. Immediately. Shane showed me the best places to hide them.

I dropped a tab in my shake each morning. Whatever I imagined for that shake to taste like then that tab worked it's magic. Strawberry shortcake and double fudge swirl was my favorite. The best thing that I appreciated from Shane was her listening to my foster stories, and she sharing hers. She truly understood foster life. She was the first person I felt comfortable around to share my personal secrets.

Yet, I craved more. I wanted to know who the other girls were from Cydra Dorms #1, #2, and #4. I wondered how they were coping here. However, that was forbidden. You were only allowed to engage with students from your own dorm house. Too many crazy rules and secrets existed here... I couldn't wait to return to Earth and see my family and pursue my dream, which was to attend Winfrey University and study pre-med and engineering.

After winter finals, Shane, a group of girls—Lee, Evie, Tonya, and Wynd—from our dorm, and I decided to go on an evening hike. They were fosters too. Our entire dorm were made up of foster, homeless, or runaway girls. The have-nots were finally being treated right.

The temperature that evening was fifty-nine degrees. We came across a crystal, tequila ocean and sat on huge rocks on top of Cydra Nine Peak to watch flying dolphins. They jumped more than two hundred feet in the air. A few flew towards us and allowed us to pet them. They had large, purple eyes and made cooing echoes. Their glistening black and white bodies reminded me of an Appaloosa horse's coat pattern.

Evie wandered off from our group. After fifteen minutes, we heard her yell out, "Hey guys, I found a cool cave. Come check it out!"

I'd started getting off the warm rock when Shane grabbed my arm and whispered, "Stay."

Jerking my arm away from her, I said in a stern tone, "It sounds interesting. This is the first time in months we've been outside our prison walls without stalker robots or teachers watching our every move. We've earned this. Come on. It'll be fun, Shane."

"You know we're only supposed to stay within the perimeter."

"What's the fun in that?" I whined.

"Go ahead. I'm going to watch the dolphins for a while," she said, pulling her knees closer into her chest. "Just be careful, Rain."

"I'll be fine," I said, looking behind me as I jogged backwards waving at her. "I have all my new martial art moves we've been learning to try out, if I need to."

Before I reached the cave, I heard piercing screams. All of the girls ran out as a swarm of drazosnappers flew behind them. Their coarse hairs fired from their squirrel-sized bodies and shot through the air, targeting the girls until they collapsed.

The drazosnappers with their six dangling legs pounced on them and started draining them with their twirling, golden pinchers at the end of their tails. As they opened their mouths, thick, burgundy venom dripped from their spiky fangs—they pierced them several times on their faces, arms, and thighs.

I stood still, trembling. Although I'd read about them, I discounted them being real. Shane came up behind me and softly spoke in my ear, "Move slow and be quiet… they sense rapid movement and loud noises. Follow me."

We had almost reached the path back to the dorms when I stepped on a branch. A loud crunch echoed in the wind, and a drazosnapper spotted us from the sky. Before Shane could punch in the code to open an entry way through the force shield, it punctured my thigh with its flailing tail and fangs. I screamed and a flood of tears followed. It felt as if thousand bees and jellyfish stung me all at once. We made it inside our fortress. Shane kicked the front half of its body off of me while the other half of it ignited into flames, banging up against the shield, until it ceased moving.

Shane dragged me to the closest infirmary, located in Cydra Dorm #4—a dorm that was off limits to all underclassmen cadets. I dropped down onto the medical table. My breathing quickened and my heart began to race. No staff were present. She flung cabinets, drawers, and a refrigerator door open to search for the antivenom. Medical supplies and medications cluttered the floor. My vision blurred. I saw her stab two long needles in my thigh and chest. They stung for a while.

"Sorry, I had to do that before the toxin reached your heart. You're going to be okay," she said.

I closed my eyes and woke up a few hours later. I felt better, but had to pee. Shane waited next to me. "Thank you for saving my life. I should've listened to you and avoided the cave excursion."

"Glad you're okay." She squeezed my hand.

"Where's the bathroom?" I pleaded.

"Down the hall to the left."

"Thanks." I looked down and ran my hand over my bruised and swollen leg.

After I went to the bathroom, I must have become disoriented, as I entered a different room instead of the infirmary. It was oversized, cold, and full of miniature glass aquariums with pale tadpole and octopus-looking creatures, swinging their multiple blue and orange tentacles as they floated. I squeezed my eyes shut and opened them up. The creatures remained. I felt my leg muscles tightening. I heard footsteps behind me, and I whipped around.

"What in the hell are all these, Shane?" I demanded.

"You weren't supposed to find out like this, Rain," she said with her head lowered. "I couldn't let you die because you've been my friend."

"Shane, you didn't answer me. What are these things?"

"Embryos... Cydrastearean embryos."

"For what?"

She looked away and mumbled, "You and the other girls... humans. Your date to have your Cydrastearean embryo implant is scheduled during the summer before your senior year. That's the magic year when a human body is ready for the delicate, medical procedure."

"Hold on. Are you telling me that I'm going to be a surrogate for one of those slimy, octo-tad little monsters?"

Clearing her throat, she said, "Cydrastearean embryo is the correct term, an extraordinary alien being."

I marched around her slowly and stared at the glass cases and began processing everything.

"Now, it all makes sense. That's why Rubee wasn't selected. Only *rejects*, like me, fosters or homeless girls are picked. I always wondered why most of the girls in our dorm came from foster homes. We can easily be erased. Just dangling a prize in front of us is all it takes. Then comes the isolation, forcing us to keep our mouths shut, feeding us those awful meals and shakes to prep our bodies, and lastly impregnating us. Boys would never be selected for Cydra—they're wombless."

"You summed it up well," Shane said. "Cydrastereans have been collaborating with your elite leaders in the highest sectors for years. In exchange for our advance tech secrets and other mysterious techniques, they sacrifice their young girls with no family ties—those who won't be missed—to us. They're disposable."

"So, what happened to Evie, Wynd, Lee, and Tonya means nothing to you?" I asked, staring into her motionless eyes and balling up my fists.

Rocking back and forth on her heels, she projected in a rigid tone, "In all wars, there are casualties. This is the battle to save our species. Evie and the other girls knew the risks of going outside the perimeter, which is lectured to us every morning at breakfast, as you know them—they chose not to follow the rules. I can tell you how sorry I am, if that'll make you feel better."

"You know what, Shane, don't even worry about it. You're beyond clueless... This program is a freakin' *roundup* of forgotten girls. Hottie Dr. Woolfe and his pack knew who they wanted all along. Guess what? I'm not keeping my mouth shut. This is all *ending* tonight. I'm killing every last one of those embryos. So, don't get in my way. If I have to hurt you, then I will," I said as a stream of sweat ran down my neck and back. My heart started racing faster and faster.

"Rain, please stop! You don't understand everything. Cydrastearean females can't carry to full-term anymore. The planet's water poisoned the female's wombs, and genetic defects began to emerge. Before the poison impacted the protected queens, they were able to produce thousands of eggs."

Glaring at her, I screamed, "I don't care about Cydra history!" I stomped away from her.

"Just hear me out... In vitro fertilization procedures were conducted. Later, Cydra scientists replicated Cydrastearean eggs in labs. We've been doing this for the last ten years, ever since we discovered that young human girls are our last and best hope to host our embryos to survive. Due to the violent births by our species, the fatality rate of humans is inevitable, which is why we are steadily recruiting."

Facing her, I cocked my head. "Um, wait, *you're* a Cydrastearean? You look like me."

"Yes, we can *shapeshift* into any living thing. I'm sorry you feel how you do. I wish there was another way, but I'm afraid there's not." She frowned.

"Shane, you could've told me—you had so many chances to, but you didn't. You and your kind are heartless and so selfish. Girls only serve as incubators and then they die, after giving birth to your creepy spawn. The option to return to Earth was always a lie, right?" I stumbled back a step.

"The way you feel about Cydrastereans now would've been the same if I had told you earlier. I had to keep my *secret*. I was assigned to you before we boarded the ship. I sensed something special about you, Rain, and I wanted to be a friend to you for as long as I could. Yes, the specialized education and scholarships were only bait to keep you all here long enough until it was time, but guardians are truly rewarded when the contract is signed and again upon the death of their cadet, due to unforeseen circumstances. Your government are professionals in cleaning those things up."

Rolling my eyes, I replied, "I can't believe all of this. You and your friendship have both been fake since we first met. You don't understand friendship at all!" I roared.

"No, that's not true." A single tear streamed down her cheek.

Crossing my arms over my chest, I eyeballed her. "Oh, yes it is. You know everything you just told me is wrong, Shane."

Dr. Woolfe busted through the doors. "You two shouldn't be in here. Shane, I'm so disappointed in you, sister."

My eyes blinked and widened. "He's your brother?"

She nodded.

Caressing his perfect, bronze chin, he said, "Shane, you know that we're going to have to kill her before she talks."

Shane stared deep into my eyes and then looked over at him. Her left leg swept out, and he fell backward. She turned around and focused down the hallway. A blue syringe zoomed in a crooked pattern through the air. It landed inside of her open hand. She flicked the top off, bent down, and punctured the side of his neck without a blink.

Stunned, I stared at her. "I didn't expect you to do that. So, you're telekinetic, too? What did you give him? He looks dead."

"I injected him with Prolunvan-517. He's in a short-term coma and will awake tomorrow night. He'll be okay. Listen, switch Jetters with me. We're nearly the same size. I have extreme flame throwers in the back."

Slipping out of mine and into hers, I asked, "Are you serious?"

"Just press this button," she said as she yanked off a hidden auburn, oblong-shaped necklace from around her neck. "Touch it. It won't hurt you."

I was reluctant to do so, but I did. A warm, orange light illuminated my entire hand.

"All of your information has been captured. You'll have access to all of my financial affairs and other things." She smiled. "It also has a mini flash drive inside. You'll be able to download everything we've been doing here. There's a tracker inside as well, which will alert Captain Batwana and allow her to locate you soon. She'll help you and transport you back to Earth, once she views this footage. Don't ever allow anyone to take this from you."

"Come with me, Shane," I urged.

"No, Zamaun—my brother—won't stop. Someone has to end this. Rain, you're right about everything you said about my kind. Cydrasteareans have been thoughtless—we've caused so much death to humans for way too long. Your story about your last two placements before ending up with Mrs. O really made me realize what you were forced to endure. I'm sorry. Now, go." Her eyes teared up. She pushed me with a slight wave of her hand, causing me to slide almost twenty feet away from her.

In a firm tone, I said, "I'm going to stop this! No other girl deserves to go through this deception to find out she's only being trafficked. We have a right to control our own bodies."

"Yes, and you will now."

"Shane, I was wrong. You're a good friend. Thank you." I gathered up bottles of sangria~isopropyl—a highly explosive liquid—from the other room and returned to douse all the aquariums. I pushed the button on

Shane's Jetters to light them up, and I flew out of the infirmary to find Captain Batwana.

Now, I had a new mission—maybe this was why I was chosen for Cydra—and I was departing earlier than expected with no plans to ever return.

THE END

Theme Song: "Freak Show"
Artist: Ingrid Michaelson

CAMP RED ROBINS

amp Red Robins, buried deep in the Piney Woods of Mazula, Texas, shut down last summer because of what my buddies did. The best part of attending camp for them wasn't the swimming in Lake Yonder, horseback riding, baseball, tug-of-war, or archery. It was choosing a live target to prey on. They always picked out the weakest kid upon arrival. This year the trophy went to Clawde Gaustad.

He was assigned the name, Gaustad from the Dead, by us. Clawde had some type of weird skin disease that caused his Casper-the-Coward flaky skin condition to sunburn fast. While all of his bunkmates went around shirtless in shorts, he wore jeans, a wide-rimmed girly hat, and long sleeve shirts in the heat. He hunted for shade most of the day and spent his evenings near the lake.

His skin wasn't the worst thing that Gaustad had to put up with. It was his boy boobs. My friends would hang his sport bras out on tree limbs on a tall pecan tree outside the cafeteria every morning. The entire camp, some counselors, too, laughed at him jumping up and down to retrieve them.

Everything jiggled on him, even in clothes. One of the guys would always run up behind him and give him a wedgie. They were always thinking of creative things to do to him, such as placing stickers inside his tennis shoes, tossing a snake in the shower as he was bathing, and sprinkling itching powder all over his sheets and clothes.

On movie night on the north side of camp, where the entire camp gathered every Friday, I remembered that I forgot my lucky cap halfway to the site. I jogged back to my cabin. I heard someone sniffling loudly. I guessed who it was.

I grabbed my hat from the side of the bottom bunk and headed towards the door until something caused me to halt and turn around. I took in a few deep breaths and scooted backwards. I climbed up to Gaustad's bunk. He had the sheet pulled over him. I tugged at it a few times. He rolled it back a few inches under his eyes.

"Please don't make me lick the toilet seats again," he mumbled with huge tears pooling inside of his puffy eyes as his hands trembled.

For a moment, I thought about all the torturous things that had been done to him—I participated mostly on the sidelines. I folded the brim of my hat in my hands. "You gotta start standing up for yourself. If you don't, then guys like them are going to keep doing things to you, man."

Descending the metal steps, I placed my LA Rams football cap on my head and reshaped it with my hands. Before my fingers touched the doorknob, I felt hot breath, mixed with burning cedar, tickling the back of my neck. I pivoted around slowly, thinking it was Gaustad, but he wasn't there—nothing was. I waved my hands all around.

Quiet laughter ignited from Gaustad, and then his laughter intensified and grew louder and louder as he sat up from the bed.

"What's so funny?" I asked and headed towards him.

Jumping off his bunk, he said, "Being the camp freak has finally paid off for me."

"You're not making a lot of sense, Gaustad," I said, squinting my eyes.

"Let's just say, I finally made a friend who has more friends than you. They're probably already at the party right about now," he explained, pulling a bag from the closet.

"I haven't seen you with any friends this entire summer," I replied with my arms crossed over my chest.

"That's because you can't see them, but they can see all of you. I told Herbie who was mean to me. Herbie and his buddies know what it's like to be teased, poked fun at, and embarrassed. They were part of the first campers here, almost thirty years ago," he said while zipping his bag up.

"You're full of it, and where do you think you're going this time of the night?" I asked.

"If you think so," he said with a half-smile. "And I'm packing."

"Camp isn't over for two more weeks," I barked.

"Oh, it'll be closed tomorrow, especially after Herbie and his friends get done. They'll finish what I never could begin."

THE END

Theme Song: "Object of My Desire"
Artist: Starpoint

BILLIE'S GIRL

Bright lights flooded into my bedroom. Centaur law enforcement officers shattered my windows with their front hooves. I fell out of the bed and landed on all fours on my cement floor.

The leader galloped into my room. He wore a shimmering necklace decorated with military medals. He had a shoulder-length golden, spikey mane. He pounded his front leg in the middle of my back and shouted, "Billie Longhorn, you're under arrest!"

"For what?" I asked, squirming around on the ground and trying to breathe. It felt as if two horses were sitting on top of me.

"You murdered Percelus Star," he accused, his voice deep and gruff.

He pulled a cigar from his leather cross-body strap.

"No... no, that's not true. I just left her a few hours ago. I would never harm my Percey. I love her!" I shouted.

"Save it, big guy, for your execution date. You just violated the primary law here with your confession of having a relationship with her. It's all been recorded," the leader replied as he lit a cigar. Then, he pressed a button on his necklace.

He kneeled and whispered in my ear, "Your kind should've never been allowed into our land. It was just a matter of time before one of you couldn't control your thirst." He blew large puffs of smoke in my face and stood back up.

"Cuff him," he commanded and exited the way he'd entered.

Swandee Ivy handcuffs floated out of one of the officer's wooden pouches. They wrapped around my wrists. One of the officers said, "I wouldn't struggle if I were you. Any abrupt movement will trigger this plant to impale poisonous thorns into your wrists causing immediate paralysis, sometimes permanent, while you inhale a burst of chloroform and formaldehyde."

Percey and I had all these crazy plans. I'd wrote out my future wedding vows to her two nights ago. If it was really true about her being dead, then all of that meant nothing. I might as well bury my heart with hers. I didn't care what the officers did to me. Once I arrived at the jail, I was placed in a small room with the handcuffs still on. I kept my hands still. I replayed my day over in my head.

I knew we were young, but I purchased an engagement ring for Percey that morning from Ms. Beatrice Feathers, a snow fairy, who designed one-of-a-kind rings from the singing willow trees and special stones she collected from Villacian Lake.

I'd fallen in love with Percey when I met her, almost a year ago. I didn't think she could ever love someone like me. After all, I was a werewolf-kitsune, and she was a mermaid-fairy. We both knew that our love affair would be challenged by everyone here in Kamelea Forest, so we kept it a secret.

There was a truce made many years ago to allow werewolves and were-hybrids to live among the Kamelean creatures—fairies, mermaids, elves, witches, fauns, unicorns, goblins, genies, centaurs, and other hybrids. The only condition was my kind were prohibited to have any inter-creature romantic relationships with the Kameleans. We were perceived as untamed predators who would only bring destruction and elimination to their tranquil habitat.

My ears sensed footsteps almost thirty feet away, and I looked over my shoulder. The leader from earlier and one of his officers strolled into the room, carrying in a large box. I kept my eyes fixed on them as they circled the table.

"I know how this works. I've seen enough movies to know that I'm not answering any of your questions until I can make my call and have a lawyer present," I said.

"We just need to hear you confess how you murdered her and why, Billie boy, that's all. I promise you'll receive the lesser punishment." The leader snickered.

I remained silent.

"Why do you want to make this so difficult? We know you did it, and so do you," he said.

He slid a large, black plastic box on the table towards me.

"What's this?" I asked, looking into his jittering eyes.

"Open it up, and find out."

Focusing on the cuffs, I said, "I don't think I would get far trying to see what's inside there with these things on."

"Uncuff him, Officer Gweneth."

The vines unwrapped themselves from me, floated up in the air, and back into her bag.

I opened the box up and nearly pushed it off the long table.

"Why would you show me something like this?" I growled. The hanging pictures on the walls vibrated at the force of my voice. I hunched over and buried my face in my hands for a few seconds. Rolling tears ran down my arms as I lifted my head up. My three turquoise, bushy tails with honey-amber, razor tips slithered out towards Chief Watkins. My eyes locked onto his.

"Put those tails away or else," he commanded, tapping his fingers against his FN P90 laser rifle.

I retracted each one, slowly, smiling at how they made centaurs cringe.

"Keep that nonsense out of my house!" He stomped his hooves to the ground, rearing back. "It's evidence, and the crime points to you, Billie. Nobody else. Your DNA is all over her, and her sliced up tail on ice. My officers found it in your basement. I know how killers keep small souvenirs of their victims, but this is a first. Just sick!"

"I'm telling you both that I didn't do it. I was about to..."

"What?"

"I'm not saying anything else until you give me what I asked you for."

"Billie, your past isn't squeaky clean. Why don't you just give us what we want? You'll get some sleep and maybe some dog food before bed." He laughed, resting on his back, manicured hoofs against the glass door.

"Listen, chief—"

"Chief Watkins, filthy wolf." He snarled.

"Please, honor my request."

He stared at me for a few minutes and huffed.

"Officer Gweneth, give him his phone call."

I called my Godmother, Rosalynne Downey, who was a lawyer for our family. I explained what I could over the phone to her. She arrived in less than an hour as I endured vicious looks from Chief Watkins. He and Officer Gweneth gulped down a few cups each of water during the wait time, but offered none to me. Percey's bloody, mutilated tail kept playing in my head. I slammed my fists into the table, leaving two large dents.

"You're paying for that!" Chief Watkins ordered. "Officer Gweneth, add that to Billie's murder report."

She pulled out a small notebook from her pouch and scribbled his request down.

The door flung open.

"Billie, I came as fast as I could," Rosalynne said.

"Thanks for coming."

Slamming her briefcase on the table, she said, "Your mom and dad are getting on the next flight out of Romania."

"So, who's in charge?" she howled.

Chief Watkins approached her and said, "I am, Ms..."

"Ms. Downey, and I'm requesting time alone with my client."

The chief looked at his officer. "All right, you two have ten minutes, starting now."

When they left the room, Rosalynne opened up her briefcase and pulled out two writing pads with pens. She wrote out,

"Billie, I know that they're listening, so I'm going to ask you some questions. I need for you to answer by writing them down, okay?"

I nodded.

"I have to ask you this question."
"Yeah, I already know, go ahead."
"Did you murder Percelus Star?"
"No."
"Are you connected in any way to her murder?"
"No."

I exhaled.

"Do you know who would want to harm her?"
"I don't."

I ran my hands through my thick, ebony mohawk.

"Anyone wanting to harm you?"

"I haven't done anything to anyone."

"That doesn't matter. Can you think of anyone who didn't want you two together?"

"Most of those who reside here. I never wanted to live here. My kind has always been feared and viewed as worthless animals with no intelligence. I was planning on leaving that night I met Percey. Her love made me want to stay, and her support made it a little easier to tolerate this place. I still had plans to find us a home, where I didn't have to worry about nasty stares and whispers. One day, we were going to have a family."

"Billie, you're right. Life is hard here. I put up with a lot in my law office. You made a choice to love her, which takes so much courage, even if it meant your life could one day be on the line. Most of our kind only form safe relationships. So, I'm guessing that someone discovered you two were dating."

She tapped her pen against her pad.

I shook my head and paused for a minute or so before I responded.

Shrugging my shoulders, I wrote,

"Probably, someone in her family?"

"Okay, I'm going to need to question all of them."

"When do you think court will start?"

"Soon, you know how things are handled here. I'm thinking before the end of the week. Billie, this is the first murder in this community. It'll be public by morning. After all, her family are important figures in the Kamelea Forest."

"Rosalynne, you believe me, right?"

"Of course, Billie. I practically raised you. I know you're not perfect—who is? I definitely know that you're not a murderer. I'm going to prove that. I'm sorry about Percelus."

She grabbed my hands and squeezed them.

I took in a deep breath.

"You know, I was going to ask Percey to marry me."

"Oh, Billie."

She began to tear up.

"Thank you for sharing. I'm going to talk to the judge in the morning about your court date."

"I really appreciate you being here for me."

The door opened. "Time is up. So, you're going to give us that confession now?" the chief barked.

"No, sir! Please assist my client to his cell, and I hope I don't hear of any unnecessary roughness by any of your officers."

He smirked and requested for the cuffs to be put back on me.

She stood up and gathered up everything and placed it back inside her briefcase. "I'll talk to you soon, Billie." She watched me until I turned the corner to go downstairs.

The cells were partially full. When I arrived at mine, I thought I would be solo until the chief opened it up, and a head of a gopher-like critter with huge, light blue rotating eyes popped out from under the covers of the top bunk.

Chief Watkins shoved me inside the cell and uncuffed me. "Billie, you may have a lawyer, but we got you. There's no way you're getting off. I'll make sure of that. Once and for all, your kind will be banished from here. Your kind never belonged here. I tried to warn them, and they wouldn't listen back then. I bet they will now."

"Too bad you feel that way about me and the rest of us. We can't help what we are, and we're not all alike," I shot back, baring my fangs.

"Whatever, just know it'll be the death penalty by public execution when the time comes. Mark my words, Billie Longhorn!"

I stared at him through the bars.

He galloped down the hall and vanished.

My only regret was that Percey was murdered because of me. I wasn't afraid of death. I turned around. The critter in the top bunk was hanging upside down by his long tail, swinging back and forth.

"Ole Chief Watkins. He despises any creature here that doesn't look as pretty as him."

He jumped down. He stood about three and a half feet tall, and I towered over him. He extended his hand, as a blob of yellow slime slid to the floor, and greeted me. "Hello, my name is Herbert Gusselhammers."

I shook his hand and replied, "I'm Bil—"

"Billie... I know who you are. By the way, you're the first to ever shake my hand with no hesitation. Anyhow, my brother told me stories about you standing up for others without a second thought. You're becoming quite the legend around here... so why are you here?"

"For murder."

Herbert backed up, crawled into his bunk, and slid the covers halfway over his head. "Please, please don't eat me."

"I'm not going to eat you, at least not right now... just kidding." I laughed, but it was a hollow sound, as I thought about how I would never see Percey again. My smile vanished.

He pulled the covers off and sat up in bed.

"Who are they saying you murdered, if I may ask?" He adjusted his oversized, rectangular glasses over his eyes.

I slid down the wall to face him, "I'm accused of killing my girlfriend, but I didn't. Someone else did, and when I find out who, then I'll probably be in here permanently—after I rip him into several pieces while consuming half of him." I told him everything about my last night with Percey. I didn't care if I was being recorded. I needed someone to know how much I cared for her. My nearly dead heart was once sealed in a tight coffin. When Percey came into my life, she smashed the wood box and revived my heart before it stopped beating.

Herbert took a few gulps before replying, "Somebody who feels that way about someone isn't a murderer in my book."

"Thanks." A single tear slid down my cheek.

"You know that there's never been anyone murdered here, right?"

"Yes, I'm aware."

"If you're found guilty, then you know they're going to make a big example out of you."

Taking in some deep breaths, I replied, "I know."

"Well, I hope you have a good lawyer. You're going to need one. I know what it's like to be framed."

"Why are you in here, Herbert?"

"I got in a fight with a drifter."

As I rested on my bunk that night, I counted Herbert's snores—they rattled the metal bars. I thought about when I'd first met Percey at the Half Moon Dance. I found a great spot way up and behind some swaying branches of a hundred-foot juniper tree. I saw her fluttering a few inches off the ground to the beat of an oldie, "Xanadu" by Olivia Newton-John. Shimmering, rainbow orchids with rhinestones outlined the edges of her translucent wings.

She didn't think anyone was watching, but I was. Her glistening ruby hair floated around her body. She heard something above her and spotted me. She zipped straight up to me and asked why I was staring at her. I could hardly answer her. We ended up talking all night as we listened to music by the Blue Foxes.

WITHIN A FEW DAYS, I WAS STANDING IN A PACKED COURT ROOM. There were signs waving in the air with written messages in thick, red ink on white poster boards that read:

KILL ALL WERE BREEDS! CAGE THEM ALL! CHOP THEM UP AND TOSS THEM IN THE FIRE!

Those messages weren't anything new for me. They would always exist as long as hatred breathed. As I entered the court room, I noticed Chief Watkins talking to the judge, a lanky goblin-genie with an orange Bandholz beard and ghostly, green luminescent eyes. Rosalynne stood up to greet me. The judge's penetrating eyes remained on me until I took my seat.

"How are you?" she inquired, rubbing my arm.

"Okay, ready to get this over with." I slowly scanned the room.

"Has anyone harmed you during your stay?" she asked.

"No."

"Listen, I was able to interview Percey's family and friends. I don't think you should take the stand," she mumbled under her breath.

"Why? I want to."

"Billie, nothing personal. However, I was told some concerning information about your relationship with Percey."

"What were you told and by whom?" I growled.

"Her best friend, Cameron Stone, shared that she heard you two arguing and that you stormed out of the pub last night."

"So what? Couples argue," I snapped. "Cameron always protected Percey. I know she loved her like a sister. I bet she's really taking it hard."

"I understand. It's what Cameron shared with me, and the prosecutor is calling her up as one of her witnesses."

"What did she say?" I asked, feeling my heart racing.

"Cameron said that you told Percey to leave her family to run away with you, and if she refused, then you would hurt someone in her family, which establishes motive."

"What?" I stood up. "That's a lie."

She pulled on my arm lightly and guided me down to my chair. "Billie, please," she begged.

I sat, my heart beating fast and hard.

Closing my eyes and counting backwards, I said, "Wait... I did tell her that if she didn't tell her parents about us, then I would. I was only bluffing. I was going to propose to her that night until she decided to break up with me... I want you to call me up to the stand."

"Billie, I have a plan and a hunch. There'll be no need to call you to testify. Trust me," Rosalynne whispered.

Rosalynne and the prosecutor, Wilma Sphinx, a cat-witch shapeshifter, gave their opening statements. The jury was mostly made up of colorful goblins, fairies, and too many centaurs—werewolves' worst enemies—who'd traveled in from different districts of Kamelea and other distant forest lands.

The prosecutor called Cameron to the stand.

"Please state your first and last name to the court," Ms. Sphinx requested.

"Cameron Stone."

"How did you know the victim, Percelus Star?"

"She was my best friend—she told me everything."

"How long had you been friends with the late Ms. Star?"

"Over seven years."

Cameron started crying.

Ms. Sphinx snapped her fingers and a box of tissue appeared and floated in front of her.

"Take a few dear... do you need some time?" she purred, twirling the ends of her sapphire hair with her long, glossy nails.

"No, I'm fine," she sniffled, blowing her nose with one and dabbing her eyes with another tissue.

"Last Friday night at approximately 9:30 p.m., where were you?"

"I was wrapping up my shift at the restaurant."

"Are you referring to Big Herb's Tavern located on 1213 Twig Avenue?"

"Yes."

"What is your occupation there?"

"I'm a waitress."

"Who was at Big Herb's that night, anyone in the court room, maybe?"

Rosalynne shouted, "Objection, your honor! She's leading the witness."

"Objection sustained. Ms. Sphinx, you know better."

Dropping her hands from her hair, she hissed, "Very well. Ms. Stone, who do you recall seeing at the restaurant that night?"

"A few regulars, Percelus and Billie. I remember them sitting upstairs on the patio, overlooking Tanzza Square."

"Were you their server?"

"Yes."

"Did you hear them talking about anything?"

"I did. I was standing behind the open door about to serve them their virgin drinks, but I paused."

"Please tell the court why you stopped, and what you heard them discussing."

A teardrop glided down her face. She held her head up and said, "Billie was really yelling at her. He was telling her how he was tired of hiding their relationship. He told her that if she didn't tell them soon, then he was going to tell them."

Standing up, I released a high-pitched growl, I said, "Come on, Cameron, you know that I've never yelled at Percey!" I felt my fangs piercing my tongue. Taking in a couple of deep breaths, I retracted them.

"Order, order!" The judge demanded, slamming his gavel down a few times.

Rosalynne motioned me to sit back down with her eyes. I followed her instructions. I leaned over to her and whispered, "I just don't understand why Cameron would lie about me like that." I pushed some papers away from me and tuned into every word that came out of Cameron's deceitful mouth.

"Did you hear Percelus's response?"

"Yes."

"What did she say from your recollection?"

I shook my head. My glowing, crimson eyes remained on Cameron.

"She told Billie that it would be best for them to break up. She just wasn't ready and didn't know if she ever would be. The next thing I knew, Billie stormed out, almost knocking me over and the drink tray out of my hand. I was afraid if he would've stayed that he might have hurt Percelus.

Well, I guess my greatest fear came true..."

"My dear, what?" Ms. Sphinx asked, patting her on her back.

Cameron pointed her finger at me, and more tears followed. She squealed, "Billie Longhorn killed Percelus."

"She's a liar!" I yelled, lifting the table off the ground partially and back down.

"Mr. Longhorn, I don't want any more outbursts from you in my court room. Understand me?" the judge commanded.

Rosalynne popped up, "Yes, your honor, he understands you." She turned to me and mouthed, "Billie, no more!"

Ms. Sphinx smirked at me, clicked her heels, and said, "Thank you, Ms. Stone. No further questions, your honor."

I lowered my head down on the table.

Rosalynne reviewed her notes before approaching the bench.

"Ms. Stone, you said that Billie was yelling at Percelus, correct?"

"Yes."

"Are you certain?"

She looked down and mumbled, "Yes." Her forehead dripped with sweat.

"I have your correct timecard right here in my hand, Ms. Stone. Your boss, Mr. Gusselhammers, delivered it to me this morning. Now, answer me correctly, Ms. Stone."

Ms. Sphinx shot up and yelled, "Objection!"

"Overruled," the judge said, "I'd like to see where this is going."

"The time clock must be wrong!" Cameron fired back.

"No, I don't think that's the issue here, Ms. Stone." Rosalynne replied, taking a few steps towards the stand, waving the timecard in her hand. "Now, why don't you tell the court about that night. The truth this time, Ms. Stone."

Cameron started panting really hard and shapeshifted into a were-hyena.

The jury members and entire courtroom, including the judge, prosecutor, and chief all gasped. Rosalynne and I did, too. We had no clue. She'd hidden her true identity well. I never smelled *were* on her. She must've been taking some kind of untraceable magical pills to conceal her scent.

She started clapping. "I guess you got me, Ms. Rosalynne. I punched out early that night, and I stuck around on the rooftop to hear everything. I waited for Billie to leave. I thought I was going to get away with it. What gave me away?" Thick, green saliva spilled from both corners of her mouth and plopped down onto the floor near her hairy legs and feet.

Rosalynne replied, "There were some discrepancies with the paw prints found at the crime scene. I sensed something was off, but I wasn't certain until your public display of what you truly are, Ms. Stone. The paw prints were a close match to Billie's, but not a hundred percent. Your honor, may one of my lead forensic investigators scan her?"

Ms. Sphinx screamed, "This isn't the protocol of our court system!"

The judge waved both Rosalynne and Ms. Sphinx to meet with him in his private chamber. They all returned in less than five minutes. Ms. Sphinx strode to her table, threw file folders inside her open briefcase, closed it, and flew out.

The judge gave Rosalynne a nod. Her investigator completed the high tech, ultraviolet scanning quickly, and the results followed. Rosalynne handed Chief Watkins the printout, and he read the report.

"Ms. Stone's DNA is a perfect match to the crime scene." Grinding his teeth, he started crumbling the form in his hands.

The judge demanded in a stern voice, "Now, now, Chief Watkins, hand over that evidence right now." The judge extended his hand as Chief Watkins approached him with his head lowered. A few of his officers surrounded the bench, preparing to arrest Cameron.

She started shifting back to her human form and said, "You know that Percelus didn't love Billie."

"What did you do, Ms. Stone?" Rosalynne questioned, pacing across the courtroom floor.

Licking her gray tongue along her upper fangs, she stood up and replied, "I did what was inevitable."

Taking another risk, I asked the judge, "Your honor, may I ask her one question, please?"

"Mr. Longhorn, I've never allowed the accused, now the unaccused, to ask a question," the judge explained. "However, with everything I've witnessed today, I'll allow it this time. Proceed."

As water pooled in my eyes, I said, "Cameron, you didn't have to hurt Percey. Why did you do it?"

"Percelus knew better and broke the most important Kamelean Law of all. So, she had to be punished. I had to make sure she was out of the picture for good, permanently. So, I got rid of her. She couldn't ever love you, Billie, like I could. I was supposed to be Billie's girl. Me! I punished you because you didn't choose me."

"Cameron, I could never love someone like you, even if I'd never met my Percey. I never clicked with you. I only tolerated you. I knew Percey adored you. I wish she would've paid more attention to you, and how jealous you were of her," I said and turned my back to her.

"Arrest her, immediately," the judge ordered, banging his gavel on his desk and breaking it in half.

Upon leaving the courthouse, I knew I didn't belong here, and I needed to figure out how I was going to make future plans without Percey in my life. I'd experienced true love for just a moment, and knew I wouldn't ever again.

THE END

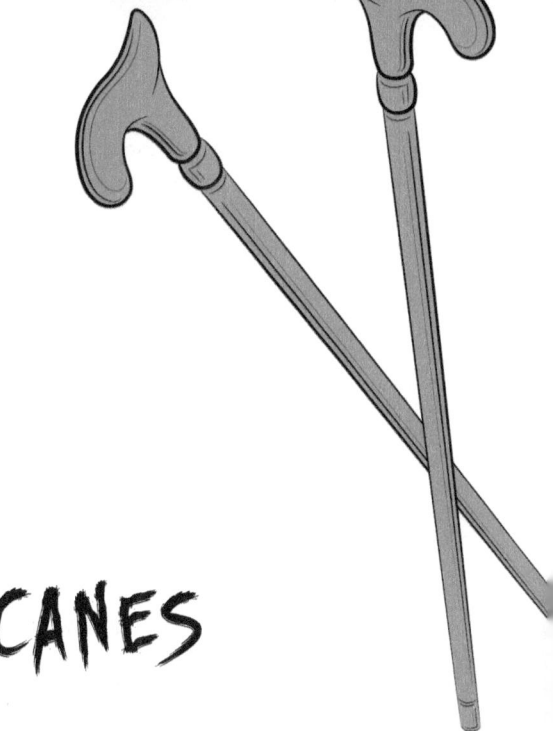

Theme Song: "Hush"
Artist: The Marias

CANES

I wish she'd never told me that last story now. We would've been graduating together from high school tomorrow morning.

My best friend, Jessie Andrews, loved to freak me out with her creepy stories every time we had a sleepover, either at her house or mine. I knew they weren't true, but they still made me always check under my bed, inside my closet, and behind the backseat at night, whenever Mom picked me up from softball practice.

A rainbow-colored whistle necklace lived around my neck. I know that sounded cheesy. I figured if something ever did crawl up to my window ledge or scratch the inside of my closet door, I could at least blow it to alarm my parents or older brother.

They would rush to my rescue before I was either eaten or slashed to pieces. A metal flashlight remained in my top bedside drawer with weekly battery checks. I usually kept the bathroom light on with the door halfway open at night because of Jessie's stories.

"Drip, Drip" was one of the scariest stories Jessie ever told, I *thought*. You know that one, right? Quick refresher, just in case you don't.

Buster Canes escaped from a local jail. Tricia King was Buster's final victim. She was the drill team captain at Walker High School in SugarBee, Texas. Tricia craved winning and didn't care if someone else got hurt in the process. Tricia's parents attended a party on her fatal night.

He broke in while she was showering to blaring ballads by Air Supply. Buster hid under her bed and licked her hand throughout the night. He pretended to be her toy poodle, Mercedes. She never checked under her bed.

Tricia kept hearing eerie dripping noises. She finally found Mercedes hanging from a soaked bloody rope in a hallway closet with the words,

YOU SHOULD'VE CONFESSED!

Written upside down and bleeding down the wall near her limp dog.

Buster crept up behind Tricia. He stabbed her thirteen times in her chest with a glistening butcher knife and hung her in the closet on a hook next to Mercedes. He etched his initials on the sides of her face.

Within six months, the local police discovered five other drill team girls' bodies, all dressed up in their stained uniforms, buried underneath Buster's basement in the summer of 1978.

The judge referred him to China Ridge Psychiatric Hospital for a complete evaluation. He ended up slitting his wrists and knocking himself off in his room the first night. The guards found a knife poking out of his mattress.

That story gave me restless nights for the next three months. I became addicted to checking under my bed often with my flashlight. I made sure my feet and hands remained inside of my covers and never hung over the bed at night—and I still practice that to this day.

Right after Ms. Whitman's eighth grade science lab on Friday morning, Jessie ran up to me in the hall and begged me to spend the night at her house on Saturday. Cupping her hands around my *Swamp Thing* suspenders, she whispered, "I got a good one to tell you." Walking backwards and checking behind her every few steps, she shouted, "You won't be disappointed, I promise!"

Although most of Jessie's stories gave me night terrors, I always wanted to hear her next one. Sometimes, I even requested multiple doses. She'd probably told me her versions of "Drip, Drip," "Infestation," and "Hook Man" more than ten times.

Every time she did, she changed it up, whether it was a guy or woman killer, the location, a couple, friends, summer, or fall. I guess that's why I craved listening to her stories. She always pulled me into her creepy worlds in different ways.

I had a cousin's birthday to attend Saturday night, but I blew it off and told Mom I had this intense science presentation about the parenting processes of seahorses compared to jellyfish to prepare before the following Wednesday. She gave me an instant pass—Mom was a chemistry professor at the local university.

Rudolph, my nosy brother, dropped me off at Jessie's house that evening. As I was about to close the door with my backpack around my shoulders, he asked, "Why do you keep torturing yourself like this? You always end up freaked out when you hang out with her. She's so weird."

"She's not. Eat my shorts!" I kicked his car door closed with my foot and stormed towards Jessie's front door.

Sticking his head out the window, he yelled, "Whatever, loser! I promise you one day that girl is going to tell you something that you'll never forget."

He drove off, shooting the bird out of his window.

Before I'd even touched the doorbell, Jessie opened the door and pulled me inside. "Don't let him get to you. We're going to have a good time tonight. Forget him." She pulled me in tight to her for a side hug.

I shook my head in agreement, and we beelined straight to the kitchen to scoop up some prepared sandwiches, sodas, cookies, and chips.

She snuck a few cigarettes out of her mom's Marlboro cigarette package off the counter near her *National Inquirer* magazine. She placed everything except the cigarettes inside a party tray. She slid the cigarettes down her padded, puke-yellow training bra.

"Are you nuts, Jessie?" I squealed.

Rolling her eyes, she whispered, "Take a chill pill. She has a lot of packs lying around, and she never counts them. Let's go."

Her parents were watching an *As the World Turns* recorded VHS tape in the living room. They were so tuned in to that soap drama that they didn't even notice us zipping past them, giggling up the stairs to Jessie's room.

Slasher and horror movie posters decorated all her walls. Jessie knew a guy from Gigi's Video Rental, and she scored expired posters from him every summer.

We stuffed our faces, danced to her new *Purple Rain* cassette, and sung into hairbrushes. I nearly choked with my first attempt to smoke; I inhaled when I should've exhaled. I dropped the lit cigarette on her checkered bedspread.

"Oops, I'm sorry," I blurted out, slamming my hand down to pat it out.

"No big deal," Jessie said as she swooped the cigarette up, pressing its end down on the windowsill, and flicked it inside her trashcan across the room.

We heard a knock at the door.

Jessie grabbed a Charlie perfume bottle off her dresser and sprayed it in the air.

"Everything okay in there, girls?" her mom asked.

"Yep, we're good," Jessie replied, blowing out a puff of smoke from her mouth and laughing.

"Jessie, I hope that's not perfumed, cigarette smoke again that I'm smelling outside of your door."

"No, ma'am."

"Well, goodnight."

We stared at each other, took in a few deep breaths, and chuckled.

"That was a close one, right?" I said.

"Sure was."

After Jessie took a shower in her bathroom and I did the same down the hallway, I was ready to be scared. When I reentered her room, lit candles covered the tops of her dressers. She sat in the middle of her bed with a flashlight shining under her chin. Two yellow, glow-in-the-dark skeletons pinned to her ceiling swayed in the air above us. I crawled on her bed and sat with my legs crossed, facing her.

Looking all around the room, I said, "You definitely get bonus points for eerie room setup."

"Thanks, I needed to set the mood just right for this story," she mumbled. "Ready?" Her eyes grew wide.

I nodded with my legs shaking.

"You know, I never told you why Buster murdered those girls... His mom was a hit and run. Tricia was the driver, and her drill team girlfriends were in the car with her that night. Buster's mom survived, but not without any scratches. The doctors thought she would be paralyzed for the rest of her life. She told Buster what he needed to do in order to reverse her paralysis."

"What?" My legs stopped shaking.

"To kill each girl, so she could regain the use of her legs. After he offed one girl, his mom could feel tingling in her toes. Each time he got rid of another one, more feelings returned to her legs."

"No way!"

"Oh yeah. Now, get this, once he ended Tricia's life, she could walk, but needed major help. She had a hunched back. She used two canes to balance herself. When her son was found guilty and she was told he committed suicide in his cell, Old Lady Canes became a recluse and never left her house again."

"Seriously?"

Jessie nodded.

"What happened to her?"

Moving in closer to me with the flashlight still shining under her face, she replied, "Her neighbors ended up finding her after they saw letters overflowing in her mailbox. They smelled a strong stench in the driveway. She was stiff as a board with her two canes resting next to her. That wasn't the best part." Jessie's eyes narrowed as she scanned the room.

"What do you mean?"

"There were secret swords hidden in the canes' shafts—a string of miniature colorful bells were embedded down each one. Many wondered about her past life... They say that her tormented spirit awakens after anyone tells her tale and doesn't believe."

I cleared my throat and remained silent.

"She'll drift into that person's room and slice them up with her crazy canes before daybreak!"

Jessie pulled two case knives from behind her and slammed them together—making creepy, clanking sounds. "Hope Old Lady Canes doesn't visit us tonight," she whispered.

I jumped backwards and fell onto her fluffy yellow carpet.

"Why did you tell this story?" I asked, shivering.

"Oh, stop being a drag. It's just a silly story I heard some older girls sharing in a bathroom when I went out of town with my mom two weekends ago." She raised her arms in the air and wiggled her fingers in front of her face. She clicked the flashlight on and off a few times.

"Whatever, Jessie. I feel bad about what happened to Buster and his mom, Ms. Canes." I sighed.

"Wait, you really believe their wacko stories, don't you?" Jessie frowned, cocking her head to her left. She stood up on her bed, bent over, almost touching her toes, and swung her arms back and forth. "Look, I'm

Old Lady Canes... help me find my dead son." She burst into obnoxious laughter and fell back on the bed and ended up on the floor.

"You shouldn't make fun of the dead," I said as I grabbed my toothbrush and exited the room. It was almost midnight. I left her bathroom door slightly open, leaving the light on. Jessie blew out all the candles. She slept at the head of the bed, and I slept at the opposite end.

As I was turning over, Jessie echoed, "Don't get sliced by Old Lady Canes." She burst into uncontrollable laughter.

"Stop being so mean." I yanked headphones from the inside of my backpack on the floor, placed them over my ears, and hit the play button to listen to my Wham and Michael Jackson mixed tape. I pulled the pillow from underneath me, and placed it on top of my head.

She laughed under her breath and scooted under her blanket.

The next morning the sunshine tumbled in. The sun didn't wake me up. I felt something wet underneath me. I knew it wasn't Aunt Flo. With my eyes still closed, I ran my hand down the mattress. Opening my eyes, I held my hand above my face. It looked like blood.

I shot up from the bed. Jessie wasn't there. Her covers were turned down. The upper sheets and headboard were painted with the red goo. I slid down to the floor. The skeletons were shredded to pieces on the ground.

Under the bed was the first place I searched for Jessie. I begged in a wobbly voice, "C'mon out. I know you're just trying to scare me." I lifted her comforter up off the floor, and she wasn't there.

When I stood up, I noticed a lot of the gunk smeared on her white accordion closet doors and its handles. I slowly went over. "Jessie, I know you're in there. The joke is over. You really got me this time. Come out!"

She didn't. I took three more steps up to the handle and extended my trembling hands. My legs almost buckled. I forced the doors back with both of my hands and attempted to scream. Nothing came out. I recalled my whistle. I popped it inside my mouth and blew it.

Jessie's body was split down the middle and hanging from her wooden closet rod. It dangled back and forth as her guts oozed down and flopped onto the floor. Three words were etched deep on her forehead and cheeks:

O.L.C. WAS HERE!

A gold and purple bell rolled out of the closet and stopped in front of my feet.

THE END

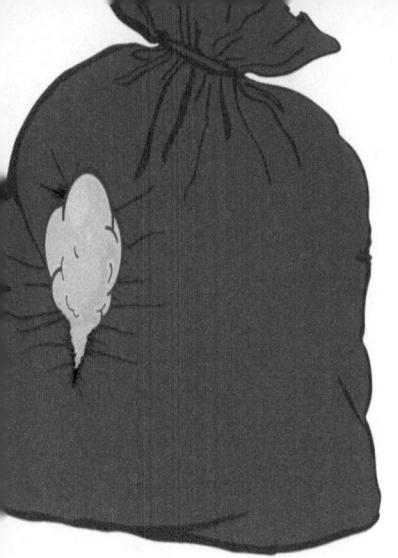

Theme Song: "Every Breath You Take"
Artist: The Police

THE BAG

Rain and dark clouds blew in out of nowhere that afternoon when the last school bell rang. Bernadine's raincoat and boots were warm and dry in her closet at home. She darted out of the back door near band hall and used her plastic science folder as her umbrella. Water puddles were everywhere. She dodged most of them, but the heavy rain soaked her clothes.

Almost a block from her house, she noticed a fat black, plastic bag under a flickering lamppost near the Ghanton Brothers Tire Repair Shop. She thought she saw it move.

The rain slowed down, but a steady drizzle continued. She raked her wet hair from her face with her pruned hands.

A faint moan erupted from the bag. It sounded like a trapped animal. She crept slowly up to it. Yet, she didn't get too close. The moans grew louder, and the bag started crawling towards her. Stepping back, she turned around to hightail it away from there. A soft voice called out, "Please, help me. Please!"

She froze up for a few seconds. The voice repeated its plea. Scanning the streets left and right, she saw no one. The business buildings were all closed. It was if everything was shut down—it was only four in the afternoon.

A gush of wind pushed the bag closer to her, where it touched her leg. Shaking from her feet and up, she didn't want to turn around, but she did. No one was there. Then, she felt a light tap on her shoulder. Her chattering teeth echoed in the air. She placed her hands over her mouth to calm them down. That soft voice returned. "Help me, please!"

Closing her eyes and counting backwards from ten, she slowly carouseled her body around to the bag and stared down at it. The bag wiggled more and more. She swallowed hard and stooped down. She dug her Harley Quinn-shaped, character pocketknife out of her jeans pocket.

Taking in a couple of breaths, she stabbed the top of the bag and glided the knife away from her until a large opening appeared. Blue cotton popped out. Using her knife, she pushed the cotton back with it to see if something was hidden underneath. The voice shouted, "Thank you for helping me!"

Two long, arms—painted in white, shoe polish—shot up. Its crooked, cadaverous hands with red, jagged nails grabbed her trembling wrists. She tried to stand up and jerk her arms away, but the tight clasp this thing had on her made it impossible. Her eyes widened, and she screamed. There was no one around to come to her rescue.

"Good...night," the voice whispered one word at a time, and it snatched Bernadine inside its bottomless pit. It burped. "*Naughty girls are always the easiest.*" The bag zipped itself as if it had never been ripped open, and inched its way back under the dim lamppost.

THE END

V.H.V. GROUP

Dear Diary,

It's been five years, seven months, three days, and thirteen minutes since he stole my twin sister, Destiny, from me on our sixteenth birthday. I had no idea that "Karma Chameleon" by Culture Club would be the last song we would dance to together.

The moonlight beamed down on him. I saw him watching us from the patio, leaning against the deck railing. I couldn't make him out. He wore a black cowboy hat pulled way down to shield his face. His fingernails tapped to the beat of the music.

I wondered why he picked you and not me. Maybe it was the red leather off-the-shoulders dress and Dorothy glittered-up pumps you wore that night.

Your thick, feathered bangs would make Tootie from *Facts of Life* do a double take. I was sure you sprayed on two bottles of Electric Youth, which probably grabbed his attention and everyone else's at the party.

None of that really mattered. He had no right to take you from me or our family. Why did you get in the car with him? I tried my best to convince you not to go. While retracting your hand from mine, you said, "We're just going around the block to *talk* for a few minutes and then to the store to get more snacks."

Talking for you was always code for making out with a guy. In this case, with a real undercover douchebag.

"Promise?" I begged with a crack in my voice as I glared at him, clenching my fists.

You nodded your head and said, "Stop being a worrywart. We have the whole night together." You adjusted the ruby rhinestone key earring in your right ear—my gift to you earlier.

He kept his head down with a half smirk painted on his face. His red convertible zoomed away as your arms flew up and danced in the cold air.

One hour past and then three. You were still gone—I felt something was wrong. After all the guests left, Mom and Dad exited their bedroom and asked where you were. It was after midnight. I tried to pretend I didn't know anything, but you always knew I wasn't the best liar out of the two of us. What were you thinking, Destiny? That was just it: you weren't.

I coughed up my confession, and Dad called the police station to make a missing person's report. Mom organized a search party with her bingo and Avon friends within hours. After two months, the volunteers drifted away until it was just Mom, Dad, and me.

A heavy knock on our front door echoed throughout the house a few days before Halloween. I knew what that meant, and by looking at Mom and Dad's defeated faces, they knew, too.

An hour after the policemen told us that the DNA matched yours, we traveled down to the morgue to identify you. I was told to wait in the lobby. Mom handed me her purse and butterfly scarf that smelled like you, a faint fragrance of Electric Youth. After thirty minutes, Mom ran out sobbing, and Dad followed her. He told me to gather up Mom's things and meet them at the car.

Standing up, I froze for a moment. I couldn't leave that place without knowing. I needed to know. I also wanted to see what he'd done to you. So, I stormed through the swinging doors.

The police officer stood about twenty feet from you.

"Little lady, you don't want to see her like this," he muttered, holding his hands up.

Tears rolled down my puffy cheeks. I shook my head, and he stepped aside.

Before I reached the table, sour flower water that had been boiling all day in the sun penetrated my nostrils. I double wrapped the scarf around my nose and mouth while tying it firmly behind my head. I peeled the sheet back.

Your face and body were sunken in, as if you had been deflated. Only a few strands of your black and bronze hair were left. Your fingernails were all split apart, and coffee stained. I saw the key earring still in your ear. Most of the rhinestones had fallen out.

Then, I noticed two black markings that looked like mini craters a few inches apart under your earlobe. I rubbed my finger across them. I jerked it back and wiped off some crusty stuff that spurted out onto my pants leg. I slipped your earring off and stuffed it inside my pocket.

Bending down, I whispered, "Destiny, I miss you every day, and I love you so much. I'll never forget you. Why did you..." I stopped and covered you up.

The officer handed me a handkerchief. I wiped my face. He escorted me out.

A lady wearing black jeans, a T-shirt with **V.H.V.** initials pasted in large letters on her chest, and golden cowboy boots with glistening silver tips sat on a bench a few feet from the door. She looked up at me.

As I walked past her, she said in a raspy tone, "I know where he is."

I stopped, and didn't turn around.

"Yes, you heard me right the first time." She came up behind me.

Turning around, I asked, "You know where who is?"

"The guy who killed your sister, but first you have to meet me here, and I'll explain everything to you. Tonight."

She extended her hand towards me with a card—her contact information and address were written on it.

It read in bold print:

V.H.V. Group, 1317 Rabbit Hill Road.

"What makes you think I'll consider your offer?"

"I believe you want to know the truth. By the way, there will be a few others there, too."

She pulled out a cigarette pack and Storm-shaped character lighter from her back pocket, popped one in her mouth, and lit it up. She blew out three puffs and sauntered away from me. She looked back at me before reaching the door and whispered, "You won't be disappointed."

Wiping my wet face with the back of my hand, I shoved the stranger's card in my back pocket.

That night came fast. My parents drifted off to sleep early on the couch. I snuck out my bedroom window. I placed the car in neutral to back it out of the driveway and started the engine away from the house. I had my whistle and pepper spray on me. I drove more than forty miles from my house to Rabbit Hill. It was hidden in the country.

When I drove up to the house with the wraparound porch, I noticed three more cars in the driveway. I parked and followed the sidewalk to the front door. The door was cracked open.

Before I even knocked, someone yelled, "Come on in. We don't bite. Have a seat."

I sat down in a cushy wicker chair. Bags of chips, fruit cups, juices, and sodas decorated the table. The others were a little older than me.

"Hi. My name is Terri. This is Vera and Rhonda."

They all greeted me.

"What's your name?" Terri asked, her Bambi eyes capturing my attention.

"Dustin."

"You don't meet to many females named Dustin."

"Nope. My mom named me after her older brother who passed

during his second Vietnam tour."

"A beautiful way to honor him and his courageous sacrifice to his country," Rhonda said, tearing up a bit.

The strange lady from earlier poured herself a drink. She made her way to the front of the room. "Thank y'all for coming out tonight and introducing yourselves to Dustin. Now, let me not be the rude one in the room. My name is Maleene, and Dustin, welcome to your first, although I hope not your last, **V.H.V.** Group meeting."

"What does that stand for exactly?" I questioned, opening up a juice.

"It stands for—" Terri began.

"Hold on now, let's not go putting the cart before the horse. Dustin is new to our group, ladies. We need to make sure we don't run her off. She may not ever return." Maleene laughed under her breath and downed her drink before setting it on the table next to her.

"Well, Dustin, we're a small outfit and growing. We only allow those in who've lost loved ones to the animals like the ones who took Rhonda's teen daughter five years ago, Vera's son two years ago, and Terri's sister last year," Maleene said.

"All of you have lost your loved ones from the same creep who took and killed my sister?" I asked.

"Oh, not by him, but others like him," Maleene hissed.

"Wait, I don't understand. What do you mean *others like him*?" I asked as my voice wavered.

Maleene stooped down and pulled out a poster-sized Texas state map and clipped it on an easel. It was saturated with blue dots in several cities.

"What do all those dots mean?" I asked, squinting my eyes and pointing at the map.

"Sightings!" Terri shouted, shooting up her hand.

"Of what?" I took a few sips from my juice bottle.

"Creatures of the night, blood suckers, vamps... vampires," Terri added with a crooked grin and a wink.

"What? No way! There's no such thing," I said, almost spitting my drink out.

"So, how do you explain the way your late sister looked on that cold slab?" Maleene asked. "There's no way her body would've decomposed that fast. Only if something supernatural and evil nearly drained all of her blood. That leaves just one unnatural thing that could've done that."

"No...no... Listen, I'm sure this is a nice group, way weird, though... Thanks for the snacks. I need to get going," I said. I yanked up my purse from the chair and sprinted towards the door.

"Don't you want to stake him? After all, he did murder your only sister... And the best part is—he's in my basement, right now," Maleene said, as she stomped her boot down into the floorboard hard, wood flakes flickering up.

I stopped. It's not that I believed in their vampire crazy crap, but if he was truly there, I needed to ask him questions.

Terri looked back at me and asked, "Don't you want to see if it's true?" She stood in the hallway, twirling on the back of her heels.

My hand ran across Destiny's earring in my pocket. I followed her. The other ladies and Maleene waited on us down the end of the hallway. Everyone had a flashlight in their hands.

"Ready, Dustin?" she asked with her eyebrows arched up high. "After you see what's down there, your life will be changed forever."

"Before I do, I have a question for y'all," I said.

"What?" Maleene asked as she leaned in towards me, bracing herself against the closed door.

"Why did my sister go with him so easily?"

"Oh, honey, he glamoured her," Terri snapped back, swinging the corded flashlight back and forth.

"*Glamoured*...what's that?" I asked with a frown.

"There's so much that you're gonna learn from us," Terri said. "Glamouring is a form of mind control a nasty vamp can place on his or her victim. Makes you fall head over heels in seconds without understanding why. Pretty much makes you do whatever the vampire commands."

"So, you're saying my sister got in that creep's car because he commanded her to with his mind?"

"Yep," Terri said, "you're a quick study." She patted me on my shoulder. "Let's go."

Maleene opened the door with one hand and whispered, "Ready?"

"I guess, but I'm really not buying into all of this nonsense, ladies, I'm sorry," I said.

"What do you have to lose?" Rhonda asked.

I thought about it, and it didn't seem like I had anything to lose. Everyone had their flashlights on as Maleene led us down the creaky, wooden stairs. In the middle of the ceiling, a body was hanging down, hog-tied with silver chains. His face looked like patches of skin had been ripped off from a sunburn gone wrong. Some bone was visible near his cheeks. He was blindfolded with a burlap ribbon. Maleene untied it. The blindfold floated down to the ground. His body twitched and danced in circles.

I gasped and cupped my mouth with my hand.

"You crazy bitch! You better release me," he screamed out.

Poking him in the back with her flashlight, Maleene pulled out a small spray bottle from her back pocket and spritzed his face, which started to smoke and bubble up. Patches of his skin melted off and slid down onto the cement floor.

He cried, "Okay... okay, please stop!"

She purred, "Play nice, we have a very special guest with us..."

"Ask him," Terri demanded.

"Did you kill my sister?" I asked, removing my hand from my mouth as my body quivered all over.

He sniffed the air for over a minute before replying.

"I remember you... the other sister I didn't choose. She smelled and tasted so good that night. I drank all I could from her before her little heart stopped beating," he said, licking his lips.

I noticed two sharp fangs slide down almost touching his bottom lips.

"Hmm, I still get turned on just thinking about her voluptuous, hot body—dead now of course. She had the perkiest—"

"Shut up!" I shouted at him. Stumbling back, I couldn't take my eyes off what was dangling in front of me and how disrespectful he was.

Taking in a deep breath, I asked, "Why did you kill her?" Tears flooded down my pulsating and inflamed cheeks.

"Because I could. Once I get out of this, I'm going to devour all of you in minutes, starting with you. I'm starving. You won't taste as good as your sister, but you and the others will do. She had that *it* factor, unlike you."

Maleene stooped down and pulled out a wooden stake from the inside of her boot. She threw it towards me. "Catch!"

I caught it in my shaky hand.

She pointed on herself where to stab him.

"Look at pathetic you. You don't have what it takes to kill me," he roared, deep laughter escaping him.

Maleene jerked up a pair of pliers from a table next to him and extracted one of his fangs. He screamed so loudly I could feel the ground move under my feet.

Without knowing what I'd done, I planted the stake inside his dead heart. Dark blood sprayed the floor.

Everyone stared at me, speechless.

"I didn't think you had it in you," Maleene said.

"Me neither," Terri said, clapping. "You're a natural **V.H.V.** girl!"

"By the way, I've been wondering what those initials mean since you handed me that card, Maleene," I said.

"**Vampire Hunter Vixens**... that's who we are. There are more vamps out there sucking the life out of our sisters and brothers. We have a lot to teach you, if you want to become one of us, Dustin," Maleene said.

"I'm totally down!"

Dustin's Entry #001

THE END

Theme Song: "I Can Dream About You"
Artist: Dan Hartman

LOVE BOO

Cowbell windchimes on the back porch swung into action, alarming me as their high-pitched echoes bounced against my windowpane.

I glanced at the time on my Princess Leia clock, and then focused my attention on the pale aqua moonbeams dancing against my Frankie Avalon and Prince posters, plastered all over of my purplicious walls.

Making my way around my canopy bed to the ledge, I leaned over with my chin cradled in my manicured hands and waited, remembering our first kiss. Almost a year ago, I met Jethro Crane under the Southern Magnolia tree, next to my second-story bedroom window. He plucked one of the flowers off a branch and slid it in slow motion on the left side of my honey blonde, curly hair before his raspberry lips touched mine.

Every night, at exactly 11:11, a thick, charcoal mist crawled down the roof inside my room, and Jethro returned to that same spot. He freaked me out the first few times he visited me—not anymore.

Bending down, he snatched up a ragged bouquet of Texas Spiderlilies planted around the tree. Each one always shriveled up and melted inside his hand. He'd hold up a bloody splattered sign—upside down—with his other hand.

In backward, crooked letters, the sign read,

"BE MY PROM DATE, RAEANN LEE CONNOR. "

I smiled when I reminisced about our memories and what could've been. Now, my heart breaks over and over again to watch him on repeat. Jethro still can't accept that he's no longer my boo.

Only a... headless corpse.

THE END

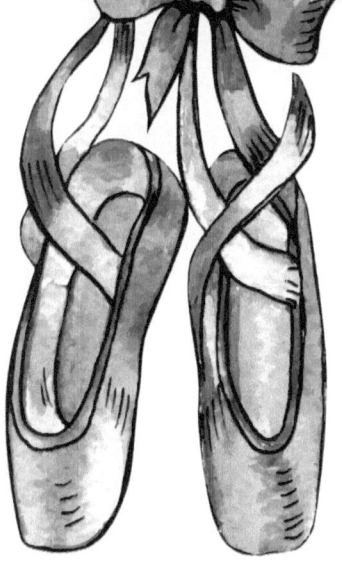

Theme Song: "Only a Matter of Time"
Artist: Joshua Bassett

DISPLAY

aint screams led me to my brother's room that night.

    Shutting the refrigerator door, I stepped out of the kitchen and climbed the thirty-seven stairs with strands of glowing, blueberry moss lighting my path.

His door was halfway ajar. He'd forgotten to lock up before he traveled to Luke's house for a *Monster Hunter: World* gaming tournament earlier. I entered and closed the door behind me.

Bloody wings fluttered slowly against a 12x12 Styrofoam board on his glass desk. Once I saw what was pinned on the board among the forty-nine different insects, I gasped, and the hairs on the back of my arms and neck stood straight up. I knew my brother, Colby, had taken something sacred that didn't belong to him.

As I removed the careless pins from her ripped ocean-blue and maroon wings with yellow glimmering polka dots, I lifted her up and placed her wilted body in my hand. I could hear and feel her tiny racing heart, beating.

She wore a shredded mahogany dress made out of leaves, which complimented her soft, freckled skin, and deep plum rose petals in the form of ballerina slippers, which wrapped around her miniature feet.

I tried to pull the strips of her dress to cover her up. She looked up at me and attempted to smile. Her eyes reminded me of a cluster of diamonds, fanned by thick fuchsia eyelashes. Before I could grab a T-shirt on the back of the chair in order to wrap her up, the door flew open.

"Drop it!" Colby yelled with clenched fists.

Charging towards me, my brother head-butted me. I fell backwards into a gaming chair, and she flew up out of my hand. He snatched her in mid-air and secured her in his hand.

"Lexi, I know what you're up to. I'm not going to let you ruin my chances to win first prize, two tickets to the *Big Texas World Gaming Con#7*, for Ms. Tucker's Eighth Grade Annual Bug Collection Contest. I'm going to get those tickets. No one will have this in their collection." He pointed at the prisoner in his hand.

Tiny tears floated down her cheeks. Her once sparkly eyes transformed to a dull shimmer. Then, a shrill cry followed. The window and the glass desk both shattered. I covered my face with my raised arms.

Colby turned his back and lowered his body to the ground. He stood and shook the crumbled glass off his board, placing it on top of his bed. Holding her up by her tattered wings, he pinned her back on that dreadful board.

"Look what you did! How many freaking times do I have to tell you to stay out of my room?" He towered over me with his index finger pointed in my face. My upper body trembled. I returned my attention to the board.

"This is the last time I'm going to warn you." He pressed his finger in the middle of my forehead and stood back up. I pushed myself up from the chair, rubbing my throbbing head, and looking to see if she was still breathing. Low whistling sounds vibrated my eardrums.

"Now, get out of here, you cray mute," he dictated.

Colby's charcoal eyes followed every step I made to his door, burning a hole in my skin. I exhaled and ambled backwards to the threshold of the doorway, replaying all the times he had either tortured or embarrassed me.

I attempted to sign to him in order to remind him of what he needed to do. I could save his life, possibly. He just rolled his eyes. He'd absorbed a few signs over the years, but overall, he refused to learn my communication, regardless of my parents getting on his case.

He pretended how it was just too hard for him. I kept a mini notebook and pen with me at all times. I retrieved it from the back pocket of my blue-jeans overalls. I quickly scribbled a written message to him. He started jogging in my direction.

Colby, you must take her back to Red Wolf Forest before midnight. Leave a note of regret and a personal gift for her clan. If you don't, then the unmerciful soldiers will come for you and...

He jerked the book from my tremoring hand.

"You and Grams's stupid rules about fairies. None of it's true. She's just a different kind of bug. Plus, she's my winning ticket. There were hundreds flying around. She chose to land in my trap. She belongs to me now," he whispered with a smirk glued on his face and dark eyes.

Balling up my notebook, he chucked it in my face. I stepped out of his room, and he slammed his door, barely missing my toes. Tonight would be Colby's payback for everything he's ever done to me and especially for taking something sacred from the Red Forest. He would receive no pity from her.

Running down the stairs, I woke Grams up; she was watching us until Mom and Dad returned from their anniversary trip. She opened her eyes. "Lexi-Girl, what's the matter? What time is it, anyhow?"

Grams rose up from the recliner, and I signed to her everything that had occurred. "Honey, there's nothing either of us can do now. Colby has done a terrible thing. He knew the rules of the fairies, and he's broken the ultimate one. Out of all the fairies he could've chosen, he chose a future queen from one of the most vicious hybrid breeds, the *Red Cap~Virikas*. He never wanted to listen to my stories... or believe. They'll be here to collect. Colby's fate will be revealed to him soon enough," Grams said with an extended sigh. "Come, we must prepare. You know what to do, right?"

I nodded. It was after eleven. We entered the guest bedroom, locking the door behind us. I made sure all the windows were locked, pulling the curtains back, so we could see when they arrived.

Shuffling over to a dresser, Grams slammed her foot against a wooden floorboard, which loosened. "Lexi, here, lift this up and grab the tin box." I handed it to her. She opened it up and pulled out three burgundy ribbon covered rings about the size of a doughnut with seven bells wrapped around each.

"Hang these on the doorknobs and place them in the middle of the windowsills. They'll protect us only. We cannot leave here until morning." I followed her exact instructions and signed to her, *what now?*

"We wait," Grams replied and wrapped her twitching arm around me as we sat in the middle of the bed, staring out the large, oval window.

It was five minutes until midnight. I heard loud buzzing and flapping wings, darting through the air. I tapped Grams's knee with my hand. She asked, "They're close, aren't they?" I nodded. She pulled me in closer.

Within seconds, the glass window was painted with a swarm of fairies, but not the nice and pretty ones you read about in most books or watch in movies. They had razor-sharp, jagged bloodstained teeth. Their claws and wings raked against the glass a few times before they spotted the rings.

Their glowing, iridescent eyes fixed on ours; they sniffed the room. Hundreds of maroon wings started fluttering faster. Their six-inch toxic, spiky tails swayed back and forth. I noticed them all wearing tiny elf-like ruby caps. They all zoomed up.

Grams and I scurried to the window and saw them headed towards Colby's room. Loud screams ricocheted all over the house. We lived deep in the woods. Only Grams and I could hear him. I paced around the room until I couldn't anymore.

Morning came fast, and we both made our way up to his room. His metal bed and mattress were turned upside down against a wall. Smelly, spoiled cooked meat odors saturated the room. We covered our noses with our hands.

There were several holes, some larger than others, all over a section of his wooden floor. Something warm and gooey fell down, barely missing my bare arm. It hit the floor and burned a quarter-size hole in the wood.

"That's flesh-eating acid!" Grams screamed. We both looked up, and she pushed me out of the way before another glob almost landed on me. "A special weapon of this fairy breed, Lexi."

Colby was pinned against the ceiling with the fairies' stingers impaling multiple sites of his skeletal body.

Most of his bloody flesh had melted off.

I grinned and my eyes shifted over to the broken, beaten board—barely standing up in an opposite corner—and she was gone. However, something was written on it in blood:

REMEMBER US... NEVER FORGET!

THE END

FINDERS... WEEPERS

I never expected what found us that one Saturday night at a place you would've never guessed. Before I tell you that part of the story, I need to share what led up to the *unfortunate* discovery.

Every summer since I can recall, Galaxy Skate World was the place to hang out with my boy, Otis Lee. It was so much more than just a skating rink. It was the best place in my backwards small town. Several disco balls covered the ceiling with colorful strobe lights and scented smoke.

There were a variety of cash contests on Saturday nights. The concession stands served the best chili hot dogs, burgers, onion rings, and homemade shakes—any flavor you could dream of. Donkey Kong,

Castle Wolfenstein, Defender, and Frogger arcade games lived there; I dominated nearly all of them.

The place felt like a magical land once you stepped in and heard bumping music by DJ Golden Boy. He always wore a gold cap, biker gloves, and over-sized shades whenever he hosted the Galaxy. He played the coolest mix jams and sold cassette tapes throughout the night. Golden Boy gave me amazing discounts. I'm sure it was related to helping him write a few knock-them-out-of-the-park English papers when he was a senior last year.

I loved the Galaxy for all it offered, but there was one person that made it the main attraction for me and probably all the boys at Emerald Junior High... Jasmine Ellington, my eighth-grade crush. She was there every Saturday night wearing large, swinging hoop earrings, tight leather shorts, sometimes with ruffles, and off the shoulder blouses. Her braided hair and feathered bangs always caught my attention. I daydreamed a couple times a day about holding her hand and skating backwards to my favorite song, "LA-LA—Means I Love You" by The Delfonics.

My Pops—maternal grandad—once told me that I possessed an old soul by the types of music I was naturally drawn to before I took my first step. I couldn't help it. The oldies was the only music played in Pops's house from sunrise to sundown. Oldie tunes made me feel comfortable and peaceful. I believe it did the same for Pops.

Anyhow, I would've given anything to be there tonight. There was a special skating contest. The winner would receive a cash prize, the chance to choose a slow song of choice, and whomever he or she wanted to skate with.

Instead of getting ready for the skate party, I was stuck loading up the trunk and half of the back seat in Mama's beat-up, 1978 Chevette, the Old White Ghost, with three packed baskets of sweaty clothes. Since our washer and dryer broke two weeks ago, my Saturday nights were spent at Walker's Washateria.

Mama didn't know when she could purchase another one. Money was tighter than it ever had been this year after Dad started hanging out with Mama's best friend, Angelica, and never returned home.

She stopped talking about Dad when she found out. My kid brother, Curtis, and I made sure we didn't bring up his name. I'd made the mistake once. That's when Mama retreated into her bedroom for the rest of the night. I passed her half open door and saw her staring at a wedding photo of them and crying. After I'd witnessed that, I made a every effort to not repeat my mistake.

Mama drove a few miles from Moonrise, our apartment complex. Walker's was usually vacant on Saturday nights. The young folks finished a few hours earlier because it was party night, and the old folks finished before dark; they didn't like to be out late. I noticed a middle-aged lady inside with pink rollers hanging on the ends of her hair. She had a nearly empty basket on her hip.

Mama parked, and I carried one basket in at a time. Curtis picked up clothes that fell to the ground and threw them in the basket, as if he was dunking a basketball in the net. He jogged in with his bag swinging back and forth. Mama propped the door open with her foot for me as she packed in the box of washing powder, bottle of softener, and her Strand book bag. I stood in the open doorway watching Curtis.

He dug into his faded denim satchel bag with colorful zippers in the front that Pops gave him one Christmas. He pulled out a couple of Dr. Strange comics I'd loaned him six months ago. Tossing them on a folding table, he leaned over, opened one up, and proceeded to read, flipping through the pages.

"Bro, you know that you could carry in one basket," I offered in a hushed tone as I stood outside against the glass door. Before he could reply that lady bumped me exiting the door, as if she was running away from something. I caught the weighty basket before I dropped it.

I noticed a small red and yellow plaid wallet on the ground next to my foot. I bent down to pick it up. As I stood, I waved it up in the air and yelled, "Hey Miss, you dropped this."

She looked at me for five seconds before she opened her car door, jumped in, and sped off on the gravel road in a half donut spin. I tucked it in my back pocket, thinking she may come back for it later.

"You got it Earkie, right?" Curtis snickered.

I unloaded the entire car while Mama loaded the washers. Standing in front of the large windows across from the line of white washers, I watched the cars drive by and heard distant echoed laughs. I knew exactly where most were headed.

"Earkie, Earkie!" Mama called, clapping her hands. "Where's your mind?"

"Nowhere, Mama," I replied as I slipped my hands inside my front pockets and rocked back and forth on my heels.

"Mama, I know... he's thinking about locking lips with *Jassss-mine*," Curtis blurted out, chuckling under his breath and holding a comic up in front of his traitor face.

"Shut up," I said. The rocking stopped.

"Make me," Curtis fired back, dropping the comic down.

"Now, you two stop it. Earkie, who's Jasmine?" Mama asked with a slight frown.

"Nobody," I said as I stared Curtis down and mouthed, "Your big mouth is going to get it later."

Mama separated the last pile of clothes and said, "Earkie, no one is getting nothing later. I need you to take these stained, gym shirts of yours. Go wash them out in the back in the laundry sink before I toss them in the washer with the rest of the clothes."

I grabbed them from her, including a scrubbing brush, slanting my eyes toward Curtis.

He did the same.

"Stop it, now, you two," she demanded with both hands on her full hips. "Earkie, you need to focus on your studies, if you're going to ever get in Harvard University. You're too young to be thinking about girls. I'm sure she's no different than any other of those fast tail girls around here. Keep your mind on your books instead of trouble, you hear me?"

"Yeah," I said, casting my eyes away from her.

"What did you say?" she questioned, sternly.

"Yes, ma'am." I replied.

Curtis giggled.

Mama eyed him, and he stopped and resumed his reading. She removed her book, *Valley of the Dolls*, from her bag and her Walkman—she placed the headphones over her ears and hit the play button. She'd been reading it off and on since Dad left. She rested in one of the plastic chairs.

I shuffled towards the back. The walls were covered with a pasty dark green and brown powdery substance. It smelled wet, like a combination of heavy chlorine with a hint of stinky armpits that hadn't been washed in a week.

Large, flickering oval hanging lights swayed above me. I went over to the big sink and turned on the squeaky, tarnished faucet and placed one shirt at a time under the running water, just like Mama taught me.

I heard a soft tap on the half open window above me. It was Otis. We'd been best friends since we first moved into our old house before Curtis was born. I turned the water off and tossed my last shirt to clean to the side. I pushed the window up wider.

Otis found a plastic paint bucket. He turned it over and sat on top of it. Rubbing his hands together and staring into my eyes, he said, "Hey, man, I came to rescue you from this nonsense. You gotta come tonight. Your girl is looking too fine."

"Wait, how do you know that?" I leaned closer to the window.

"I just left there, and I have proof right here." He tapped his chest on his thin Pac-Man windbreaker.

"What?"

"Polaroid pics—I bought them for a dollar." Otis pulled out two pictures and waved them in front of me while blowing kisses in the air.

"Let me see," I begged.

"Hmm, promise me that you're going to come with me."

"Otis, you know I can't leave. Mama would kill me. Even if I did, Curtis would give me up in seconds, if she didn't figure it out for herself. I can see it now. I'm about to take Jasmine's hand and lead her to the dance floor," I said, rocking my head to the side and closing my eyes.

"I can see it, too," Otis said.

"Suddenly, I'd feel someone squeezing my shoulder. Turning around, Mama would be right there. She'd drag me out of there by one of my ears. Then, I'd face the aftermath at school on Monday," I said, opening my eyes.

"Oh, man, that's messed up, but you're probably right. Your mama is like an Alcatraz guard. You sure you don't want to sneak away for a little bit? It'll be worth her prison sentence," Otis said.

"Nah, I don't think I'm going to risk it." I sighed, watching the water trinkle down the faucet's neck. I heard something scratching. I looked all around.

"Earkie, what's up? We doing this or what?" Otis stood up.

"Nothing. I thought I heard something. You're going, and I'm staying here," I said, taking in a long breath.

"It won't be the same without you. I know you would've won the contest tonight and got your big chance that you've been dreaming of for so long."

"Maybe, Otis." I breathed in deep again.

"Oh, I know that you would've won top prize with these babies as an incentive," he said as he handed me Jasmine's pictures.

"You know it." I smiled, unable to take my eyes away from her photos.

"Catch you later, Earks," Otis said as he ran towards his Huffy bike.

"Tell me who she ends up dancing with," I yelled and tucked the pictures in my back pocket.

He saluted me and replied, "Will do."

Otis peddled away into the night. A light rolling fog came out of nowhere, and I could barely see his headlights. It started misting, too. I pulled the window down, just leaving a small crack.

After I finished scrubbing my last shirt with the hand brush, I delivered them to Mama. Grabbing my Sherlock Holmes book from her bag, I returned to the laundry room, hoping to read in silence without interruption from Curtis. Though I knew I would mostly daydream about sweet, sweet Jasmine. I jumped on the counter and leaned against the window. After five minutes of reading, the noise from earlier returned.

I felt a vibration against my legs and found that the scratching was coming from the cabinet. Placing my book on the counter, I scooted off. I attempted to open up the wooden doors, but they were stuck. So, I yanked on the cobwebbed knobs a couple of times until they finally flew open. I fell back a little bit, but was able to recover my balance.

A deep, red glow came from the back of the cabinet. I pushed away cleaning supplies and found a cardboard box. I pulled it out by its floppy lid. The glow continued and at the same time the light fixtures above started swinging back and forth. I sat the box in front of me.

Looking down inside it, I noticed lots of crumbled pieces of newspaper. I grabbed them and threw them out behind me. The red glow faded. I gingerly picked up what was left waiting for me—a sealed tan, rectangular box, about the size of a shoebox, with red and yellow diagonal squares and squiggly lines on the sides.

It wasn't heavy. I felt some paper on the back. I turned it over. It was a folded piece of notebook paper taped on the bottom. I peeled it off slowly and this is what it read:

IF YOU'RE THE UNLUCKY ONE TO FIND THIS, THEN BY NO MEANS RUB THIS THREE TIMES. DIRE CONSEQUENCES WILL ONLY FOLLOW YOU...

Before I could finish the last word, Curtis jerked it from my hands and ran over to the opposite side of the room. "What's this?" he asked, twirling it around his hands.

"Give it here!" I shouted and charged towards him.

He read the message and started tossing it up in the air.

"Stop it. I don't even know what this is yet, Curtis," I said in a firm, yet shaky voice.

"Hmm, rub it three times. If I didn't know any better, then I think there might be a genie inside of here," he said with a big smirk painted on his face.

"Nonsense. Genies aren't real. Now, I'm not going to tell you again. Hand it over. I found it," I demanded.

"Finders... Keepers. It belongs to me now, loser," he said, sticking his tongue out with a burst of laughter. "Don't you remember the "Aladdin" story from *One Thousand and One Nights*?" he asked as he flipped the box back and forth in his hands.

"Yeah, I remember. So what? It's just a weird box, and someone is playing a joke with that note," I replied.

"What if it's not a joke and there's a live genie in here?" he said, squinting one of his eyes and tapping it three times with his index finger. "I got some wishes."

The glow returned brighter than before. Curtis dropped the box to the ground. "Ouch, that thing is hot!" He examined his hands. They looked sunburnt.

The box turned on its side and spun around thirteen times. It opened up. Thick, gray and red smoke crawled out of it up towards the ceiling, waving back and forth.

Both of us just stood there... speechless. The smoke encircled the entire room and shut the door softly and locked it. I heard the clicking noise. The smoke returned to the center to both of us.

It danced around. The smoke transformed into something that resembled one of the monsters in my comic books. It didn't have any legs, just a speckled black and red muscular torso with gargantuan arms and hands. Stacks of silver rings decorated all of his fingers with gold bracelets up to his elbows. Red flames danced in between his hissing, snaky dreads. His broad face sported a long, golden handlebar mustache. His skin seemed to sizzle as it moved. His teeth consisted of rows of double, silver fangs. He had one black eye and a glowing, teal eye with bushy white caterpillars for his eyebrows, which inched across his forehead.

For once Curtis was without words. He stood frozen, gawking up at the creature. Its eyes darted between the two of us. My mouth dropped.

Curtis peed himself twice, I think. His lips trembled.

A deep roar exited the beast's mouth, and he asked in a super deep Barry White voice, "Who freed me?"

I stepped back and tripped over the cardboard box. He came towards me and stared into my eyes. One of the snakes flicked it's slimy forked tongue on my throbbing cheek. He took in a long sniff of my braided hair.

"It wasn't you," he mumbled, shooting me a hostile stare.

The creature flew to Curtis and took in a huge whiff. Curtis closed both of his eyes so tight that tears streamed down. "You... you're the one who let me out." He bowed his head all the way to Curtis's feet.

"Master Curtis... they call me, Alonzo. You may ask me for three wishes, and I'll grant you anything in the world or out of your world, if you so wish, Master."

Curtis's mouth stopped shaking.

"Master?" Curtis asked, opening one eye.

"But of course." Alonzo remained floating at his feet.

Opening his other eye, Curtis asked, "Wait, so you're like a real-life genie—I meant, my real-life genie?"

He rose up and looked down at him. "Correct, Master Curtis. You can wish up anything you desire, but you can only have three wishes."

Curtis sat down on the cement floor and stared up at the genie. "Now, why just three wishes?"

"That's the way it's always been. I cannot answer that unless it's your first wish, Master Curtis. Is it?"

"Nope, nope!" he shouted.

"So, what will it be?"

"Curtis, be careful," I begged.

Alonzo glared daggers at me, stroking his snaky dreadlocks with his enormous hands.

"Master Curtis, wish away. I need to have them all at once—that's the rule. All you have to do is state this out loud to me: Oh, Alonzo the Great, my first wish... second... third... Grant them to me now."

"Wait, Mama, won't let me keep the stuff I wish." Curtis frowned and expelled a deep huff.

"No need to worry. I've already taken care of her," Alonzo whispered, swaying from side to side.

"What did you do to our mama?" I demanded, standing in a fighting stance.

"I placed an itsy-bitsy, sleep spell on her, so she wouldn't interrupt all the fun Curtis is about to wish up. Time will freeze, and she'll never know. She may be a little tired, but that's all. It's harmless, I promise," Alonzo replied in laughter and a crooked smile followed.

Curtis thought for a few minutes before he poured out his wishes.

I thought maybe he would wish for us to have a better life, take away Mama's bitterness, and bring our dad home, but I was mistaken. Curtis wasn't going to share this stage.

"Oh, Alonzo the Great, my first wish is to fly in a cape like Dr. Strange, second wish is to have a million comic books, and third wish is to meet the Lone Ranger. Grant them to me, now!"

"So, it shall be for Master Curtis," Alonzo announced. He raised his hands up in a triangular position and blew a line of black dust towards Curtis's body.

Curtis coughed a few times, wiping his face with his hands. All of a sudden, he levitated off the ground and a red, velvet cape appeared around his body, barely touching the tops of his white Converse tennis shoes.

Alonzo flicked his index finger to raise and widen the window large enough for Curtis to exit. He zoomed out. He returned after several minutes and floated around me.

"This is so cool. Can you believe this, Earkie?" He pressed his hands down his cape.

"No, but I see you flying. Your wishes suck!"

"They're my wishes, not yours," Curtis barked.

"Earkie, don't be a sore loser. Come, Master Curtis, look over here." The genie pointed.

I crossed my arms over my chest and watched them.

In the corner, there were stacks and stacks of comic books as tall as the ceiling. Curtis flew over and flipped through several, reading different parts. I just kept watching. I picked up a few of the comics, and I could smell the fresh ink. It wasn't an illusion. They were real. I browsed through a couple.

After two hours of Curtis enjoying his new mega collection, and I have to admit me too, Alonzo beckoned Curtis to come. Within seconds, a cloud of white smoke appeared, and the Lone Ranger, dressed in his famous outfit and with his horse, Silver, emerged.

Curtis couldn't say anything. The Lone Ranger was one of his favorite heroes. They talked for a bit, and Curtis even road his horse around the block before returning back to the laundry room.

Alonzo asked, "Are you happy with all of your wishes, Master Curtis?"

"Oh, yes!" He stroked Silver's mane while floating up in the air.

"I forgot to tell you something," Alonzo said, the words rolling off his double tongues as they ran in different directions between his fangs.

"What?" Curtis asked, looking back at him.

"You must now pay me three golden coins for the wishes I granted you."

Curtis landed on the ground and gave him a death stare. "Hold up, what are you talking about? Those were my wishes. You didn't say anything about money. Plus, wishes are free."

"Nothing is free, nothing! You didn't ask me if there would be a fee for your wishes," Alonzo said, gliding his fingers over his bushy, moving eyebrows. He peeled one off of his sweaty forehead. It squealed like a drove of pigs. He dangled it above his immense mouth and popped it inside—another fluffy caterpillar appeared above his head and flew down next to the other one.

I closed my eyes, blinked a few times, and replayed everything in front of me.

"You didn't mention that they would cost anything," Curtis argued.

"I don't have to tell you anything. The wishes I grant are short-lived," Alonzo replied.

Within seconds, all the comics, Curtis's cape, the Lone Ranger, and Silver all disappeared. Alonzo stretched his long fingers, flames shooting from the tips, as he requested, "Hand me over my payment now. No payment will result in me consuming all of you."

I went up to Curtis and pushed him behind me.

"Excuse me, Big Alonzo, but there has to be another way to work this out," I petitioned.

"I'm afraid there's not. Step aside or you, too, will be inside my belly. I'm very hungry. I haven't had any little, juicy boys in years. They're unique delicacies and very tasty." He laughed through his pointed nostrils, rubbing his glowing stomach.

"Come, Master Curtis. It's time to pay what's owed to me."

"This isn't fair," I snapped.

"Earkie, my boy, I'm afraid you're right. It isn't, but greedy fools always get what's coming to them in the end. After all, you said you couldn't stand the lazy idiot a few nights ago in your bed," he said with a malicious chuckle.

Curtis stepped in front of me and mumbled, "Earkie, did you mean it?"

"How did you know what I said? Curtis, I take it back... all back. I didn't mean it," I moaned.

"I know things after I've listened to conversations, and you meant every word. It's time, Curtis. You enjoyed your temporary wishes—now, it's time for me to enjoy my treat—you. Come, now!" Alonzo commanded.

A few of the snakes grew larger.

"Earkie, it's okay," Curtis whispered with tears in his eyes.

"No, it's not okay. You can be a big pain in the rear end, but I love you."

"Thanks, Earkie. I'll be seeing you around. I caused this."

Curtis left me and ran towards the open window. He jumped on the counter. As he was reaching up, Alonzo's shadow swept past me.

"Get out, Curtis!" I yelled. I ran behind the genie.

Alonzo turned around and roared, "Stop this nonsense!" His rotten egg breath pushed me down, and I slid on the floor with my back hitting a wall. I tried to stand up, but I couldn't.

He bent down, opening up his mouth wide enough to fit an eighty-pound boy. Curtis screamed and blocked his face with his raised arms. Alonzo slurped him down with one gulp. A long burp which lit a flame in the air followed. He vomited up Curtis's Florida Gator's baseball cap.

I started balling hard and pulled my knees into my chest.

"Tasty, just like I remembered," he said, licking his fingers and lips. "So, I don't usually do a double. However, if you would like three wishes, then I could arrange that for you. Maybe money for your mom or something pretty for her to wear. Oh, no, I know... an unforgettable date with that little sweet thang, Jasmine. I'll even throw in an extra hour just for you and a Persian bouquet of pink lemonade roses. She'll dig them."

I paused and thought that would be a dream come true. However, I'd just witnessed what happened to Curtis. I wasn't about to give into this sidewinder genie. I needed to outsmart him to survive, just in case he had some other dirty deed planned. Instead, I told him something that he didn't expect.

"I command you back in your box!"

"What did you just say?" he roared, beating his chest with his closed fists.

"You heard me, now get in here." I stomped both of my feet.

The genie's body slithered on the ground towards the box, which repaired itself in seconds. I picked it up, snatched up Curtis's hat, and placed it inside the cardboard box. I unlocked the door and found Mama folding the last batch of clothes. She still had her headphones planted over her ears.

I led her over to a chair to sit down. She peeled her headphones off and embraced me as I handed her Curtis's hat. I told her everything that happened, which would've been unbelievable to most, but Mama believed me for some reason. We cried together for a while.

A few weeks passed by. We had a closed casket funeral for Curtis with his favorite picture—him and a Lone Ranger look alike at a local fair two years ago. We never told anyone the truth of what had really happened to Curtis. If we had, then we would've both been thrown in the loony bin for sure. We kept it to ourselves and made a pact that night to never return to Walker's and to get rid of that box.

I did end up returning the lady her coin purse, which held her driver's license with her address and two dollars in coins. It was three months after Curtis was laid to rest. The lady told me something that I was surprised to hear.

She shared that she hid the box there that night. She figured no one would discover it in a place like that, especially where she stashed it. She shared her condolences about Curtis. She told me how her older sister was also one of Alonzo's victims.

The lady added that tricky and evil genies like Alonzo feed on selfish souls. She explained to me that she'd been reading up on genie mythology and folklore throughout history at the Emerald Library for a couple of months now. I told Mama about my meeting with her. Mama didn't say a word.

Saturday night rolled around. I loaded up the car with the baskets of clothes for the last time. Mama had purchased a new washer and dryer. It was scheduled to be delivered next week. I found one of my Dr. Strange comic books tucked in the back of the trunk. My mind immediately drifted to Curtis.

He was a brat to me, but he was my kid brother. Now, I wouldn't ever get to see him grow up. Although he made the decision that night to make those wishes, he didn't deserve what happened to him, regardless of who Curtis was.

"Let's go, Earkie. Don't want to be late tonight," Mama said, turning up the radio as it played my favorite song, "LA-LA—Means I Love You."

"For washing and folding duty, Mama. I don't think so," I mumbled, looking out into the sunset.

She smiled, drove up to blaring music, and parked in front of a familiar building.

"Mama, you hate the Galaxy. Why are we here?" I asked, turning my head to face her.

"I'm not going inside, but you are," she said and patted my shoulder. She leaned over to hug and kiss me.

"Thanks, Mama. I really needed this. It's been a long time," I said.

"Yes, I know," she said, grabbing my arm. "Go and enjoy yourself."

I nodded.

Opening the back door, to retrieve my jacket from the back seat, I noticed a small roll of wrapping paper, tape dispenser, and a pair of scissors on the floor. Mama's book bag had tipped over. As I went to stand it up, I saw it... the wooden genie box.

Popping my head in the passenger's open widow, I whispered, "Mama, what's that doing in the car? I thought you got rid of it for good. We talked about how we didn't want it to end up in the hands of anyone else again." I could feel my heart speeding up.

She looked at me without speaking a word and then said, "Earkie, you weren't supposed to see it. I know what we discussed. I need to take care of something first. After I finish this, I promise, I'll destroy it."

"Tap your breaks for a minute... what are you talking about?" I frowned. I could hear Otis calling out my name in the cold air a few feet behind me.

"He and Angelica took Curtis away from us. Curtis would be alive right now, if I hadn't needed to travel with you both to Walker's, where he met that messed up genie. They caused it... So, tonight, I'm gifting the box to her and taking her away from him."

THE END

Theme Song: "Son of a Gun (I Betcha Think This Song Is About You)"
Artist: Janet Jackson Featuring Carly Simon & Missy Elliott

HEMLOCK'S SECRETS

I bet no one has ever told you about *shadow twisters*, right?

They're eccentric trees that grow best in deep, fertilized soil, where rotten bodies sleep. You can find plenty of them in the Hemlock Cemetery. Most people don't know the differences between regular trees and *shadow twisters*. They think they're just trees and harmless, but that's where they're wrong—especially when one is removed from Hemlock without proper precautions being taken.

I tried to tell my careless brother not to steal anything else, most certainly not a twister. He laughed at me. He owned a home in the country. His closest neighbor lived several miles away from him.

About a month ago, near midnight, he drove to Hemlock in his

1986 rusty Ford truck and dug up a tree to plant in his backyard for extra shade. Butterflies, birds, squirrels, bees, grass, and flowers disappeared from his yard almost overnight. The leaves stayed stock-still in that tree, even when breezes came through.

After only three days, the dirt around the transplanted tree bubbled up during the daytime. It resembled coffee grounds. Zig-zag markings decorated its trunk. On the seventh night, all the tree's wooden limbs broke off. The waiting quicksand devoured them.

By the time I went up to visit him, the summer before my freshman year of college, his yard smelled as if hundreds of dead rats—doused with the cheapest perfume you've ever encountered—had baked for hours under the blazing, Texan sun. Wiggly and twisted, thorned and hairy, burgundy tentacles sprouted out a hole in its trunk that resembled a mouth.

"Travis, don't you smell that awful stench?" I asked, as I exited the glass sliding door, holding his bottled beer in my hand.

"I don't smell anything," he said, walking up barefoot and leaning in to touch one of the branches.

My brother was oblivious to everything going on around him, and that's when I knew the twister had placed him under its wicked, wicked spell.

"Travis, stop!" I begged.

"Why don't you mind your own business and sit the beer down next to my chair?" he snapped.

I honored his wish.

"Fine, you think you know what you're doing? You know *nothing*—you will soon enough," I said, sitting down a few feet from his chair and crossing my arms. I looked away from him.

"Ouch," he yelled out.

I turned my head back towards him. Two tentacles wrapped around his wrists and a third one extended towards his throbbing veins in his palpitating neck. He jerked his arms away and the tentacles retracted back to their original positions—they swayed in the wind.

"Did you see that? That damn tree just bit me," he shouted. Sweat streamed down his temples and saturated his beard. He massaged his wrists with his hands for a minute.

Wiping some draining blood off his neck with a rag he dug out of his back pocket, he returned back to his lawn chair and sat down, sipping on his beer. He stared the tree up and down. Within a few minutes, his glass bottle crashed onto the patio.

He stood straight up from his chair and vomited out the most piercing scream I'd ever heard. The broken glass trembled on the ground.

My eyes locked on him.

His entire body transformed into a crispy, charcoal statue. First, his toes curled back—then each one crumbled away. His legs, arms, torso, and head all did the same.

I already knew I couldn't help or touch Travis.

It was too late.

After all, he'd invited the *curse*.

He became a pile of gathered dust, which floated up in the air and encircled the tree.

Then one of the tree arms unzipped itself, and his gritty remains slithered down the tree's throat. It took in a deep gulp and swallowed.

I contemplated calling the police, but dismissed that crazy idea. Who would actually believe my creepy story about a *shadow twister* consuming my brother? I figured Travis's disappearance would be reason enough to celebrate for most who knew him. So, I never called.

When I woke up the next morning, the tree and its stench had vanished.

I drove up a few days later to Hemlock and found the same tree that Travis had stolen back in its original spot.

The twisted tentacles were gone.

It looked normal.

Yet, fuller and completely satisfied.

THE END

Theme Song: "The Voodoo House"
Artist: Rick Springfield

CORDELIA, CORDELIA...

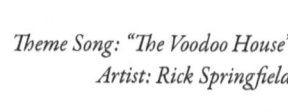

Taylor Rose, the cheerleader captain of Sycamore Junior High, didn't believe in haunted houses—until tonight.

She entered the Brydstein House on a dare from her best friend. You know the house—the one located in the wooded abyss at the end of Hanging Hill County Road.

Many swore they could hear cackled screams and echoes coming from that abandoned place. Some swore it was the ghost of late Loola Brydstein crying out, in a slow, raspy high-pitched moan, "Cordelia... Cordelia, where are you?" throughout the nights of the full moon.

You've heard of Loola, right? She was the old lady who lured a group of kids to her house one Halloween night. They were frozen at the sight of the candy feast on her huge picnic table in the backyard. Their bellies were so full that they could hardly make it back home.

When each of them woke up the next morning, none of them could talk or hear. I believe only one remains alive today to share the whole story, which she wrote down in a journal, years ago, about why Loola did what she did.

Taylor knew most of the story, but didn't care. She was committed to complete her mission. So, she tramped all through the house in her blue converses and red and white cheerleader outfit with a flashlight. She coughed each step she took from the dust tornadoes encircling her. Stained white sheets covered the furniture.

She found a curvy, dusty staircase, and she ascended, avoiding the decayed steps. The doors were all locked. She shone her light up towards the ceiling and noticed it was saturated with thick swinging cobwebs.

There were no signs of Loola until she heard a muffled scream coming from one of the doors followed by a scratching sound. Something cold and slimy ran its skeleton-like finger along Taylor's bare shoulders. She jumped and dropped her flashlight.

Standing at the edge of the stairs, a gush of wind pushed Taylor down. She tumbled down to the first floor without a scratch—thank goodness for her awesome acrobatic skills from the last seven years in gymnastics.

Taylor bounced off the floor and dusted herself off. She whispered to herself: *There's nothing scary about this old house.* Just as she turned around to face the open front door to leave, the door slammed shut and each lock slid in place. She took five steps back, clamping both of her trembling hands at the ends of her skirt. She felt something sharp rake down her back.

As she whipped herself around to see what it was, a cobwebbed blanket rained down on top of her. She tried to pull it off, but the more she struggled, the more it seemed to squeeze her tighter. It was as if it was gluing her down to the wood planks underneath her.

Taylor heard something running towards her covered face, like tiny footsteps. She looked to her right and saw a cobalt blue spider, about the size of a kitten, with striped yellow and red legs scurrying towards her.

It used its jagged fangs to rip through the web and crawled up her long ponytail and pierced her scalp several times. She screamed and shook her head back and forth to try to throw it off. She even tried wiggling out of the web. The strands felt like steel.

Each time she shook, the spider bit her again and again. Her eyes widened and mouth trembled. The nasty critter crawled down to her face and pierced her cherry glossed lips with its pulsating fangs.

Taylor barely saw it creep away towards a tall vapory, thin figure wearing a long, ebony high-collared lace dress with a floppy red ribbon tied around her flamingo-like neck.

Her appearance became more transparent the closer she approached Taylor.

A wide, warped smile curled upwards, showcasing her black gums. "I bet your little friends won't be pestering around my house anymore. They'll be too petrified to enter after they hear about your unfortunate demise. Tsk, tsk... you should've never disturbed me tonight. Now, come along, Cordelia... our work is complete, for now."

Cordelia ran up Loola's laced thigh, twirled around her abdomen, and climbed onto her shoulder. Her eight icy, blue eyes were the last thing Taylor saw before her own heavy-lidded eyes closed, permanently.

No one from Sycamore Junior High ever went creeping around the Brydstein House again. If you don't believe this really happened, then check out the place for yourself one night. Don't be surprised if you hear a faint cry floating in the air calling out, "Cordelia... Cordelia... Cordelia..."

THE END

Theme Song: "Bad Moon Rising"
Artist: Creedence Clearwater Revival

NIGHTRUNNER

*C*hosen...

Have you ever really thought about what that word actually means? Honestly, I've never had any reason to.

Why is one person picked off while the other person isn't? Think about it for a moment. In the *Grimm Tales* and *Friday the 13th* movies, most characters are plucked off one by one, leaving only a few survivors, if any at all.

Some would argue that it's luck if you end up surviving.

Let me tell you this about being a survivor—in my case, it really sucks. I wish I could erase what happened that weekend, but the memory will contaminate me forever. Hell, some things are just not unseen. Ever. No matter how many therapy sessions you attend, anti-depressants or sleep medications you consume... those memories stick, becoming a permanent file that you'll never be able to delete.

Your senior year of high school is supposed to be full of amazing memories, so you can share stories with your future kids and grandkids, right? Not mine. I didn't even get the chance to graduate. Sometimes when I close my eyes, I see it coming for me. I don't sleep much, especially at night. My insomnia wasn't triggered from being dumped the day before my senior prom, but because I was forced to watch my older brother get slaughtered in front of me.

It's true what they say, how your life can change in an instant. Believe me, I had no freakin' idea any of this was about to stroll into my life and cause *major* heartbreak.

Hey, before I go any further, let me first introduce myself to you. My name is Myles Bolanos, pronounced *Bow-lan-nose.*

As you probably deduced, I was a seventeen-year-old senior ready to depart from high school to begin my college dreams in Cali, outside of my small town, Chiminee Springs, Texas. However, all my plans started changing way before then.

I had prom night all detailed out. I'd scheduled a limousine, ordered my boo, Ash, a special corsage from an online flower shop based in Barbados, picked up a sweet tux from the mall, and made reservations at the fanciest steakhouse in town. The best part, I'd booked a room at Penelope's Bed and Breakfast.

Okay, don't judge me, Ash and I'd been dating for a bit, and you know we'd never... I figured prom would be our magical night, you know what I'm saying. I'd been super patient and never wanted to come off as the pushy type. Plus, guys who do that are just dicks.

Anyhow, I got the *R/J* Room. I bet you're wondering, what's that? Well, it stood for the Romeo and Juliet room—lovers only. I viewed all the rooms online and knew this was the one. This room came with everything heart-shaped—the balcony, windows, bed, rose petals everywhere, pillows, lights, bathtub, and complimentary chocolate strawberries with a bottle of wine.

Bubba Hawkins, a cool friend of mine since kindergarten and Boy Scout buddy for almost seven years, had made fake IDs for Ash and me a few weeks before. He even threw in a slow jam playlist of Bruno Mars, Taylor Swift, and Kem.

I worked two jobs last fall to save up enough to make this a prom night my girl would never forget. My brother offered to cover all the expenses. I turned him down. He knew how important it was for me to take care of this on my own. Enough about all that, let's get back to the story.

It all started going downhill for me on Friday afternoon after three. I found out I'd scored a fat "D" on my last AP Economics quiz, right before the last final. I refocused my mind on my girlfriend, Ash, and the big night I had planned for our last prom at Vikings High.

Shuffling towards my locker, I noticed something yellow sticking out the side. I dropped my backpack to the ground and pulled it out. I must've nicked my finger on the corner; a small trace of blood smeared the edge as I unfolded it. I pressed my bleeding finger against my jean leg and read silently to myself:

Hey, Myles, I didn't want to tell you this way, but I figured it would be best like this. I know how you feel about me. I just don't feel the same about you. So, I decided to cancel us out before prom tomorrow night. It just wouldn't be right to go with you.

—Ash

I read that letter a dozen times before I crumpled it up in my hand and tossed it in the trash bin. I counted each beat from my pounding heart, lowering my chin against my throbbing chest. As I looked up, I saw Ash turning the corner, strutting towards me in those tight purple, ripped jeans I'd always salivated over and wearing her favorite baseball cap. I'd brought her an Oregon Ducks hat last Valentine's Day, along with a duck-shaped, lemon-flavored cupcake I had Mama's Lil Secrets Bakery make, especially for her with green duck-stud earrings hidden inside. It was an idea I'd stolen from one of those crazy reality television shows.

This was my chance to squash all this nonsense between us. However, she wasn't alone. My best friend, Jesse Styles, had his pinky finger wrapped around hers. My chest unzipped itself as my heart tumbled out and slid down my legs. I tried to say something, but nothing came out. I thought back about when I'd first met Jesse.

Keeping it real and all, I'd rescued him when he'd transferred from another school, right after our first snowfall in late November. No one in Ms. Kirkpatrick's fourth grade class had talked to him that entire morning. His red corduroy jeans were ten inches above his ankles and his blue plaid, long-sleeve shirt barely stayed buttoned up over his plump stomach, whenever he took in deep breaths.

Jesse had almost tripped twice over his untied tennis shoes. At lunchtime, I noticed him sitting at a table alone with his head down, doodling in a notebook with a short pencil as the other kids snickered all around him, stuffing their mouths with food. I swear I could hear loud monster growls coming from his table.

Maybe his parents had forgotten to give him lunch money, or he'd left his lunch in the car. I stood up from where I was sitting and plonked down in the chair next to him. I opened up my paper lunch bag and gave him half of my peanut butter sandwich. Other kids joined us.

We hit it off pretty quick once I started talking about *Halo* and *Warcraft* video games. Jesse and I were inseparable until he landed his first kiss in eighth grade—everything started to change right after that with our relationship. Our game playing days and sneaking into movies at the Chiminee Hippodrome on Saturday nights were terminated after he lost thirty pounds and discovered girls.

I guess I can't say too much about that. My entire attitude about girls changed when Stacie Jackson pulled me into the empty band room and gave me my first French kiss, the summer before my freshman year.

During our sophomore year, Jesse went on to become co-captain of the football team and drama club, which made him an instant girl magnet. Regardless of all that, he had the balls to go and steal the one girl I had to work so hard for. I'd finally won Ash Barrington's attention last summer at a cheer camp during the annual welcome party.

Ash and Jesse were both laughing and began to lean in to kiss until she noticed me standing there in the middle of the hall. Ash tore her hand away from his and stopped twelve inches in front of me.

"Hey, man, we thought... I mean, I thought, you had volleyball practice today," Jesse said, clearing his throat, slanting his eyes towards Ash, and taking a step away from her.

I stared into his twitchy, gray eyes, thinking about how I'd stood up for him more than once.

"Coach cancelled," I snapped. "The prom decorating committee requested more time to decorate the gym."

"Sorry you had to find out like this, Myles. I was planning to hit you up later tonight to tell you," Jesse whined as a smarmy smile curled up on his unshaven face.

"No... No, you're not!" I shouted. "And you, Ash, *break-up by letter*, really? How weak is that?"

"I don't want any trouble," Ash squealed, stepping behind Jesse, clutching his upper arms.

Mumbling under my breath, I jerked my backpack up and adjusted it around my shoulders, and said in a gruff tone, "You two think I'm going to do something to both of you because my so-called best friend hooked up with my girl—excuse me, ex-girl—behind my back. How long has this been going on? You know what, save it, Bonnie and Clyde. Hope you two kill it at prom, deuces!"

Sprinting towards the metal back doors, I kicked both of them wide open with my foot and got out of there as fast as I could. I scrammed towards the graveled parking lot. Then I pressed my key fob, jumped into my Jeep, slammed the door, and sped out of the parking lot with a trail of smoke following behind me. I kept replaying the first day Jesse came into my life. If only I'd never befriended him back then, it would be me holding Ash's hand right now and taking her to the prom. I stepped on the gas pedal harder.

"I've Done Everything for You" by Rick Springfield blared from my satellite radio. I can't even tell you how fast I was driving as I wove in and out of traffic on the highway and exited onto Whistler Bend.

Red and blue lights danced in my rearview mirror. I heard a high-pitch siren over my music. I shook my head, slowed down, and came to a complete stop. I turned my radio off with my right hand and placed it back on the steering wheel. My heartbeat's rhythm shifted from being dumped to being pulled over by a state trooper.

I watched him from the side mirror. One black cowboy boot stepped on the pavement as the other followed. He adjusted his gun belt around his waist and bent down to place his ebony cowboy hat on his head. Sliding his *Top Gun* shades onto his bearded face, he shut his door. He looked up at the sun and then towards a field of pink and yellow wildflowers before he approached me.

Touching the button, I rolled my window down, and I turned off the ignition. The officer asked, "Boy, do you know how fast you were driving?"

Facing him, I said, "Nope." I noticed his badge read, "Bloom."

He ripped the shades off his face and yelled, "I'm going to ask you one more time... and you best answer me correctly, or I'm going to drag your ass out of there so fast that you won't have time to blink twice." I felt a light splash of his spit landing on my upper lip.

I turned my head away from him and gripped my steering wheel tighter. A drizzle of sweat ran down the back of my neck and squiggled down my spine. I bit the inner lining of my bottom lip, playing back my dad and late Uncle Satchel's lecture about what to do, if I ever was stopped by a police officer.

Looking the officer in the eye, I replied in a shaky voice, "No, sir!"

He scanned me from head to toe and said in a stern voice, "Better. Hand me your driver's license and registration. Keep your hands in my clear sight."

I handed them over to him and then put my hand back on the steering wheel. He took them and went back to his vehicle to run my information. I thought about burning off, but before my hand found the ignition button, I smelled cherry-flavored smoke coming from the empty passenger's seat.

There was only one person who would leave that scent around and that was Uncle Satchel who'd always had his pipe in his mouth while rocking in his checkered yellow and brown chair in his living room, telling me stories about his summer trips visiting his brother in the Big Easy. He was probably the most superstitious person I'd ever known. I rubbed my eyes with my hands to make sure I was seeing what I thought I saw the first time.

A wavy, translucent figure in the shape of Uncle Satchel floated a few inches above the seat. He mouthed something to me that I didn't understand. I knew what he was attempting to tell me. He was warning me not to do anything I would later regret. I closed my eyes and when I opened them again, he was gone. I wondered if he'd really been there. I sniffed my shirt—the scent was still there.

It felt like an hour before the trooper came back to me. He returned my license and registration. Leaning inside my window with his shades on, he said, "You know, I clocked you driving fifty miles over the speed limit. You could've gotten hurt or worse."

After he'd issued me my ticket, he said, "I hope I never stop you again for speeding. Next time, I won't be nice." He lifted a chain from around his neck. It reminded me of a girly locket. He opened it up and pointed at a young girl's picture.

The officer said, "This was my only kid. She'd lost her life from a hit and run on this very road, years ago, trying to rescue a stray dog. The dog lived." I noticed a single teardrop fall from his shaded eyes. I swallowed hard. He slapped my side door with his open hand, backed up, and retreated to his vehicle.

I waited until he drove off, then I slowly pulled away from the curb and went home. On my way, I thought more about Ash and Jesse. I tried to figure out when he'd made a move on her, and then it hit me. I'd had a flat on our way back from the basketball game against the Belmont Bears four months ago. Jesse had pulled up from nowhere and offered to take Ash home. Like an idiot, I agreed. It was really cold and windy that night. He had that look in his predator eyes when she climbed out of my truck, and her cheerleading skirt flew up.

I should've known he was hungry. I dismissed it. Why would I ever have suspected my best friend of moving in on my girl? He was always a smooth talker. I just never imagined him cutting me like this. He'd beat me when he became co-captain, and now he'd done it again. I stumbled out of my car, grabbing my bag.

Mom's car was gone, which meant she'd been called in to work the emergency room tonight, again. Dad ended up divorcing Mom when I was in junior high. He couldn't compete with what he termed, in his opinion, as her second marriage—WoodPeak Hospital. Dad lived almost twenty-five minutes from our house. He came by the house often, especially when Mom was working. I spent time at his apartment at least once a week.

I heard some kids playing some hoops across the street. I looked up at the tarnished basketball goal above our garage and thought of my brother, Dallas. His playing style reminded me of Jordan and Bird. I loved attending all of his games. He had been the star basketball player at Viking.

As I got older, I realized he must've been really high on something bad when scouts came out to watch him for that big game. Dallas had moved like a loose noodle. Before the end of the first quarter, he collapsed to the floor and seized out. He was rushed to the emergency room.

Dallas ended up dropping out of high school before the end of his senior year. He could've probably had a full ride to any Texas university. He gave his basketball dreams up and dove straight into truck driving school, after he saw a commercial on television one night.

I never understood why he just withdrew himself from a game he loved so much. When I asked him what happened that night at the game, he'd started yelling, throwing stuff all around his room, and dropped down to his knees—he cried in my lap for more than an hour. After that, I never asked him about anything else related to his basketball break-up.

Coach Silvers had tried to recruit me my freshman year. As soon as he saw me dribble a ball, he threw his hands up in the air and broke his plastic clipboard in two pieces. I had my eyes on high school cheerleading, and it came natural for me, plus all the girls. I practiced gymnastics when I was really young and started lifting weights in the seventh grade, so I made a great male cheerleader. I knew this would catch Ash's eye.

On my way to my bedroom, I saw the bulletin board with the picture collage of Ash, Jesse, and me. I jerked that board from the wall—some of the beige paint came off with it. Peeling all the pictures off the board, I looked at a few before I ripped them up and trashed them all.

I thought burning them up would be even better. Before I pursued that, I found the bears, T-shirts, and garters that Ash had given me during our time dating. I also found stuff from Jesse over the years. I knew I would probably miss some stuff, but I was driven to gather as much as I could. I tossed all that crap in my Morbius fan-made metal trashcan. I grabbed the matchbox out of the kitchen drawer and lighter fluid from the garage.

While hugging the can, I opened the backdoor and shut it behind me. The sun was about to go down. I flipped that barbecue lid up and threw everything inside. I doused it all with a little lighter fluid and scratched a match on the side.

Tossing the match on it, I stepped back a few inches, holding my trashcan in front of me like a shield. The red and orange flames shot up high for a few seconds. I stood there just staring and watching their faces melt away. I'd been crushing on Ash since sixth grade and Jesse knew that. After thirty minutes, everything was gone. I made sure to close the lid.

Returning to my room, I thought I would feel better after ridding myself of everything related to her and him. Yet, I didn't. I kept seeing them walking and holding hands. The cheaters had hidden their secret from me. I felt like the biggest dumbass in the world. I should've seen it sooner. There were clues, and I missed each one.

I heard my cell phone beeping. I didn't even check it. I fell back on my bed and drifted off to sleep around nine. Continuous cell phone dings woke me up. I rolled over and pulled my phone from my backpack. I noticed that I had a few text messages from Bubba. Most importantly, I had two missed calls from Dallas.

Looking at the time, I noticed that it was almost four in the morning. Bubba could wait. I knew that he was only wanting to play a game remotely. I hadn't heard from Dallas in three weeks. Dallas never called twice, so I knew something was up when he didn't leave a message. I got up to peep out the window. Mom's car was still gone. I called him up.

His phone rang a few times and went straight to voicemail. I left him a message to call me back as soon as he could. I texted Bubba, and just like I thought, he was up gaming with some guys in Chicago, London, and Canada—he texted me right back.

Bubba begged me to get on so he could ditch his London partner. I told him to just keep playing and text me his score, if he didn't get too busy. He told me to text him all the details about my personal after-party with a few winking emojis and a standing ovation GIF. I texted him back to tell him I got dumped and would catch him up on everything next week in school.

After I showered and wrapped a towel around my waist, I swiped the mirror with my hand to clear the condensation and stared at myself. *Why did Ash fall for Jesse?* I thought we were solid. I fell for her hard, maybe too hard. I'd dated different girls—none made my heart feel the way Ash did. I mean when I kissed her I never wanted to stop, you know what I'm talking about?

I never expected a betrayal like this. I punched the glass and cracked it. My right knuckle started bleeding. I rinsed it off under cool water, poured some alcohol over it, which made me cringe for a bit, and wrapped some gauze around it.

Car lights shone through my curtains. I threw on some shorts and a shirt. I cracked my door open and saw my mom coming down the hall with her head down. Her white coat was tossed over her shoulder along with her stethoscope.

Her disheveled scrubs and hair confirmed her exhaustion. I stepped back in my doorway and closed the door. I was sure that she had dealt with enough from Friday to Saturday, and hearing about my day wasn't important.

Crawling back into bed, I picked up my phone to check the time. It was after seven in the morning, and I saw a text from Dallas—he would be in town after noon today for a short rest before his next run mid-week. He couldn't have planned it better than this. I knew I could get all my stuff off my chest with Dallas.

I texted Bubba back to see if he was still up and playing. He said he was still on, and I got online to play a few sessions with him. I was out around eight, dropping the gaming controller on the floor.

When I woke up, it was after one, and I saw a blurry image of Dallas. He sat in a chair in front of me. I sat up in bed.

"Ready for your big night with Ash?" he asked with his arms crossed over his chest and a huge grin on his face.

"Jesse's taking her," I said.

He uncrossed his arms and frowned. "What! What do you mean?"

"They've been creeping around, and I found out yesterday."

"That's messed up... Pack a bag," he demanded, throwing my Vikings cheerleading bag in my lap.

"For what, Dallas?"

"Don't you worry about all that. Now, get ready. See you in thirty."

Scratching my head, I asked, "What about Mom?"

"I got you."

He snatched the sheet off me and exited, closing my door behind him.

While brushing my teeth, I noticed my bandage needed to be changed. I cleaned my wound and redressed it with my free hand. I found some folded jeans with a T-shirt on the top of my laundry basket in the corner and slid them both on.

As I was packing my bag, I noticed my closet door was slightly open. I didn't recall opening it, so I pushed it closed. No more than two minutes after I'd finished packing, the closet door squeaked open again, and I heard something heavy drop to the ground.

I slowly placed my hand on top of the doorknob. My brother's basketball varsity jacket, which he'd gifted me after his discharge from the hospital, had fallen onto the floor. I turned on the swinging light and didn't see anything inside, only a few swaying empty hangers.

Bending down, I grabbed it and was about to hang it up when from the kitchen, Dallas yelled, "Pack a jacket. A cold front is coming in later tonight to where we're headed."

I retrieved the jacket, pulled the string to turn off the light, shut the door, and that's when I noticed hand-sized red markings on the white door.

They resembled the numbers 119. I ran my fingers over the numbers, and they lifted off the door in ashes and disappeared into the air. I heard a faint and raspy whisper call out: *"Myles...beware... of... 119..."*

My body shivered all over. Grabbing my bag, I tossed the jacket over my shoulder. I looked back at the door, but it was completely blank. I closed my eyes and opened them—still nothing. I sprinted out of my room, and shut the door behind me.

I passed my mom's door. It was still closed. I knew she would be out for a while. Dallas left her a note on the kitchen table. I snatched a banana off the counter and poured a glass of orange juice with my unsteady hand.

Through the window, I saw Dallas's beauty, his solid metallic blue eighteen-wheeler truck parked at the side of the house. He called her *Optima Prime*, and her name was written in cursive on his door surrounded by huge red and silver flames—the flames wrapped around both sides of the truck and back. He was wiping her down with a towel when he noticed me and waved me to come on. I peeled the banana and chewed it. Then, I drank down the juice in one swallow and sat the glass in the sink.

Picking up my bag, I locked up and climbed up into his truck. The seats were leather and firm. I threw my bag behind me with my jacket on top. As he drove away, Dallas pointed at my hand. I gave him an in-depth summary of everything, including the possible Uncle Satchel ghost visit. I decided to leave the strange door experience out.

Dallas listened. I think he believed that I saw Uncle Satchel from the questions he asked me. I wasn't sure where we were headed. He wouldn't tell me. We stopped at a small diner. It was almost seven and sixty-five degrees out when we finished eating.

"How much farther?" I asked, yawning, as I stretched my arms before sliding back into my seat.

"Relax... We're almost there," Dallas said and patted my head with his hand before we drove off.

Scrolling through my phone, I got on ClickTime and saw pre-prom photos. They, Ash and Jesse, were all smiles and hugs. Dallas leaned over. He snapped his fingers and demanded I hand it to him. I did, and he dropped it in a compartment on his side door.

We drove more than a hundred more miles and came upon a gravel road in a deep wooded area. Dallas started slowing down and pointed towards a building with a crazy name in purple and white neon lights, Beaver's Drive-In. It was a big three-story white building with no windows, and it didn't look like much on the outside. I noticed two huge movie screens on both sides of the building.

The temperature had dropped twenty degrees. I grabbed my jacket. Dallas pulled a heavy black sweatshirt over his head and jumped out of the truck. He locked her up. I walked over to his side with my hands shoved in my pockets and asked, "Can I have my phone back?"

Dallas lit up a cigarette, took a few puffs, wrapped his arm around me, and said, "Not tonight."

I still didn't know what we were about to enter. He gave a low-key laugh as he blew smoke up in the air. The parking lot was packed with cars, RVs, and trucks—more cars continued to pull in. I noticed that it was mostly guys entering the door and that's when it clicked for me.

A cherry red Ram truck pulled up in front of the entrance. A lady jumped out. She wore super short denim daisy dukes with pink ruffles, sparkly snow-white cowgirl boots, and a low-cut top, through which you could see her black, lacy bra. She bent over to wipe something off her boots and winked in our direction. As she stood back up, she pulled a purple sucker out of her pocket. She slowly peeled the wrapper off and inserted it in her mouth.

Dallas placed his hand under my mouth to close it and handed me a handkerchief from his back pocket to wipe my drool. I wiped both sides of my mouth and balled it up in my hand before stuffing it in my pocket.

A sudden gust of wind caught her long, curly dark brown hair with silver highlights. The numbers 119 were tattooed on the back of her neck. I remembered what I'd seen on my closet door, but whispered to myself that it didn't mean anything. How could somebody as hot as her be trouble, right? My breakup was really messing with my eyes.

She removed the lollipop from her mouth, fluttered her long eyelashes, and kissed one of the bouncers on his cheek. She slapped him on his rear with her hand, never taking her eyes off of us. Licking her glossy pink lips, she twirled the candy in her hand like a mini baton. The bouncer opened the door for her as she pranced inside.

Dallas and I were only a few feet from the door. The bald-headed bouncer with tats all over his muscular arms asked for our driver's licenses. Dallas jumped in front of me and handed his license over to him. The tall bouncer with a curly man-bun glided a wand down our outer and inner legs, hips, arms, chest, and back. He waved Dallas in. I took my license out of my wallet and prayed it would pass the test. I really wanted to see more of what was inside—especially of the Cowgirl.

I took a few steps towards Dallas. The bouncer stopped me with his Thanos hand on my chest. He peered at my license while his eyes stared me up and down. He started shaking his head and whistled his buddy over who was checking others in. I was guided to step to the side. He took a rope and hooked it to separate me from the entrance.

Dallas came over to me and asked, "Do we have a problem?"

The bouncer who had my license looked at him. He crossed his guns and didn't respond to Dallas.

So, my brother said, "I don't think we're going to have a problem."

Rolling his eyes, the bouncer held out his hand. Dallas slipped him a hundred-dollar bill. The bouncer then unhooked the gate. He let out an obnoxious guffaw and said in a low voice, "Just messing with you, kid, enjoy everything... I mean, everything..."

The place was bigger than it looked on the outside and it was packed solid. Loud music blasted. I could feel the wood floors vibrating under my feet. There were poles, ropes, swings mounted in the mirrored ceilings, themed bars, several disco balls of various sizes, heavy smoke, and flashing colored lights. Girls, girls, and more girls. They were dressed way less than Cowgirl. I'm talking severely sexy lacy, G-string thongs and no tops. I'd seen topless girls in movies and a few video games, but never in person.

All right, I might as well confess now. I'm sure you've already guessed... Yes, I'm a virgin. I bet you thought I wasn't earlier, right, booking the big *R/J* room and all? Anyhow, I had it all planned out. As you already know, I wasn't living it up at prom tonight. However, I could guarantee you that Jesse would be sick if he knew where I was—what I already had and would witness.

I just stood there taking it all in for a few minutes. A few ladies brushed up against me once or twice. My eyes were wide open. I lost my blinking reflexes until Dallas came up behind me and placed both his hands on my shoulders. He leaned into whisper in my ear, "I'm going to make you forget all about that Ash tonight. First, we're getting drinks and then tats."

Dallas ordered drinks at the celebrity-themed bar. An 80s Madonna impersonator was the bartender. She asked, "What can I get you two?"

I'd had a few beers with the guys, but not a real drink. Dallas yelled over the song, "Freek-A-Leek" by Petey Pablo. He pumped his fists in the air and bounced his head sideways. I mirrored his rhythm with my own flavor.

Dallas told the bartender, "Give me something to numb me, and my baby bro, well, he needs something to make him forget about getting dumped by a loser the day before his senior prom. Surprise us, Madonna." He closed his eyes and moved his head to the beat of the music.

She nodded and started performing her bartender magic. In less than five minutes, she slid two glasses down to us. I lifted my slender glass and asked, "Is this cranberry juice?"

"That's no cranberry juice," Dallas said with a slight smile, drinking his drink. It was clear with two floating cherries.

"What are you drinking? Let me try it," I demanded.

Holding his glass up with his hand, he said, "This right here is way too strong for you, Baby Bro. This here is a triple Kamikaze." He downed it, popped both cherries in his mouth, and requested another one.

I took a few sips, and it was a tasty mix of cranberry and peach juices. "Hey, this is nice, what's it called?" I continued to drink it down.

"Red-headed slut," Dallas screamed, scooping a handful of peanuts in his hand and throwing them in his mouth.

"It's really called that?" I asked and laughed out loud. "Perfect, Madonna, thanks."

She turned around, bowed, and smiled.

Dallas looked at the bartender, and she slid down another one towards him, but he didn't catch it first—Cowgirl did. She leaned backwards, drank it, and slammed the glass down. She slithered around his entire body and pressed her backside against his.

I finished my drink and kept my eyes on the show.

She whispered something to him and kissed him on the mouth. Cowgirl then turned around to face me and ran her hands through my curly hair. Her lips were lined up with mine. My heart felt like it was going to shoot all the way to Mars. She outlined my quivering lips with the tips of her black nails and kissed me close to my lips.

"Yep, you've forgot all about her," Dallas said with a huge smile.

"Who?" My eyebrows shot up.

"Exactly, give us another round, please," he requested.

Cowgirl smiled and started heading back towards the dance floor.

"Hey, what's your name?" I shouted, rubbing my hand across my mouth. I could taste mango and cherry Now and Later candy.

"Cowgirl... will do just fine. See you two later."

"Hey, I never told you my nickname for you."

"You just did."

I stroked my chin with my hand and thought about what she just said.

The dense smoke swallowed her up in the crowd fast.

"Dallas, thank you, man," I said.

He looked over at me while rotating his glass in his hand and he asked, "For what?"

"For bringing me here. I really needed this," I said with a slight slur.

"Think you've had enough already," he said.

"Nah, I'm just getting started," I replied.

"I'm cutting you off, soon. Come on, let's go get those tats."

Dallas and I went up the spiral stairs to the second floor, where he knocked on a glass door.

Yanking on the end of his shirt with my hand, I asked, "Hey, this isn't your first time at Beaver's Drive-In, is it?"

"What gives you that idea?" he asked and grinned.

"You know your way around here, Dallas." I said. "By the way, why is it called Beaver's Drive-In, anyhow?"

"Some friends told me that the owner, Beaver Womack, owned a drive-in, but wasn't making enough to cover expenses, so he decided to keep the name and opened up a dance club with perks," Dallas said with a single wink and opened the door for me.

There were a few people getting tats. I flopped down in a black leather recliner and Dallas did the same next to me. I'd always wanted a tat. I looked on the walls and saw some awesome designs and symbols, such as the Mandalorian, vampire fangs, and college logos. There were too many for me to make up my mind.

"You know what you're getting?" I asked Dallas.

"Sure do. I've been wanting this for a while," he said.

"Hold up, don't you already have some tats?"

"Nope," he said, tying up his shoulder-length, wavy hair up with a rubber band and pulling off his shirt.

"Wait, you told me you were getting one last year."

"You know, I thought about it, but I wanted to wait to get one with you," he said.

"Aww, man, that really means a lot to me, for us to bond like this."

He looked at me for a minute and said, "Myles, there's something I've been meaning to tell you for a long time..." His eyes looked teary. He wiped his face with his open palm.

Focusing my eyes on his, I asked, "What?"

"Later, okay... later. Here, look through these albums—you might get inspired." He handed me two big tat books.

I flipped through them for more than fifteen minutes before I came up with an idea of what I wanted on my chest—a black heart with a chain wrapped around it, and two red light sabers linking the chain ends together. I thought the needle pain would be the worst, but I was sure the alcohol would help, and it would hit me all at once in the morning.

What I didn't know then was that I would experience a much greater pain than that. Dallas looked over and gave me a thumbs up. I endured the drilling until the tat artist finished and bandaged it up. He handed me a paper list of instructions of all the dos and don'ts. I folded it up and placed it inside my back pocket.

As Dallas's guy finished up his tat on him, he beckoned me over to check it out. I studied it for almost five minutes before I spoke. Smashed up black letters with no vowels decorated his lower forearm. A detailed silver dragon tail with specks of crimson wrapped around his upper arm and neck. The head of the Chinese dragon rested in the middle of his back. I tried to make out what the letters meant:

FGHTFFYRDMNS

"Okay, I give up, what does it mean?" I asked.

Pausing for a few seconds, he answered, "It stands for... *Fight off your demons.*" The tat guy bandaged him up, too. Lowering his head, he sputtered out, "I'm gonna release all of them tonight."

"That's pretty deep, Bro." I stared into his eyes and noticed his jittery hands. "You okay?" I placed my hand on his shoulder.

"Yeah," he said, squeezing his nostrils together with his thumb and index finger. "Come on, let's go. Thanks, guys, for the great work."

They gave us high fives and started cleaning their tools. Dallas paid the cashier, and we went downstairs. More people kept piling inside. We found a table by the middle of the stage.

"Cool spot, Dallas."

"I reserved it when you told me your prom plans were off."

A waitress took our order, two beers, waters, and a large bowl of mega flaming nachos with various peppers, cheeses, and beef. The main show was in twenty-five minutes. I watched girls swinging upside down all around me. The waitress returned with our order. I popped a nacho in my mouth and guzzled two bottles of water down.

Dallas laughed at me and said, "Guess I should've warned you."

"Would've been nice... Hey, your tat, what was that all about?" I picked up the beer bottle and pressed it against my tingling lips to take a few sips.

Dallas drank his beer in one gulp. He waved another waitress over and requested more beers. I felt that he wanted to tell me something heavy, but wasn't sure he was ready to. His eyes locked on his tat for over a minute before he spoke to me.

"Myles, I did something unforgivable and never told anyone." He scooted down in the chair and dropped his head.

The waitress returned and placed the beers on the table.

I scooted my chair closer to him. "Hey, you know you can trust me, right?"

He lifted his head, and I saw tears pooling around his eyes. "Yes, that's why I'm telling you. I should've told you everything when you first asked me that night. I figured you were too young to know what kind of brother you had, so I waited."

"Dallas, I love you. No matter what," I said without a blink.

"You might change your mind after you learn the truth."

"No... I won't." I frowned.

He took in deep breaths and shared, "That night before the big game, Jet Wilson and I got really drunk at a party. His brother told Jet not to get in the car. He did, and I jumped in the passenger seat. We burnt off."

Dallas went silent on me for a while.

I prodded him. "What happened?"

"We hit her in Jet's Porsche... and left her bleeding out. We didn't stop to help her or call 911. Jet sped off. I called his brother. His dad got rid of the car and told us to never breathe a word to anyone."

"You kept this with you all this time?" I asked, my voice cracking and legs trembling under the table.

"I had to. I told Jet the next day, a few hours before the game, I needed something to help me forget. He gave me some kind of drug cocktail that caused me to fall out and have a seizure on the court. The doc told me I nearly went into cardiac arrest. I wished I had died that night, Myles."

Slamming the bottle down on the table, I cried out, "Dallas, don't say that. You weren't the one driving." My watery eyes fixed on his.

"I was there. I'm just as guilty as Jet. I didn't do shit to save her. I could've said something. I was part of a young girl's murder, and I chose to leave her there... to die. So, I'm going to write my confession and deliver it to the police department after I sober up."

"You sure you want to do that now? You can't... I won't let you!" I sniffled.

"Myles, I've got to... It's the only way I can get rid of my darkness..."

Raising my voice, I asked, "What about Jet? Where is he? He should be the one to confess. He was the one behind the wheel, not you. It was his fault!"

"Don't know. He ghosted me several months back," Dallas muttered, casting his eyes away from me as teardrops hit the table.

I hugged him. We got some stares from others. I didn't care.

"You should've told me sooner," I sighed with my hand resting on his shoulder.

"Nah, I had to do this in my own time. You know... I see her crossing the road in my dreams almost every night—sometimes, I swear I've seen her on the side roads during my truck runs—and I see the blood, all the blood splattered on the road." He wiped his wet face with the back of his sleeve. I patted his shoulder.

Something pushed me to ask, "Dallas, what was the road and the girl's name?"

His wet eyes scanned the floor. He looked up at me and said, "Whistler Bend and Caroline Bloom. I learned her name on the news that night. I could never forget her scared face in those headlights. Why you wanna know?"

"The cop who gave me a ticket earlier—his name was Bloom and that's where I got pulled over. He showed me Caroline's picture."

"Damn, what are the odds of that?" He shook his head. "You see? That's my sign to finally tell the truth and turn myself in for my crime." He sighed and sniffled.

Before I could reply, two hands touched our shoulders. We turned around, and it was Cowgirl.

"Hey fellas, y'all okay?" she asked. "There's only one rule at Beaver's Drive-in."

"What's that?" I asked, swiveling an empty bottle side to side.

"No tears, ever. Only good times here," she said as she wiped under Dallas's eyes with her thumb and tilted his chin to the side with her hand. She bent down and pressed her plump, moist lips against his for a kiss. I timed it. The kiss lasted at least two minutes and thirty-seven seconds.

Opening his eyes, Dallas muttered, "You're right." He reached for another beer and started drinking. Lights waved across the room and the black curtain started rising for the big show. "Pour Some Sugar on Me" by Def Leppard pumped out of the speakers.

Purring, Cowgirl asked, "How about a three-way private party, out back, fellas?"

Dallas's bottle almost slipped out of his hand. He caught it by the neck before it did.

I knew Cowgirl had her eyes on Dallas, and I didn't roll that way. Dallas knew that, too. He needed the distraction now, not me. I planned on enjoying the performance.

"Hey, I'll be back Myles, so we can finish our convo, all right? I'm going to find you somebody tonight," he said, shoving some money in my hand and grabbing a beer off the table. Cowgirl wrapped her arms around his waist.

They weaved through the crowd and vanished. The show became a blur to me as I thought about everything my brother had just laid on me. I was determined to convince Dallas to not confess. What would that really accomplish? Caroline was gone. I didn't want to lose my brother. I needed him in my life, and I knew he needed me, especially now.

Eyeing my watch, I noticed more than an hour had gone by. I watched another show and looked at the time again. It was almost midnight. Something told me to go check on Dallas.

I slid my jacket on slowly. I abandoned the club scene and headed for Dallas's truck. I opened the passenger door and noticed black, velvet panties draped on the steering wheel and shorts over my headrest. Cowgirl's boots were tossed on the dashboard. Climbing up the step, I heard some deep moans and screams. I began to back down with a slight smile and thought, *she must be really something*.

Before my foot touched the ground, the entire truck rocked hard and caused me to fall onto my back. I recovered fast and jumped up. I rushed up inside the truck and noticed blood swimming down the metal floor towards my tennis shoes.

Running towards the back of the cab, I pushed a beaded curtain back with my hands. It felt ice-cold inside the trailer. I could see my breath in the air. Before I tell you what I perceived holding my brother's bloody, nearly skinless, body up in the air, you may want to sit down—it was hard for me to believe.

I saw the tattoo glowing on the back of this monster's neck, as its hair stood straight up in the air. That is when I knew it was Cowgirl. She'd lassoed her long, jagged barbed tail around my brother's neck.

"Run... Myles!" Dallas gurgled as blood squirted from his mouth. He gasped and closed his eyes.

I noticed a flare gun on the floor, so I picked it up and pointed it at Cowgirl, pulling the trigger back. She heard the click and jerked her head around to face me. Her eyes rounded, and she snapped her wrist, throwing me against the wall. The gun fired towards the roof.

Landing in a pile of Dallas's skin, I watched her mouth open wide, spraying blood orange vomit all over him, which started to dissolve his body. She unhinged her jaw, swallowing what was left of him.

My mouth, arms, and legs were frozen. Tears shot from my eyes, and my heart felt like it was about to explode. She glared at me with her red eyes and melted mascara pooled around them. Her tail retracted. She crawled over to me with her hooved feet and serrated claws. Her nose split wide open as she rose up off the ground. I tried to move, but couldn't.

She stood over me. Her darting eyes focused on my bandaged hand. Her bloody claws pinned my chin up against the wall. She bent down, flicking her long, lime tongue and licked my hand, leaving behind slime that smelled like day-old vomit. "Pure..." she hissed. Moving across my chest, she took in a big whiff and popped up crazy fast, sliding backwards on the bloody floor towards the corner.

Snaking up the metal wall, she tore it wide open with her claws. She looked back at me, and she said in a choppy whisper, "He had it coming." Her tongue dragged across her protruding fangs, and she jetted out.

I scurried over to the large hole to make sure she was gone. I saw her running at cheetah speed into the darkness. I plummeted down to my trembling knees and took in everything. Tears raced down my cheeks.

After a few minutes, I heard sirens. Cop cars and an ambulance encircled the truck. I was briefly questioned and told I would be taken to the police station for more questioning. I retrieved my phone and bag from the truck. An EMT took my vitals and gave me a medical assessment as the cops examined the inside and outside of Dallas's truck.

"You were lucky, kid. Many don't walk away like you after something like that," the EMT guy said. He took the blood pressure cuff from around my arm. He told me my blood pressure was up some and handed me a thick towelette to wipe my face and neck. I told him my head was pounding. He gave me medication in a paper cup and a water bottle. He instructed me to lay down on the gurney inside. He assessed the scratches on my face and dabbed ointment on them.

"Wh-what do you mean?" I asked.

"Listen, I'm not supposed to tell you, but this isn't the first time I've seen something like this. No human could cause a truck or person that kind of damage."

I knew that much. I wanted to know what that thing was.

He looked around his vehicle and over both shoulders and whispered,

"Two questions: Did you know the victim, and did the victim hold a secret?"

"Yeah," I nodded. "What did this to my brother?"

"A *nightrunner*… It's a descendant from the reaper shapeshifter family. There are many. They're strategic assassins who work for the restless spirits realm. *Nightrunners* can transform into anything and can be over-the-top alluring when they need to be. Some beckon their victims here. This place is well-known for high death tolls because of them."

"Really?" I sat up.

I didn't want to believe him, but how else could all this be explained?

"Yes. They're extremely nasty creatures who search for the guilty who have committed unspeakable crimes against innocents. They wait for the victim's death to be witnessed by a loved one, so the witness can endure suffering, an eternal punishment. A *nightrunner* will only spare the witness, if he or she is pure or protected by something."

"Protected?" I asked.

"A protection bag, usually made up of salt, shreds of silver, thin metal horseshoe strings, and holy-water, soaked lily petals." He took a few steps back.

"I don't think so."

"Check all your pockets." He focused on me.

The last pocket I checked was an inner jacket one I'd never noticed before. I pulled out a tan crisscross tied pouch. I untied it and all those elements stared back at me.

He pointed his finger at it and said, "There, I bet that *nightrunner* hightailed it away from you once she knew you possessed that."

"I guess so." I closed the bag up and placed it in my front jeans pocket.

"Don't worry about going down to the station. It's only routine. This town knows all about *nightrunners's* Modus Operandi. Be safe out there." He handed me a card with his contact information. I thanked him.

Stepping down from the ambulance, I looked back at him and asked, "How do you know all this stuff about them?"

He turned around to face me as he started cleaning up. "Someone told me about them when my life was also spared, years ago. Somebody was definitely watching over you tonight, kid."

I knew it was Uncle Satchel. He must've placed the bag in the jacket pocket when I went to see him for his last Christmas. After that night, I now know that losing Ash and a friendship were trivial compared to the permanent removal of Dallas from my life—something I would have to deal with on my own. I knew who saved me that night too, and I had to continue to live. I had a lot to learn about *nightrunners*... and I definitely had a future date with Cowgirl.

THE END

CONCLUSION

Thank you so much for choosing to read **FRIGHT BITES**. I hope that you enjoyed. Miracle would be ecstatic to hear which story or stories were your favorites. Feel free to leave a short review on Amazon, post a pic of you posing with **FRIGHT BITES** on social media, or direct message Miracle, if you would like. She truly enjoys hearing from readers and fans. Until next time, keep reading spooky and amazing books!

"Every time you leave a *positive* review for an author, you become the little voice that whispers in her or his ear... 'Don't you quit!' So, give a review to the authors you enjoy. It doesn't have to be long... just say you enjoyed her or his book."

~Author Unknown~

GRYSELDA'S SECRET MESSAGE

Now, let's have some fun. Solve the clues below with information dotted throughout **FRIGHT BITES**. Then, transfer the numbered letters to their spaces below to reveal a quotation from the Bard of Avon, William Shakespeare. Read the first letters going down from the answers to discover the character who spoke these words.

1. Like Percey in "Billie's Girl"

__ __ __ __ __ __ __   -   __ __ __ __ __
16 5 7 26 44 11 38   15 44 8 7 2

2. Author of **FRIGHT BITES**, Miracle ____

__ __ __ __ __ __
44 20 24 3 30 12

3. Planet S-709 in "Roundup"

__ __ __ __ __ __ __ __ __ __ __ __
9 17 38 7 44 23 18 27 44 7 5 44

4. Therapist in "Stilts" with a fruity name

__ __ __ __ __
1 37 7 7 45

5. Curtis's bro in "Finders... Weepers"

__ __ __ __ __ __
27 44 7 10 34 49

6. Mega superstar of the "Night Tour"

__ __ __ __ __ __ __ __
28 14 21 25 7   7   47 33

7. "Darla's" brother, J.R. ____

__ __ __ __ __ __ __ __ __
4   41 13 19 39 14 43 27 7

8. Centaur Chief in "Billie's Girl"

__ __ __ __ __ __ __
43 44 3   10 30 12 23

9. Michaelson, inspiration for "Plucked"

__ __ __ __ __ __
11 31 13 7   30 38

10. Judee Lee ____ of "Wake"

__ __ __ __ __ __
3   20 35 36 49 7

11. Location of "Night Runner"

__ __ __ __ __ __ __ __   __ __ __ __ __ __ __
46 29 41 48 8   31 49 37   42 6   7   34 31 32 50

12. Ghostly resident of "Camp Red Robins"

__ __ __ __ __ __
40 27 7   22 8   5

Be sure to check Miracle's website for this **time-sensitive** contest and future ones. Good luck!

SIGNING OFF FOR NOW,

−GRYSELDA

"Just Creepin' It Real"

16	33	50
■	■	49
15	32	48
14	31	47
■	30	46
13	29	■
12	28	45
11	27	44
10	26	43
9	25	■
8	24	42
7	■	41
6	23	40
■	22	39
5	21	■
4	20	38
3	19	37
■	18	36
2	■	35
1	17	34

PLAYLIST
SONGS THAT INSPIRED
FRIGHT BITES

"Sign Your Name" : Terence Trent D'Arby (Sananda Maitreya)

"I've Done Everything for You" : Rick Springfield

"Judy's Turn to Cry" : Lesley Gore

"Oh What A Night" : The Dells

"Talking to the Moon" : Bruno Mars

"DJ Got Us Fallin' In Love" : Usher Featuring Pitbull

"Shivers" : Ed Sheeran

"Little Bitty Pretty One" : Frankie Lymon

"Memories" : Maroon 5

"He's the Greatest Dancer" : Sister Sledge

"All I Need" : Radiohead

"Eye of the Tiger" : Survivor

"Something About You" : Level 42

"Bad Moon Rising" : Creedence Clearwater Revival

"Object of My Desire" : Starpoint

"Jessie's Girl" : Rick Springfield

"Freak Show" : Ingrid Michaelson

"Here I Go Again" : Whitesnake

"Freek-A-Leek" : Petey Pablo

"Pour Some Sugar on Me" : Def Leppard

"Fever" : Peggy Lee

"We Are Never Ever Getting Back Together" : Taylor Swift

"All Out of Love" : Air Supply

"Every Breath You Take" : The Police

"Love on the Brain" : Rihanna

"The Voodoo House" : Rick Springfield

"Beautiful Monster" : Ne-Yo

"Fresh" : Kool & The Gang

"Maneater" : Daryl Hall & John Oates

"Losing Sleep" : Boyz II Men

"Buttons" : The Pussycat Dolls Featuring Snoop Dogg

"Welcome To The Jungle" : Guns N' Roses

"Centerfold" : The J. Geils Band

"LA-LA (Means I Love You)" : The Delfonics

"Hush" : The Marìas

"I Can Love You" : Mary J. Blige

"Levitating" : Dua Lipa

"Bust Your Windows" : Glee Cast Featuring Amber Riley

"Losing My Religion" : R.E.M.

"Xanadu" : Olivia Newton-John

"Superman (It's Not Easy)" : Five For Fighting

"Girl on Fire" : Alicia Keys

"Save Your Tears" : The Weeknd

"The Wild Boys" : Duran Duran

"Killing Him" : Amy LaVere

"Gunpowder & Lead" : Miranda Lambert

"Legs" : ZZ Top

"Pretty" : Ingrid Michaelson

"Creep" : Radiohead

"Janie's Got a Gun" : Aerosmith

"Torture" : The Jacksons

"Cell Block Tango" : Chicago (the musical)

"Baby Be Mine" : Michael Jackson

"Karma Chameleon" : Culture Club

"Jealous" : Ingrid Michaelson

"Truth Hurts" : Lizzo

"Somebody's Baby" : Jackson Browne

"Another One Bites the Dust" : Queen

"Don't Talk to Strangers" : Rick Springfield

"I Put a Spell on You" : Nina Simone

"Share My Life" : Kem

"Nothing but a Good Time" : Poison

"Cold Hearted" : Paula Abdul

"Send in the Clowns" : Judy Collins

"Give Me the Night" : George Benson

"Son of a Gun (I Betcha Think This Song Is About You)" : Janet Jackson
    Featuring Carly Simon & Missy Elliott

"I'll Be over You" : Toto

"Lost in Love" : New Edition

"Mother" : Ingrid Michaelson

"Nightime Hunger" : Overcoats

"Animals" : Maroon 5

"Unpretty" : TLC

"What Goes Around... Comes Around" : Justin Timberlake

"Oh Shelia" : Ready for the World

"Close Your Eyes" : Kim Petras

"Precious Hewie (Haunting Ground)" : Rod Herold

"Always in My Heart" : Tevin Campbell

"Rock You Like A Hurricane" : Scorpions

"Voices Carry" : 'Til Tuesday

"Only a Matter of Time" : Joshua Bassett

"I Can Dream About You" : Dan Hartman

"The Way It Is" : Bruce Hornsby and the Range

PREVIOUSLY PUBLISHED WORKS

Hemlock's Secrets first appeared in Sirenscallpublications.com Issue #57, © Spring 2022

Breathless first appeared in Sirenscallpublications.com Issue #58, ©Summer 2022

RoundUp first appeared in Castle of Horror Anthology Volume 6: Femme Fatales, © January 2021

The Latch first appeared in Sanitarium Magazine, © February 2021

Prowler first appeared in Sirenscallpublications.com Issue #53, ©Spring 2021

Summer of 1989 & V.H.V. Group first appeared in Sirenscallpublications. com Issue #54, ©Summer 2021

Pachooee first appeared in Sanitarium Magazine Issue #4, ©August 2021

Cooties From Mercury (original title: *Human Eaters*) first appeared in Sirenscallpublications.com Issue #50, ©Summer 2020

NightRunner first appeared in The Wicked Library Podcast #1006: Season 10, ©May 2020

Love Boo first appeared in Sanitarium Magazine Issue #3, ©August 2020

Darla first appeared in Sirenscallpublications.com Issue #52, ©Winter 2020

Wake first appeared in It's Not All Rockets and Ray Guns (Anthology Book 1), ©2020

Plucked first appeared in Sirenscallpublications.com Issue #51,

ABOUT THE AUTHOR

Miracle Austin is a Texan gal who works in the medical social work arena by day and in the writer's world at night, including the weekends, as a YA/NA author. *Doll* is her debut YA supernatural, coming-of-age novel with diverse themes intertwined; it won second place in the Young Adult category in the 2016 ***Purple DragonFly*** Awards. She loves horror, collecting T-shirts, Marvel/DC, sparkles, unicorns, 80s music, *Stranger Things*, and daydreaming up stories to share with her awesome readers who already know her and new ones, too.

Find Miracle online at:
www.miracleaustin.com

Twitter & Instagram: @MiracleAustin7
Facebook: Miracle Austin Author
Email: shadesoffiction@miracleaustin.com

"Don't Stop Believing!"

#StrangerThingsForever #YouCantSpellAmericaWithoutErica
#Enough #CantStopWontStop #ROPESHOVELHOLE #BOOM

"Just remember that Dumbo didn't need the feather, the magic was in him."

—STEPHEN KING

ALSO BY MIRACLE AUSTIN

Trilogy:

Doll
Doll 2: The Revealing
Doll 3: The Hunting

Anthology of Diverse Tales:

Boundless

Coming Soon:

FRIGHT BITES: VOLUME 2